At Home In
Persimmon Hollow

Gerri Bauer

Franciscan
MEDIA
Cincinnati, Ohio

Cover illustration and design by Candle Light Studios
Book design by Mark Sullivan

LIBRARY OF CONGRESS CATALOGING-IN-PUBLICATION DATA
Bauer, Gerri.
At home in Persimmon Hollow / Gerri Bauer.
pages cm. — (Persimmon Hollow legacy ; 1)
ISBN 978-1-61636-863-0 (paperback)
1. Single women—Fiction. 2. Frontier and pioneer life—Florida—Fiction.
I. Title.
PS3602.A9355A83 2015
813'.6—dc23
2015008015

ISBN 978-1-61636-863-0

Published by Franciscan Media
28 W. Liberty St.
Cincinnati, OH 45202
www.FranciscanMedia.org

Printed in the United States of America.
Printed on acid-free paper.
15 16 17 18 19 5 4 3 2 1

*To my husband, Peter D. Bauer,
for his love, support,
and for always believing in me.*

*   *   *

*And to my parents,
Edward M. Giovanelli and
Catherine Rose Puccio Giovanelli,
for instilling in me a love of reading,
and so much more.*

Chapter One

Central Florida, August 1886

A fine man, indeed. What had that woman in Jacksonville been thinking? Agnes Foster sighed. She didn't need this discouraging first encounter, not when she was already tired, bedraggled, and disappointed in her new surroundings. The Persimmon Hollow train station was nothing more than a log shelter in a hot, isolated wilderness. It was definitely not what she expected.

Wilting in the thick air, she stared at the sullen stranger who'd met the train. She was almost sorry she'd agreed to chaperone young Billy, the only other traveler to get off in this middle of nowhere. That impulsive offer of chaperonage, which she'd proposed at the Jacksonville train station, meant she now had to deal with this unfriendly ox of a man seated before them on a placid, grayish-white horse. He sat straight-backed and frowning, gripping the reins as though impatient to depart as soon as he could finish his business. *No humility in this man's stature,* Agnes thought, before she reminded herself not to judge. But it was hard.

She felt for the rosary in her skirt pocket and searched her heart for charity. The touch of the smooth beads of the Lourdes rosary, a gift from Mother Superior, grounded her. But it remained a

1

challenge to feel charity for the grim-faced man before her. She already knew his name was Seth Taylor, even though he hadn't introduced himself. She already knew Billy was his nephew, despite the way Mr. Taylor hadn't responded to Billy's hello or to Agnes's how-do-you-do. He hadn't even removed his well-worn Stetson hat. He hadn't made any acknowledgment of Agnes or Billy at all beyond a stony glare. Whatever in heaven was wrong with him? A stubborn mule would be easier to reckon with.

The woman on the train who'd entrusted Billy to Agnes's care had been right about one thing, though. Seth Taylor certainly was fine looking. But good looks didn't make up for rude behavior. And his behavior made her suspect his character was as poor as his manners.

Billy kept silent and stood with slumped shoulders and a lowered gaze. In his neat city attire of trousers and collared shirt, he seemed out of place in the wilderness of tangled forest growth. He scuffed the sand with one shoe while Seth just stayed on his horse, lips pressed together and face shaded by the overhang of his hat.

"Telegram from your aunt reached me this morning," Seth finally said to Billy. "Said to meet the train. Said she was shipping you back because you're too much for her to handle. Starting right now, you best forget your foolhardy ways. They'll get you nowhere here. Now get on and let's go." He indicated with a nod of his head that Billy was to sit behind him on the horse.

"I'm surprised the telegram even got here before you did," Seth grumbled. "Guess it's too much trouble for city folk to ask a man if he minds that his life's about to change."

Agnes's displeasure bristled in proportion to the crestfallen look on Billy's face. Her own discomforts fueled her impatience with Seth's sour words and disinterest in his nephew. The man was as sorry as the place she'd landed in.

Persimmon Hollow wasn't anything like the description in the advertising circular, the one she had read so often that the folds in the paper were worn thin. The palm-log station house was small and empty. The bare, sandy lot around it stretched in a bleak circle. The advertisement's etching had depicted a larger station that seemed airy and appealing, with happy travelers standing inside and out, and horses and wagons filling the lot. The scene before her was desolate.

Her high-collared blouse, full wool skirt, and long-sleeved jacket chafed her skin under the sun's intensity. Tendrils of hair escaped her scarf and stuck to her cheek, damp from humidity. Every time she took a step or shifted position, more soft sand trickled between the laces of her high-top shoes. And never in her life had she heard such a loud buzz of insects and odd critters' noises in broad daylight. Her ears were more attuned to the clip-clop of horses' hooves on cobblestones, the sounds of vendors calling out their wares, and children playing on the sidewalks of busy city streets.

Worst of all, no one had arrived to escort her into the heart of town. Her patrons and new employers, the Misses Alloway, had written that they'd send a wagon to meet her. Well, she'd walk into town before she asked the surly Seth Taylor for help. That is, if she could figure out in which direction town lay.

The contrast between then and now, between the life she had been forced to leave and this new unknown, was almost too much to bear. *Stiffen your spine, Agnes,* she told herself. She thought of

Mother Superior's encouragement and prayers and of Fr. Tom's advice to put herself in God's hands and follow his will. Yet right now, those thoughts only made her long for home, St. Isidore's Home, the only home she'd ever known.

Had she really been gone only a few days? It seemed like forever. Even the train's stop in Jacksonville seemed like it had been weeks ago. Yet it had been mere hours since the shrill whistle and the screech of brakes had awakened Agnes when the train halted in the north Florida city. There, the station had been alive and busy. Here, the standoffish silence between Seth and Billy stretched as interminably as the sun's rays. She closed her eyes against the glare and thought back over the journey that had dumped her, alone, in the barren, sandy wilderness of Persimmon Hollow, responsible for a child she didn't know, apparently abandoned by her new employers, and forced to deal with a man of questionable behavior. She was far, too far, from home.

*　*　*

Jacksonville, 8 hours previous
Agnes's skirt caught on the edge of the train seat as she awoke, shifted, and looked out the smudged glass of the sooty window. At last, a town of substance. For so long there had been nothing but rows of pine trees that stood like soldiers at arms, with green, spiky shrubs bunched at their bases. The view had been the same through the night under the light of the moon. It was just past dawn, yet Agnes already felt a daytime heat. Her throat was dry and scratchy, and her small canteen was empty.

She wondered what city they were in. More than half the train car's passengers had disembarked at Charleston or Savannah, and a goodly number of the rest were now getting up and gathering their bags. She dug the advertising circular out of her satchel and compared the etching of the Persimmon Hollow station with the building she saw through the window. Not even close. The etching depicted a small but bustling log depot with forest in the background. This station was red brick, solid, and large. Wood buildings crowded around it, and a platform thronged with people ran alongside the track.

Agnes stood up and yanked on the window to open it. A blast of warm air greeted her. She could almost feel her hair under her scarf springing in disarray, tresses that escaped tickling her cheeks. She tucked the curls back in and hoped the combs that secured her hair in a twist at the nape of her neck would stay where they belonged.

"Sir," she called to the conductor, who stood just below the window and helped people down the steps from the railroad car. "Is this Florida?"

"Yes, miss," he said and looked up at her. "But not your stop. That's eight hours down the track. This is Jacksonville. We'll be here for thirty minutes if you want to freshen up." He glanced at the watch he wore on a chain. "You still have a good twenty-five minutes."

Agnes headed for the women's entrance to the station. She neatened up, grabbed a few sips of coffee in the station house dining room, refilled her canteen, and was back in her seat just as the conductor called, "All aboard."

Eight hours to Persimmon Hollow. Eight more hours to a new life, with the horror of what had happened tucked away, a thousand miles away. She drummed her fingertips on her satchel as she waited for the train to start moving. Despite what had happened, she couldn't help but remember all the good things she'd left behind. She felt like the woman she saw on the platform outside, the one with fatigue on her face but a brisk pace and a firm hand on a frowning boy. Going somewhere with purpose, but not happy about it.

Another boy who trailed the glum youngster yelled in a voice that carried above the din. "When you coming back, Billy? You ain't gonna stay down there forever, are ya?"

The woman blocked the boy from running back to his friend and instead ushered him up the car steps and onto the train.

"Hurry, William!" she urged. He broke away from her, clumped up the aisle, and then, despite all the open seats, slumped into the seat facing Agnes, immediately turning and leaning out the open window.

"I ain't staying down there!" he called to his friend. "I don't wanna go, and I ain't staying!"

"Hush, William," the woman said. She smiled apologetically at Agnes. "Pardon him, miss. His manners aren't always so unbearable. He's being stubbornly difficult about this journey."

"He's no bother," Agnes said. "I'm used to being around a lot of children."

The conductor blew his whistle and yelled, "Leaving the station!" The train engines started to rumble louder. "Oh! I must go!" the woman said. She turned to the boy and put her hands on his shoulders.

"William, you listen to me. You behave for the conductor and do not get out of your seat until this train reaches Persimmon Hollow. Understand me? Your Uncle Seth will be there to meet you at the station. Do you understand?"

The boy stuck out his lower lip and kicked at the train seat.

"William, this is no time for misbehavior. I want your promise to…"

"I'd be glad to keep an eye on him," Agnes interrupted. She stood up and reached her arm toward the woman for a hand-shake. "I'm Agnes Foster, Persimmon Hollow's new teacher. I'll make sure he gets safely into the hands of his uncle."

The train inched forward and stopped. The woman's eyes widened. "Oh, bless you, thank you," she said, touching her hand to Agnes's and smiling. Agnes knew she made a trustworthy impression on people. Hadn't she been told that a hundred times? Something about her heart-shaped face, clear hazel eyes, and wide mouth that was quick to smile combined to put people at ease. Her whole face smiled, not just her lips.

The woman gave William a kiss on the head and hurried toward the car's exit.

"His uncle is named Seth Taylor, my brother-in-law," she called over her shoulder, then stopped at the doorway and spoke hurriedly. "He'll be easy to identify. A handsome man, with the rugged look of an outdoor life. Black hair, and green eyes the same as William's." Then she exited and was gone.

The boy had waved to his aunt and friend until the people on the platform were so far in the distance they appeared as small as the specks of dirt on the window. The train rounded a bend and was swallowed by pine forest. He flopped down in his seat.

"I ain't gonna stay," he announced. "Uncle Seth ain't gonna make me stay. I bet he don't want me coming any more than I want to go."

He stared at Agnes with defiance. "And my name's Billy, not William."

"How old are you, Billy?" she asked.

"Twelve," he said.

"I've heard twelve-year-old boys are big eaters. I have a tin of meat and some cheese, far too much for me to eat. Would you do me a favor and help?"

He shrugged, but there was a look of interest in his gaze.

Agnes peered into the frayed bag that held her worldly belongings: an extra skirt, two aprons, two shirtwaists, a shawl, a few small towels, an extra scarf, a brush, her Bible, her *Catechism*, and a small vial of Holy Water. Her fingers flicked over the circular she had stuffed back in the bag. Then she found the small lunch tin and the cookies Polly had baked as a going-away present. Her bright, young Polly. She was so close in age to the young fellow across from Agnes. Tears started to blur her eyes. How she wished they could have finalized adoption papers before she'd had to flee.

"Look what I found!" she exclaimed in as bright a voice as she could muster. "Sugar cookies!" Billy sat forward, and his eyes brightened.

"For dessert," she added.

She spread out small cloth towels and gave him a hefty portion of meat and cheese. She forced down a few bites herself, but her appetite had stayed behind when the rest of her set out for Florida. The more Billy ate, the less disturbed he appeared. He settled into his seat and gave Agnes a quick grin. She remembered how good it felt to lend a helping hand to others. She looked upward and murmured a quiet thanks.

"You've been in Persimmon Hollow before?" she asked. He nodded affirmatively as he munched on sugar cookies.

"Has your Uncle Seth lived there long?" Again, a nod.

"After we eat, would you tell me a little bit about the town? This is my first time going there. All I know is what I learned from an advertising circular."

Billy swallowed and nodded.

"Sure," he said. "Wait 'til you hear about my Uncle Seth. He's a real swell guy. I wanna be like him when I grow up. Well, I mean, like everybody says he was before he got mean and mad at everybody and...uh...I mean...uh..." He stopped, as though remembering a warning about what he could and couldn't talk about with strangers. He looked uneasily at Agnes.

"I look forward to meeting your uncle," she said. "I'm sure he's a fine man."

* * *

Agnes winced as she remembered saying those words to Billy. He'd glowed on the train when he spoke of his uncle. His disappointment now was vivid, and it irked Agnes that his Uncle Seth could be so unfeeling.

In no rush to climb onto his uncle's horse, Billy kicked a downed oak branch into the brush at the edge of the clearing. The action startled a pair of ruddy-backed birds with speckled breasts, and they flew up out of the leaf litter.

Seth's horse whinnied, neighed, and sidestepped. Seth's face and manner changed. He patted the horse's neck.

"Just some birds, fellow," he said. "Poking around the ground for lunch."

It was the voice of a man who cared for his horse as far more than a means of transportation. He spoke soothingly to the animal in a firm but low voice until it calmed. Why, Agnes wondered, didn't he approach his nephew with the same care and consideration?

She wanted to tell him that we all shoulder what God gives us, and God had obviously sent Billy to Seth for upbringing and guidance. But for the moment, she curbed herself of what Mother Superior had termed her "impatient habit of offering advice when none was sought."

The tiny group remained at a stalemate. Finally, Agnes couldn't tolerate the tension a second longer. She stepped forward and placed a hand on Billy's shoulder.

"Billy told me what a fine man you are," she said to Seth. "He has been looking forward to seeing you."

Seth pushed back his hat and glanced at Agnes as though seeing her for the first time. "Who are you?"

*One...Two...Three...Four...Five...Six...*There was no way Agnes could make it to ten.

"Someone who is no longer surprised at young Billy's occasional lapse of manners, considering the example his uncle sets," she said.

She straightened as though trying to squeeze more length from her five-foot-four frame, stepped forward with more gumption than she'd thought possible in herself, and offered a handshake. She didn't care how forward it seemed.

"My name is Agnes Foster, and I'm the new teacher in Persimmon Hollow."

He didn't grasp her hand in return. "Another one? Last one stayed for three weeks. I expect you'll be gone soon, too."

He looked at Agnes from tip to toe. "I give you, maybe, a month."

Agnes pressed her lips so tightly her jaw hurt. "I am not a quitter, Mr....Mr...."

She waited for him to fill in his last name. She knew it, but refused to extend another inch of civility. *Forgive me, Jesus, for my rudeness,* she prayed.

"His last name's Taylor," Billy mumbled. "Same as mine."

"Well, Billy," Agnes said. "I'm certain you can room with the Misses Alloway and me in town, since your presence is such an imposition on your ill-prepared uncle. He apparently has forgotten the meaning of family. I understand the Alloways have a large boarding house with several bedrooms. You'll be close to schooling at the Academy, and I understand the house is also close to church."

"He goes with me," Seth said.

"Then perhaps you should welcome him," Agnes replied. It must be the heat, she thought, that made her lose her tongue. She was hot, hungry, and tired, and already so homesick she wanted to crumple into a heap of self-pity. *Please, God,* she prayed, *grant me a little patience because I certainly can't summon it myself.*

Seth took a bandana from his pants pocket and wiped his faced with it. He let out a long, audible breath.

"You're right," he said after a pause long enough for Agnes to wonder how a person ever managed to think with birds, insects, and what-have-you making such a constant racket.

Wait. Had she heard him correctly?

"Come on with me, partner," Seth said to Billy in a voice that attempted familiarity. "Folks at the grove will be glad to see you again."

Billy perked up and straightened at the attention. Seconds later, a hawk swooped in to a tree and diverted his attention. He ran over to investigate.

A look of pain was fleetingly visible on Seth's face.

"It's not that I'm not glad to see my nephew," he said to Agnes and nodded toward Billy, who was out of earshot. "For a minute I thought I was seeing ghosts. He looks like a mixture of my brother and sister-in-law…my *dead* brother and sister-in-law. Heck, he could be my brother at that age. Or me."

The hawk flew off, and Billy sauntered back. Agnes put a protective arm around his shoulders and drew him close.

"God gives us strength to bear grief with fortitude," she couldn't help saying. It sounded smug even to her. "Preachiness is not next to godliness," she could almost hear Mother Superior murmur. "We show by example," she would say. It was as if she were standing there next to Agnes.

"Don't talk to me about God," Seth said. He reached down from the horse and beckoned to Billy, who ran and gripped his hand with joy. Seth tousled the boy's hair. "Hop on. I'll help you up." And with quick efficiency, the boy was sitting on the horse. "This is Silver, isn't it?" Billy said with delight. "You still have Silver!"

"Sure do," Seth said. "A right good horse, he is."

Seth looked at Agnes and around the empty space as though he suddenly realized that if he and Billy left, Agnes would be alone. She, meanwhile, was still amazed at the sudden transformation Seth had undergone and still grappling with the dawning understanding that Billy might be as much an orphan as she was.

"Halloooooo, hallooooo!!!" They all looked toward the tree-canopied sand trail and saw—and heard—a squeaky wooden wagon pulled by slow-moving oxen. In the cart were three people—two women and a man who guided the oxen. One of the women held a large parasol over her and the other woman's heads, and the other woman waved at them.

If this was the welcoming committee, a sorry lot it appeared to be. Agnes waved, but her spirits tumbled a little more. She wanted to abandon her charade of self-reliance and run home. But she couldn't. Her return would spell disaster for the orphanage.

She looked around as they waited for cart to inch its way closer. The train tracks ran north and south as far as she could see in either direction. The uneven, sandy trail ran east and west. It emerged toward her from a bend in a forest that was thick with a mix of trees: hickory, oak, and others Agnes had never seen before, including one with large, glossy leaves and giant white flowers. The trail crossed the railroad tracks and continued west into the forest where, in the distance, the sound of gentle lapping wavelets and the tangy scent of river water signaled the location of the St. Johns River mentioned in the circular.

Agnes ached to be back in the fold of St. Isidore's Home, in the midst of the bustle of everyday life. She wanted to be helping the Sisters of St. Francis teach, bake bread, make cookies, and look after the orphans—there were oh so many in need of a loving shelter, home-cooked meals, and the guidance of the Lord. She wanted to check on Polly, to talk with happy Sister Gertrude, to see even grumpy Sister Helen, who always shushed laughing youngsters. She wanted to fix up the small building Mother Superior had said she could live in, the one next to Mary's garden in the convent courtyard, now that she had attained maturity. Agnes bowed her head. *Dear Blessed Virgin Mary, I pray for your intercession. Help me find the strength to do God's will, to follow his path the way you did, even when that path is hot, dusty, and buggy like this one, and so far from home.*

She felt for the Miraculous Medal that she wore on a thin gold chain around her neck, under her shirt, and prayed for strength and fortitude.

Chapter Two

he wagon creaked and rattled its way over the rutted trail and rolled into the clearing. "I remember them! It's the Misses Alloway and Mr. Clyde!" Billy yelled. He slid off Silver and ran toward the wagon. Seth started to back his horse away.

The high-wheeled wagon drawn by the two plodding oxen was bare of decoration but clean and well kept. The driver, Mr. Clyde, was tall and thin and wore denim overalls, a white shirt, and a straw hat. Seated next to him on the plank seat were Agnes's employers and patrons, the Misses Alloway. One was as tall and thin as Mr. Clyde. She had gray hair pulled in a tight bun and spectacles perched far enough down her nose that she could look through them or over them. The other was shorter and plump and had pink cheeks and curly silver hair. While Agnes drooped in her wool outfit, they appeared fresh and comfortable in lighter-weight garments.

The thin woman held the parasol, while the plump one cooled herself with the fan she held in one hand. She waved at them with the other hand.

"Yoo-hoo, are you Miss Foster?" the plump woman called. "Dear me, you must be! We all apologize for our tardiness. Land sakes alive, but it's a warm day today!"

Her words tumbled out one on top of the other as Clyde halted the oxen. Billy waved flies off the animals' backs.

"How come you got oxen instead of horses pulling this, huh?" he said to Clyde. "I remember you, you own the store. You remember me?"

"Sure do," Clyde said. "The young man with all the questions. It's good to see you, son. Things are quiet down here except during your visits, and those're few and far between. And these oxen, well, they're sturdy and dependable for long-haul trips with a lot of folks or luggage in the cart." Agnes saw him glance at her one pitiful bag. The plump woman, meanwhile, cooed over Billy while the thin one welcomed him as one would a young adult.

"Billy, get over here," Seth barked.

"No need to get your feathers ruffled, Taylor," said Clyde before turning his attention to Agnes.

"Pardon me, miss, I'm forgetting my manners. I'm Clyde Williams, owner of Clyde's Mercantile, finest general store in all of Persimmon Hollow..."

"*Only* general store in Persimmon Hollow," said the thin woman in a friendly tone that softened her somewhat stern appearance. Her thin lips curved into a smile.

Clyde cleared his throat but appeared pleased at her attention. "As I was saying, I'm owner of Clyde's Mercantile, and the sometime town mayor of Persimmon Hollow, and the all-around helper to the Misses Alloway. Allow me to introduce Miss Eunice Alloway," he beckoned toward the thin woman, "and her sister, Miss Fanny Alloway. That there fellow over there is Seth Taylor, owner of Taylor Grove. Makes a habit of being unsociable."

"With good reason," said Seth.

Seth had backed up enough to put distance between the little group and himself but was still close enough for conversation. He still sat tall and straight on Silver, but now he held the reins loosely while resting his hands on his thighs. Agnes couldn't help but notice that his hands—and the rest of him—were sturdy and well shaped and that the dark, almost black, hair that brushed his shirt collar was clean. Scuffed boots and denim pants faded at the knees told her he was no stranger to work.

"This isn't the time to start fussing about the past," said Eunice. She put down her parasol, climbed out of the wagon and helped the plumper Fanny do likewise.

"This is hardly a warm welcome for Persimmon Hollow's new teacher," bubbled Fanny. "Welcome, Miss Foster, we're so proud to have you join us."

The Alloway sisters stood close together and spoke like a unified welcoming committee.

"You'll find Persimmon Hollow to be a town of upstanding citizens who have a goal of making our small community the Athens of Florida," Eunice said.

"Our father founded the town on the foundations of God, education, neighborliness, kindness, and...," Fanny continued the thread.

Seth snorted. "Billy, let's go," he said. He pressed his knees against Silver's sides and directed the horse toward the boy.

"Why, Seth Taylor, pay attention to who you are talking to!" said Fanny, but not before Agnes saw compassion cross her face. "It's us, Fanny and Eunice Alloway and Clyde Williams."

"Reckon he's forgotten who his friends are," said Clyde.

Seth ignored them, leaned over and helped Billy up onto the horse again.

"Wow, I forgot how great it is to ride Silver," Billy said. "I swear he's the biggest horse I've ever seen, and the finest, too, aren't you, boy?" He leaned forward and patted Silver's neck as Seth started to lead the horse away. "Maybe coming back down here ain't gonna be so bad after all," Billy said.

"Wait," Agnes blurted out, not ready to let Billy leave with his uncommunicative uncle, even if he was family. "I promised I'd chaperone Billy and…and…well, I almost hesitate to say this, Mr. Taylor, but I'm not quite certain that…I mean…you *did* say you would have preferred more notice about Billy's arrival. Perhaps it would be better if he stayed with me a few nights at the Alloways until you can get things in order."

She turned toward Eunice and Fanny. "Could Billy stay with us until his uncle is more prepared to welcome him? Before you got here, Billy's arrival appeared to be a bit of an imposition on Mr. Taylor."

"Is that so?" said Seth. "You, a stranger, are deciding what I'm to do with my nephew?"

"I promised to look after the boy," Agnes said, determined. "I take my promises seriously."

"I'm sure you do, lady," Seth said.

"We'd love for Master William to join us," gushed Fanny, as she continued to fan herself in the heat. Eunice nodded her agreement.

Agnes forced herself to remain polite even though she wanted to lift Billy off the horse and back into her group's little fold. "Mr. Taylor, it would give Billy time to adjust and give you time to tend to preparations. Please consider the offer."

That wasn't the whole truth. Already she sorely missed the brightness and optimism of the children at the orphanage. She

needed to hear Billy's chatter as much as she believed he needed a
warm and welcome return to Persimmon Hollow. He was so close
in age to Polly.... She thought of her precious daughter-to-be so
many miles away. Were Polly in a similar situation, Agnes would
want a caring adult to step forward for her.

"Mr. Taylor?" Agnes asked, again, for he still hadn't answered.
He continued to say nothing. In fact, he turned Silver and started
heading toward the road.

Clyde took the blade of grass he was chewing out of his mouth
and called to Seth.

"The lady asked you a question, Taylor," he said. "Mind your
manners."

Seth looked over his shoulder. Despite shooting a glance of
annoyance toward Clyde, he reined in the horse.

"I'll mind my manners when she minds her business," Seth said.

"Oh, dear, oh, dear, this is turning into a dreadful welcome,"
fretted Fanny, fanning herself even faster than before. Her cheeks
became pinker and pinker.

"Can't we all get along?" she asked. "Seth, do you need more
time to settle things at the grove? You know how much we love
young William. We're so glad he's returned to us again. It's been,
what, how many years? We'd be happy to..."

"He's returned to me," Seth corrected.

"But are you able to accommodate him?" Eunice asked and
frowned. "I heard at the store that you plan to attend the agricul-
ture fair in St. Augustine. That takes place this week. It wouldn't
be appropriate for Master William to be out at the grove without
you. The Gomezes aren't even there. Lupita told me they were
moving up to Gainesville for a while, to help her sister's family

because of a carriage accident. I understand there were some
serious injuries. She said they could be gone for months."

"Billy will be fine. Tustenuggee's around," Seth said. "A man
values his true friends."

"Even those he doesn't realize he has," said Clyde.

Agnes sighed and made one more attempt.

"Mr. Taylor, I promised your sister-in-law I would look after
Billy. Won't you let him stay in town for a couple of days, so that
we may register him for the new school session? Or would you
be willing to drop him off after church tomorrow?" She had just
remembered it was Saturday.

Agnes hoped the town was big enough to have regular church
services. She had been worried when the advertising circular
noted that the closest Catholic church was in St. Augustine. But
it had stated that Persimmon Hollow's faith communities worked
together to meet needs of all until each congregation could build
its own church.

"My sister-in-law?" Seth asked.

"Yes," she said and wondered why she hadn't thought to
mention that connection earlier. She relayed the train encounter,
while Seth examined the reins and the Alloways and Clyde
exchanged glances.

Seth's gaze locked with Agnes's. She met the intensity of his
green eyes and felt a most surprising tug toward him. His eyes
widened in a way that made her think that he, too, had noticed
something. She felt her cheeks flush, and not from the heat, as she
broke the connection.

"Okay," he said. "Four days. You get him for four days while I
take care of business out of town."

He started talking to Billy in a lower tone.

"I realize you know how to act like a man, but the ladies make a good point about you staying in town. Señora Gomez isn't here to fix meals at the grove or tend to the housekeeping. You might go hungry while I'm gone. Señor Gomez isn't here to keep an eye on you, and Tustenuggee comes and goes. You stay with the Alloways and the new teacher, and I'll pick you up on my way back."

Billy nodded and Seth tousled his hair. "That's my man," he said, and Billy sat straighter at the praise. Agnes sensed, in that moment, that Seth cared about the boy. He just needed some help learning how to show it. Oops. She could almost see Mother Superior tapping her foot with a look of exasperated fondness on her face as Agnes barged into someone else's business...again.

"Lovely," said Fanny. "It's a wonderful resolution. Come, William, help me and Miss Eunice back into the wagon, put Miss Agnes's bag in the back, help her get in, and climb aboard yourself."

Clyde had already stored Agnes's bag in the wagon bed, and he helped Eunice into the front seat. Billy slid off the horse and puffed up with helpfulness as he assisted Fanny into the wagon.

Agnes glanced toward Seth, and their gazes met again for a few seconds before she looked away in confusion. She wasn't used to such bold behavior from men.

Actually, she wasn't used to any behavior from men. She'd had scant individual contact with men except for that brief scary interlude spent away from St. Isidore's Home. She shuddered at the memory. To think all of them at the Home—Agnes especially—had believed that mysterious man's lies about lost relatives and guardianship. Agnes had been so happy to learn she had blood kin that she went willingly with him, with everyone's blessing. He had fooled them all with his false sincerity.

She pushed the memory aside. It was over. God's mercy had protected her. Everyone, well, almost everyone, at the Home had welcomed her back and reminded her that the world is filled with goodness and God's love, despite the efforts of evil men swayed by the devil.

But after prayer, discernment, and discussion with their chaplain, Fr. Tom, they decided Agnes had to temporarily put distance between herself and St. Isidore's Home, for everyone's sake. It was the best way to handle what had become a difficult situation. They feared the imposter would use trickery to legally prove he was related to Agnes and try to claim guardianship, even though she was twenty-five, because she was still unmarried. In Persimmon Hollow, she was out of harm's way and beyond his reach. Her reputation would have time to recover. Gossipy tongues would grow still in due time, said Mother Superior after word leaked out about Agnes's frightful experience. Agnes took comfort from the knowledge that money she earned as a teacher in Persimmon Hollow would help sustain the orphanage.

Soon enough, she'd be able to return and once again teach at the Home's school and find the right man who would help her love little Polly and as many little orphans and natural children as could fit into a future home. Her heart was big enough for them all.

First, though, she had to survive Persimmon Hollow.

* * *

"Who's the girl?" The round man hissed as he peered through the shrubby oak thicket that concealed him and his partner. "I thought you said nobody was gonna be here but the cowboy? And what's up with that kid? Where'd he come from? I don't want to mess around with no job involving no kid. I got my standards."

"Shut up, Barrel," said the other man as he groomed his greasy handlebar mustache with a nervous hand. "Lemme think a minute."

"She's not from around here, I kin tell," Barrel continued, ignoring the smaller, skinny man's order. "Did ya hear her talk? Huh, Lester? Did ya hear her talk? From somewhere else, I kin tell. What's her business with Taylor, huh?"

"I said shut up," Lester Little hissed louder and shifted his crouched position in the thicket behind the station house. "We got wrong information, is all. Didn't see nobody unload fence posts from that train. That means Taylor ain't out here to pick up supplies. And that means he ain't ready to build the fence yet. Gives us more time to figure out how to get our hands on his land."

"Maybe she's a mail-order bride?" Barrel continued to blabber. "Yeah, that's it. I bet he put in for a mail-order bride. I think maybe I'll get me a mail-order bride when I get my share from this job. Ain't that a fine plan?"

Lester spat in disgust and groomed his moustache.

The two men watched from their hiding place as Seth cantered down the road ahead of the wagon and its five passengers: Clyde, the Misses Alloway, Agnes, and Billy. As the travelers moved out of sight, the two men crawled out of the scrub, stood up, and brushed pine needles, sand, and oak leaves off clothing that hadn't seen a washtub in many days.

"I dunno, Lester," said Barrel, who was as round as he was tall. "You didn't say nothing about women and kids. I don't fancy messin' with women and kids. I'm gonna have to raise my fee."

"How many times do I have to tell you to shut up, Barrel?" Lester said. "You'll do what I say. Today is our lucky day. I'm mighty glad to see the young lady and the runty kid, especially if Taylor has a soft spot for 'em. We can use this to our advantage. Yup, a fine day."

* * *

"Oh, dear, the seating arrangements!" Fanny fussed as Agnes settled herself in the plank bed of the wagon as it rattled along the road.

"Clyde, why haven't you a bench seat in the back?" Fanny continued fussing. "Our new teacher is reduced to sitting on the floor. Have you a blanket? One that doesn't smell of horses or oxen?"

"Wasn't fixing to turn my delivery wagon into a barouche," Clyde said, then grinned at Fanny. "You could offer your seat to the lady."

"Really, it's all right," Agnes said, as Fanny made an audible puff of breath. Eunice clucked and said, "Clyde! At our age?" Clyde chuckled.

Agnes was accustomed to cramped spaces. In the orphanage, they doubled and tripled up in rooms, rather than turn away a child in need. She tucked her legs to one side, smoothed her skirt, and leaned against her bag, which she'd pressed up against a wood chest built against the back of the seat. The arrangement kept her as far as possible from the shotgun at the back of the wagon.

"It's too hot for a blanket. So no, thank you," she said and shook her head no to the blanket Billy had pulled from the wood box.

"Oh, you poor child, in all that heavy clothing!" Fanny said. "We will help you dress in a way that accommodates the weather, dear. I am already thinking of one of Eunice's frocks, in particular, that will look lovely with your hazel eyes. Is your hair uniformly that dark chestnut color, dear? From the little I can see peeking out from your scarf, it looks quite lovely. The frock I have in mind will show off the color nicely."

Agnes thanked Fanny. She'd wear anything to get out of the heavy woolens, whether it clashed or complemented. As long as it didn't come with a gun attached. She watched Billy roll the blanket and set it with the farrier's tools, bucket, and coil of rope next to the gun. Mr. Williams also had a rifle at rest across his lap. Seth had had a gun strapped to his belt and one in his saddle. Agnes yearned for the relative safety of a city street. What kind of a place was this that a man needed two guns with him? The circular hadn't mentioned anything about firearms.

Part of her was relieved not to be in a position for conversation. Her doubts grew in proportion to the miles that started to separate the cart and the railway station, where home was as near as the next train north. The wagon creaked and lurched over the uneven sand, bumping her back and forth with enough rhythmic regularity that she began to reconsider the cushion a blanket would offer, even if it did smell like a barn.

"I do apologize for the inconvenience," Fanny said, as she shifted to enable a near face-to-face conversation. "We wanted to bring our carriage, but it's too unsteady for this road after so many weeks without a soaking rain. Oh, look over there, dear! Look on the other side of the pines and palmettos. See how the railroad will soon extend all the way into town. We're excited with the progress. Persimmon Hollow grows bigger each day." She pointed off toward the right of the wagon.

"How nice," Agnes said, as her throat grew drier and her lips parched from the heat and dust. Billy and she had finished the last of the water an hour before reaching the station. Fanny's comment explained the downed trees and piles of shell-studded sand that paralleled the road on the other side of a thin strand of trees. Try as Agnes might, she couldn't muster the effort to say more. The heat felt like a weighted brick that pressed on her chest.

"Pardon my poor attempt at conversation," she choked out. "The trip fatigued me." And the encounter with Seth Taylor had left her more than a little unsettled.

"Oh, you poor girl!" Fanny said. "Hasten, Clyde, please. We must get this child settled."

"Oxen are moving about as fast as oxen generally do," Clyde said. "Git along, Abe and Bet, you heard Miss Fanny." Agnes was glad to see he didn't apply the lash to their backs. The wagon lurched along at the same slow pace. Seth had galloped so far ahead that the dust his horse kicked up settled before they reached it.

"I remember my arrival here. It was a bit of a cultural surprise," Eunice said, as though she had read Agnes's thoughts. "No doubt you'll come to love this town as we do."

"Surely, you will," Fanny echoed.

Agnes stared at the alien landscape as it shifted from the river valley's shady hammock of oaks and hickories to a higher, drier collection of pine trees towering over the same spiky palmetto plants she had seen from the train window. Their stiff, spiny leaves formed a low-growing mound. The scent of warm pine softened the sharp edges of the vista. The buzz of insects and birdsong traveled along with them. As they rounded a bend in the road, the thin tree barrier between the trail and the new rail bed vanished, and the two routes ran close together.

"Uncle Seth says there's Indian bones and old pots and stuff in the shell mounds that the railroad people dig up and use for the rail bed," Billy piped up. "Can't wait to get out here and see what's lying around. Uncle Seth found an eagle carving out here once. Tustenuggee gets mighty upset about the piles getting destroyed. Says they are the resting places of his ancestors. You should see some of the piles, Miss Agnes, out by the river. They're as high as a tree."

"Not everybody's in favor of using the shell mounds, but they're cheap and plentiful," Clyde said. "Doesn't seem fitting, though, to mess with the mounds that contain graves."

"Fanny and I have discussed this more than once," Eunice said. "We certainly have great need for stable road material. But we've invited a scientist from Harvard University to board with us this year or next, depending on his schedule, and give us a scholarly assessment of the historical value of the found artifacts."

Grave-digging. Heat. Insects. *St. Jude, pray for us!* Agnes gazed up into the blue, blue sky and saw thick white clouds floating in lazy peacefulness. She stared as though she expected to find answers. The wagon creaked and bounced, and dried leaves crackled as the wheels rolled over them. A dragonfly alighted on her shoulder for the briefest of moments, and the movement of a pair of bright red cardinals near the treetops captured her attention. A trickle of sweat dripped from her temple. Ahead of her waited a giant unknown. She'd often heard it said that God helps those who help themselves, but what about those in over their heads?

Chapter Three

here it is, Persimmon Hollow," Clyde said, halting the wagon. The pride in his voice made Agnes scramble to a kneeling position. She peered between Eunice and Fanny's shoulders, Billy beside her. The wagon had just inched up a long, almost imperceptible incline that she would have missed but for the way the oxen slowed down even more. From the hilltop view, a collection of buildings set along a ribbon of roads arranged in a grid spread out before her. Clyde and the Alloways beamed like proud parents.

Agnes, for once, was speechless. This was their idea of a town? It looked like pictures she'd seen of frontier settlements of the Gold Rush out West.

"That's the heart of Persimmon Hollow, the main intersection," said Fanny. She pointed toward the center of the cluster of wood buildings.

"The Academy is along the road that runs north and south," Eunice added. "We call it the boulevard." She indicated the sandy road that intersected, at the bottom of the hill, the east-west road they traveled on.

"See, if you look to the left—or north—along the boulevard, you can see the Academy's bell tower mixed in with the pines,"

Eunice continued. "We built the school just north of downtown proper. See it? Four blocks past the intersection."

"Wow, this place sure is bigger than last time I was here," said Billy. He stood up, energized, and started to drum on the side of the wagon.

Agnes thought for a moment he was jesting. *Bigger?* The heart of town was a dirt crossroads. Four blocks of wooden buildings were sprinkled along the north-south boulevard. Two blocks of buildings did the same along the east-west road the cart was on. Beyond them, in all directions, were small homesteads. Most included large lots, even acres, filled with the dark, round trees that resembled the citrus etchings in the advertising circular. In the distance, pine forests surrounded the town in all directions. The treetops whispered in the slight breeze. A row of young oaks made a pretty line up the middle of the main boulevard.

All the homesteads had small, fenced kitchen gardens within the larger boundary fences. The dooryard citrus groves were neat and orderly, with row after row of trees planted the way farms up North had rows of corn or wheat.

"Note all the citrus groves," Clyde said. "People have what's called 'orange fever.'"

"But the town is named after persimmons," Agnes said. "Which trees are persimmons?"

"They're wild, and they grow thick around springs, lakes, and waterways," Clyde said. "They grow out at Taylor's place, by the freshwater spring on his property."

"They make delicious jam," said Fanny. "And are good for fresh eating, too."

More features of town came into focus as Agnes continued

to stare. A few large wooden hotels with wraparound porches and signs out front shared space with the homesteads. Parceland Hotel. Land Inn. Putnam Hotel. Even the hotels had dooryard groves. She saw the Academy's short bell tower and was half-surprised that she didn't see more citrus on the school grounds. The wooden Academy had two stories. It sat atop a gentle rise in the midst of pines with open undergrowth and grasses. Even from this distance, the grounds had a restful and inviting look to them.

"Our father, God rest his soul, planted those oak trees you see in the center of the boulevard, Persimmon Boulevard, all the way through town," Eunice said.

"It gives town a special distinction," added Fanny.

Agnes reached for the rosary in her pocket, glad she'd kept it within easy reach instead of putting it in her satchel. The touch helped her feel connected to a stable foundation as she studied her new, unfamiliar home.

The settlement had an air of neatness about it, despite rough edges. The homesteads were tidy, each with well-tended main house, outbuildings, kitchen gardens, and fruit trees. The air was pure and clean and carried a refreshing scent of pine. Her spirits started to lift. She had had a safe journey and had been received warmly. There were worse places she could be. So what if Persimmon Hollow was a bit smaller than she'd expected. Well, a lot smaller. "O give thanks to the Lord, for he is good; for his steadfast love endures forever."

"Huh?" said Billy.

"Oh, I didn't realize I'd spoken aloud," Agnes murmured.

"She's giving thanks to the Lord for bringing us here safely," Fanny said in such a teacherly and approving manner that

Agnes almost smiled. It was easy to picture the Alloways as
schoolmistresses.

"I can see your education is indeed in need, if you didn't recognize that passage from the book of Chronicles," Eunice added.
"We'll rectify that in short order, Master William."

"Oh, brother," Billy grumbled. Agnes bit her lip to hold in a
laugh. She gave him a slight no-no nod but tempered it with a
grin. She remembered well from St. Isidore's Home that to force-
feed youngsters their lessons wasn't the best way to garner understanding or appreciation of a subject, even one as important as
the Lord's Word.

"Which house is yours?" she asked the Alloways. "And the
citrus trees? They grow everywhere here?"

"The house is right there," Eunice said and pointed to a large,
two-story wooden building that fronted the road at the bottom
of the incline. It had a wrap-around porch on the first floor and
a balcony porch on the second. The house was one building
removed from the main intersection and had one of the largest
yards of any homestead.

Like the other dwellings, it lacked the gingerbread scroll-
work, round turret-rooms, or scalloped shingles so common on
the fancy uptown houses she'd seen back home. This house was
sturdy, simple, and symmetrical, with large windows that were
tall enough for a person to walk through. Curtains rippled in the
breeze at the open windows, but otherwise, there was no sign of
activity. Everything about the house looked neat and clean and
inviting, and Agnes had a sudden urge to get there, climb upstairs
to one of the bedrooms, and rest her head for a long nap.

"It's quiet now," Eunice said. "Our winter boarders and other
winter tourists won't start to arrive for another two months or so.

Yes, citrus trees grow beautifully here, as well as the wild persimmons, and they withstand drought and our sandy soil. Citrus brings in a good cash crop. People grow oranges, grapefruits, lemons, and tangerines."

Clyde put the wagon in motion, and the town grew larger as they neared the buildings. People stepped out on porches or looked up from yard work as the wagon rolled by. More than a few shaded sun off their face with one hand and waved with the other.

"You'll meet everyone this evening, dear," Fanny said. "We've planned a little soiree. Everyone is happy that we have a teacher again."

As they neared the main intersection, a hound dog with floppy ears loped out of an open gate on the property across from the Alloways' house. The sign on the gate said "Clyde's Mercantile," and she saw that the property's main building fronted the boulevard at the main intersection. The dog lumbered toward them and gave a yip of pleasure at Clyde's wagon.

"You still got Lumpy?!" Billy exclaimed. "Oh, boy!" and before anyone could answer, he leapt out of the wagon and greeted the dog, who barked in camaraderie and licked the boy's face. The two ran off together like long-lost friends.

"Master William, we expect you at the house momentarily," Eunice called as the two ran into the mercantile's large yard, which stretched some distance behind the store and included a barn and other outbuildings.

Clyde stopped the wagon in front of the Alloways' house and got out to check the oxen.

"Now that we have a moment's privacy, I want to fill you in about that young boy's uncle, the man you encountered at the railroad station," Fanny said in a lowered voice.

"It's an unfortunate tale," Eunice added as she accepted Clyde's hand and started to get out of the wagon. "We didn't want to mention it in front of William."

"Ladies, where shall I put the luggage?" Clyde said as he picked up Agnes's small bag after he helped her and Fanny to the ground.

"The front room will be fine, Clyde, thank you," Eunice said. Agnes noticed an almost imperceptible softening in her voice as she spoke to the thin man with the lined, leathery face. He nodded and went ahead with her bag and the parasol.

"Come onto the porch," Fanny said to Agnes. "We'll sit for a spell with some refreshment, and then you can rest and freshen up." She patted Agnes's arm and tucked it into hers as she, Eunice, and Agnes headed up the brick walkway to the front steps.

The walkway was edged with short, mounded grass but otherwise the front yard was swept sand except for some flowering shrubs along the fence and a sprinkling of citrus trees.

"The Lord, I'm sure, intervened in Seth Taylor's journey," Fanny said. "The devil came close to having his way with the young man."

Agnes thought of the wary, watchful Seth.

"We didn't want to speak in front of William, particularly because he has grown to resemble his late father," Fanny said. "The likeness is striking."

Clyde came back out and tipped his hat as he passed them.

"I believe I'll call him Billy, not William, which was his father's name and could bring up sharp memories every time it is uttered," Fanny continued. "You should too, Eunice, dear, don't you think?" Eunice appeared to consider the question, then nodded yes before Agnes had a chance to mention that Billy was the boy's preference, too.

"Billy's father was Seth's brother," Fanny said. "I was startled when I saw Billy. I thought I was looking at a man brought back from the dead before the Lord's appointed time. I'm certain the resemblance caused Seth some painful moments when Billy got off the train."

She lowered her voice even more. They had reached the steps and stopped walking. Agnes didn't have a chance to affirm what Seth had said about Billy's appearance before Fanny started to speak again.

"Seth, you know, feels responsible for his brother's death. Oh, it was so tragic, my dear. Tragic. I remember how…"

Fanny fell silent, overcome with emotion, as they climbed the few steps to the porch. Eunice frowned but didn't pick up the conversation. Agnes wanted to know more but managed to keep from asking lest she start to figure solutions for people who might not want them. Her reticence surprised her, and she wondered if Mother Superior's prayers for a guardian angel to help Agnes watch her tongue had finally come to fruition.

"Forgive me, Agnes," Fanny said softly. "I need a few minutes to compose myself."

"That's all right, it's probably not my business, anyway," Agnes said, although she felt it might be, given her promise to watch Billy.

She realized now that Seth had wrestled with memories when they first met at the station house. Her imagination started to conjure scenarios before she caught herself. *How little we ever know of what's in another person's heart and mind,* she thought. She vowed yet again to refrain from instant judgments and from jumping to conclusions before she knew a full story. She remembered how harshly people had judged her before they knew the details of her plight. Here she was, about to do the same to another. *"Do unto others…,"* she reminded herself. She almost wished Seth were near so she could offer an apology. Almost.

The three women crossed the porch, and Agnes sank into one of the wicker rocking chairs. The screen door opened, and a plump, tan-colored woman with a large apron over her gingham dress and a turban over her hair walked out to meet them.

"Praise the Lord, you are finally home," she said to Eunice and Fanny and gave a nod to Agnes. "Miz Bight's ailing Grandmother Phoebe has up and died. Gone home to Jesus."

Eunice let out a moan, and Fanny dropped her fan and pressed her hands to her cheeks. "Oh, Estelle, when did it happen?" she asked.

"Soon after you left here. Parson's wife asks that you please go to the Bight homestead soon as it's fitting for you. Miz Bight is doing poorly, and Parson's wife fears for her well-being. You know Miz Bight's health is poor even in the best of times, and you know how close she was to her grandmother. Don't know how she's going to make do without Miz Phoebe there to help with the little ones."

Fanny grasped Eunice's hand. Agnes felt helpless. She made the Sign of the Cross and said a prayer of repose for the woman's soul.

"We had hoped Phoebe would be with us a little longer," Eunice said to Agnes, and her eyes behind the spectacles shimmered with tears.

"Of course, Estelle, we will go directly," Eunice said to the woman in the turban. "Is there anything prepared that we can bring?"

Estelle nodded. "I fixed a tomato salad, raised some biscuits, and sliced some of the cured ham from the smokehouse. I'll bring them out directly." She disappeared back into the house.

Eunice looked at Agnes. "I regret this, but we must ask you to help. We can't delay burials in this climate. Every hand is needed."

Agnes shook off her fatigue. "Of course," she said. Her earlier, self-absorbed concerns seemed trivial now. "What shall I do?" She rose from the chair and picked up Fanny's fan and gave it to her.

"First, pray. We have to pray," Fanny said and broke into a sob. "And we have to decorate the casket. Someone should make a daisy chain of Spanish needles. That would be pretty. What else is blooming? And food. We'll have to feed the family and other folks who come to help. Sarah Bight is too frail to bear that burden. What about…"

"Estelle has prepared food already," Eunice said, and she placed her arm around Fanny's shoulder. "Didn't you hear her?" Fanny shook her head no.

"Estelle is our cook," Eunice explained as an afterthought to Agnes.

"Oh, dear, the casket!" Fanny said. "Do you think the family needs a casket?"

"I doubt they have one," Eunice said. "Money is tight for them, and I suspect Toby Bight wouldn't have made one while Phoebe was still alive, no matter how near death she came. I doubt he has time to make it now, not if Sarah is ailing."

The Alloways turned as one toward Agnes.

"Agnes, we must go ahead to the homestead. Please go ask Clyde if a pine box has been delivered to the Bights," said Eunice, while Fanny stood beside her and wrung her hands. "If a casket hasn't been delivered, ask him to do so immediately and put the cost on our account."

"And please pick flowers. Spanish needles and others, before you come," Fanny said.

Agnes was glad to have something to do and turned to go just as Estelle came out briefly to give Eunice a cloth bag whose aroma told of its contents.

"We appreciate your willingness to help, Agnes," Eunice said as the three women went down the walkway together and then separated. Agnes heard Eunice and Fanny's voices as they went down the street and she turned toward the mercantile yard. "Her heart finally gave out," she heard Fanny say. "Where is Toby? Has anyone seen him? He was fond of Phoebe, and I'm certain he's sick with worry over Sarah. I wish her melancholy would lift. Pray that this doesn't make matters worse." The conversation faded from earshot as they moved farther away.

Agnes watched sand dust fly about her feet as she crossed the road. She walked around the corner to the front of the mercantile and was surprised to find wooden sidewalks in front of the stores on Persimmon Boulevard. They certainly made it easier to walk. She hurried into the mercantile and almost collided with a man who approached the door from the inside.

"Oh! Pardon me!" she said and then realized she was face-to-face, or rather, eyes to chin, with Seth Taylor. He was mussed with sawdust and was maneuvering a long, upright pine casket on a two-wheeled carrier toward the door.

"Is that…is that…?" Agnes pointed to the box, but her tongue twisted around the words.

"For the Bights' Grandmother Phoebe, yes," he said. "I came over here soon as I heard. Clyde always has a lot of cut lumber, and there was plenty to meet the need. All I had to do was hammer in the nails."

"Thank goodness," she said. "The Alloways say the burial must be done quickly because of the heat. Will you take it to the family? I'm on my way there to help however I can....Oh...!" She realized that, in the haste on the porch, no one had told her the location of the Bight homestead, and she had neglected to ask.

"I have no idea where the family lives," she said. In her confusion, she almost asked Seth if she could go with him. She caught herself before she spoke. She couldn't travel with him alone, without a chaperone. What was she thinking?

"I'm moving this outside, so I can put it into the wagon as soon as Clyde gets back," Seth said. "He went to fetch the parson's wife and children. Parson Pierce rode out to the Bights' in his buggy as soon as he was notified. You can ride with Clyde and the rest of the Pierces. I'd show you myself, but I'm not going."

"Oh, I see," Agnes said and followed him back outside to the quiet street. But she didn't see at all. His refusal to attend perplexed her. They stood in awkward silence and waited for Clyde to return.

"Do you not know the family? Is that why you're not going?" Agnes was surprised that anyone in a town so small would refuse to rally around a neighbor in need.

"I've got my reasons," Seth said.

Let's hope they are good ones, she couldn't help but think. She tried to study him with a side glance without him aware of it.

"What? Never seen a man before?" he asked.

She felt her cheeks flush with embarrassment. To think, this man is Billy's role model. And just where was Billy, anyway?

"Has your nephew come back?" she asked.

"Thought he was with you and the good Misses Alloway, who are so concerned about his moral fiber and upbringing," Seth said.

Agnes ignored the jibe. "We should go look for him. What if he's lost?" She spun around and took in the view in all directions. How dire for a boy to be lost in such wilderness. Worse, even, than being alone on the streets of a city, and that was bad enough.

"We should hurry!" she said, and in her haste put a hand on Seth's arm, then withdrew it with dismay at her boldness.

Seth shook his head and ignored her flustered movements. "Billy's all right. He knows every inch of this place and most everyone in it. He's young, but he's visited back and forth enough to learn his way around. Anybody he doesn't know, he will by day's end. Clyde said he ran off with Lumpy, who'll guard him with his life. Billy knows the surrounding woods and knows how to survive in them. I taught him well over the years."

His calm certainty in the boy's skills lessened Agnes's anxiety somewhat. Still...a child alone...

"He's probably snacking on citrus or eating in somebody's kitchen, playing the hungry fool," Seth said and actually chuckled. "This isn't the big city, miss. Folks watch out for young'uns here."

"Exactly," Agnes said. "Helpful neighbors. That's just as it should be. That kind of neighborliness is why everyone should attend the burial service. It's only right that..."

"Too much praying for me," Seth interrupted.

This time, she made no pretense of not staring. "Sometimes, prayer is all we have," she blurted out. "At all times, it's the best thing we have."

"Then you best do enough for both of us," he said.

The sound of the wagon reached them in the quiet of the fading afternoon. Their pained conversation fell short as Clyde pulled up with a middle-aged woman, a boy, and three older children in the wagon. Agnes was too surprised to continue talking, anyway. Not believe in prayer? She couldn't imagine life without it.

Yet part of her began to sense what the lady of the train had told her—that underneath the aloof, scruffy exterior, Seth was a good man. He certainly was an attractive one. He intrigued her. His actions betrayed concern for the same people he distanced himself from. Why? Why push people away? *Not your business,* she told herself. *And don't go making it your business either,* she added. She didn't want any closeness with a man of little faith. *Dear God, help him find his way out of the wilderness he's in,* she prayed. She added him to her prayer list, a nice safe place for him to be. The last thing she needed was a personal entanglement in Persimmon Hollow.

Chapter Four

*S*eth loaded the casket into the back of the wagon, took off his hat, and used it to dust the sawdust off his pants and shirt. Then he put it back on, raised his arm in a half-wave, half-dismissal, and went back into the store without saying good-bye.

Clyde watched him go but said nothing. No one spoke for a few moments.

"Never will figure out that man," Clyde muttered. "Miss Agnes, I'd like you to meet Parson Pierce's family," he said and indicated the slim, middle-aged woman with gray hair piled atop her head and the four young Pierces who appeared to range from childhood to young adult.

"A pity we can't meet under more pleasant circumstances," Mrs. Pierce said with a friendly nod. "Welcome to Persimmon Hollow." In her lap, she balanced a large bowl covered with a dish towel. Agnes caught a whiff of fresh-baked bread from the wrapped bundle a teenage girl held. The young woman also smiled and nodded, and her three brothers tipped their hats.

"The Alloways have gone on ahead," Agnes said. "May I ride with you, or is the house within walking distance?"

"Over yonder a few blocks, past the Land Inn, which is the large building you can see about two blocks down from the mercantile yard," Clyde said, pointing. "We passed it coming into town."

"I'll walk," Agnes said. "That way I can gather flowers for the decorations Miss Fanny mentioned. Shall I look for anything in particular?"

The Pierces and Clyde sat silently. "Afraid none of us is much in the flower department," Clyde said.

"Not at this time of year, at least," Mrs. Pierce said. "The peonies and lilacs I grew back home don't fare well here, and even the Johnny-jump-ups and petunias bloom only in winter. You could look for some suitable grasses and perhaps any wildflowers that may be flowering."

Agnes waved them off. The walk alone would give her time to collect her thoughts. Surely she'd find something in bloom along the way. The thirst she'd ignored in the wake of the crisis struck at her. She toyed with the idea of asking the Alloways' cook for a drink but discarded it. She didn't feel at home there yet. The mercantile would offer something. She weighed the need for a beverage against the idea of another encounter with Seth Taylor inside the store. Her thirst won. Maybe he'd already left out the back door. She could hope.

The interior of Clyde's store was cool and dim, and a welcome respite from the outdoor heat. She wondered if there was a Mrs. Williams and whether she would be at the counter. Instead, Billy was there. Lumpy, who was plopped on the floor next to him, thumped his tail in greeting as Agnes neared the counter.

"Can I help you, Miss Agnes?" Billy got up from the stool behind the counter and addressed her with importance. "I'm minding the store for Mr. Williams while he's gone."

"I'm so glad to see you!" she said. "I was worried you'd gotten lost."

"Around here?! Nah." He laughed. "Did you hear that, Lumpy? She thinks we got lost." He looked at Agnes and beamed. "We was just visiting with folks."

"We *were* visiting," she corrected.

He scrunched up his face. "Uh huh," he said.

She laughed. "Never too early to start. I *am* the new teacher."

"Yeah, but school doesn't start for a while yet," he pointed out. "What can I get you here right now?"

"Just some cool water, please," Agnes said and smiled at him.

"Sure! There's a well out back. I'll show you." He and Lumpy led the way through the store and out the rear door into the back yard. Seth stood at the well, but he stepped back when he saw them, looked away, and started to adjust the harness on his horse.

The well water was close to being warm, but it was wet and refreshed her. She remembered to be thankful for the simple gifts in life.

"Plenty of things are in bloom this time of year, if you know what to look for," Seth said, without turning around to face them.

Surprised, Agnes spit out a spray of water before she could lift a hand to cover her mouth.

"You eavesdropping?" It was as much a question as an accusation.

At that, Seth turned around and faced her. "It's hard to ignore nearby conversation when the only other sounds are cicadas, mockingbirds, and blue jays," he said and fixed an unsmiling gaze on her. "I don't make a habit of intruding in other folks' conversations. I like it just fine when people stay out of each other's business."

"Then why get involved in this?" Agnes asked.

"Because I heard you ask what kind of plants to seek. You can find plenty blooming. Most don't resemble what folks are used to seeing. Florida plants are different."

She swallowed. Did she stay and find out more about Florida plants or end the conversation with this man who seemed to harbor a grudge against the town, or at least against the people she'd encountered so far? But he had jumped to build the casket. An embittered man wouldn't have done so.

Flowers, Agnes decided, were safe territory.

"I'd appreciate if you would point out some blooms to me," she said.

He nodded and retied Silver's rope to the fencepost after untying it during their brief conversation. "We can start right here in the yard," he said. "Look up against the fence posts." He nodded toward the far corner, and they started to walk toward it, trailed by Billy and Lumpy.

"Uncle Seth, you gonna show her spiderwort and Spanish needles?" he asked. "What about the Cherokee bean? Those flowers are something else!"

"Spiderwort only blooms in the morning," Seth said, as he pointed to thick green flower stalks that emerged from grasslike clumps of strappy green leaves. The small flower heads atop the stalks were closed.

He squatted in front of a plant with small daisylike flowers. Clusters of it grew all along the fencepost. "Spanish needles sprout up everywhere," he said and unsheathed a knife strapped to his belt. He cut clumps of the plant and handed them to Agnes.

"Thank you," she said, touched by his gesture but again perplexed by his refusal to participate in the town's shared sorrow.

He cared enough to help her do her part, and he had thought of—
and acted upon—burial needs before anyone else had.

Seth stood up and scanned the horizon. "As you go past the
Alloways' place, cut some of the purple blooms off those tall ironweed shrubs just inside their fence."

"I'll help!" Billy said, and he unbuckled a smaller knife in imitation of his uncle.

"What about the store?" Agnes asked him.

"Oh, yeah," he said.

"I'll stay for a while," Seth said. "But there's nothing to worry
about. None of the locals will shop during the service, and tourist
season hasn't started yet. Billy, go with the lady and make sure she
gets to the Bight homestead."

"Yes, sir," he said, and he puffed out his chest and stood a bit
taller.

"See if you can find any elderberry flowers for her, too," Seth
added.

"You mean the white stuff Tustenuggee uses to make wine?"
Billy asked, and Seth nodded in affirmation.

"Who's Tustenuggee?" Agnes asked. It was the third time she'd
heard the unusual name mentioned.

"A friend," Seth said, cutting Billy off from giving any further
explanation in his stead. "You have a good day, miss," he added
and touched a hand to the brim of his hat before going into the
store.

Patience, Agnes, patience, she told herself and pressed her lips
together to stifle questions that were in danger of arising. She said
a quick prayer for strength to improve her weak spot, her lack of
patience.

* * *

Trailed by Billy, she arrived at the Bight house with an armload of feathery purple ironweed flowers and branches of tiny Spanish needle clusters. Somber men and women—all strangers to her—milled around on the porch. They turned and watched as she and Billy proceeded up the raked sand path. Dusk had started to fall, and she was beginning to feel the strain of the long, arduous day. The train ride seemed years ago.

Fanny pushed her way through the group and emerged with arms opened wide. Her pink cheeks were mottled and her eyes rimmed with puffiness. "Bless you, child, and here it is your first day in town," she said. She pulled Agnes into a warm embrace and then stepped back but kept an arm around her waist. She turned them both toward the porch and spoke to the assembled group.

"This is Miss Agnes Foster, the Academy's new teacher. She just arrived in town today."

Agnes heard a chorus of how-dos and saw people nod hello and lift hats, but the smiles were strained and eyes were sad. The pall of the death hung heavily on the gathering.

"Let's place the flowers in a bucket," Fanny said and then beckoned toward Billy, who had been quietly backing away in the direction of the other youth at the gathering. "Fetch us some water first, Billy, before you go anywhere," Fanny said. She inspected the bouquet of purple flowers interspersed with tiny, white, daisy-like petals with yellow centers. "You did well, dear," she said.

"Seth Taylor pointed out the plants," Agnes said.

The murmur of low talk on the porch fell as quiet as though a heavy blanket had been thrown over the group. Fanny opened and closed her mouth, as though she thought better of whatever she meant to say. The silence felt louder than the buzz of insects in the surrounding trees.

"But he ain't here now, is he?" a man on the porch said loudly. "Afraid to show his face?"

Billy frowned as he walked back to Agnes and Fanny from the cistern. He handed Fanny a wooden bucket of water, and she and Agnes busied themselves putting the plants in it. Agnes glanced up just in time to see a mutinous expression on the boy's face as he clenched and unclenched his fists.

"My Uncle Seth is not afraid of nothing and...," Billy started to yell. Fanny and Agnes each instinctively placed a hand on his arm. A woman on the porch did likewise to the man who had just spoken.

"Run along and join the other boys now, okay?" Agnes said to Billy, pointing to the corner of the yard where other youngsters were clustered.

Fanny thanked him for his help with the water and gave him a hug. Over his head, her glance met Agnes's. It was troubled.

Billy had only taken a few steps when a boy about his own age darted out of the crowd and ran toward him. "I know all about your uncle!" he taunted. "Your uncle is the reason a man died. He's dangerous. I know!"

"No, he's not! You don't know nothing!" Billy yelled back, and within seconds, fists flew, and the two started to fight in the sandy yard. "Let him be! He just got back to town!" hollered another boy of similar age. "Who cares!" said another. And less than a minute after the first boy yelled, every young man under courting age was involved in the melee.

A number of the adults started to talk at once, and some of the men stepped off the porch and ordered the boys to stop. "Boys,

boys!" cried Fanny to no avail. "Such behavior. Oh, mercy!" She raised up her hands in despair.

Agnes was about to step in, herself, despite the shock of having heard the words "reason a man died," when hoofbeats came to a halt in front of the yard just as she wiped her hands dry on her apron.

"That's enough, Billy, boys," Seth said from just outside the gate. "Show some respect for the occasion."

Statues wouldn't have looked more still and quiet than every person in the yard and on the porch.

All gazes were upon Seth as he slowly got off Silver, tied the reins to an oak limb, and entered the yard.

Parson Pierce recovered first.

"Thank you for coming," he said and stepped forward to shake Seth's hand.

The parson glanced over the entire assembly before he started to speak. "Let us heed the words of the prophet Micah in chapter six verse eight," he said. "He has told you, O mortal, what is good; and what does the Lord require of you but to do justice, and to love kindness, and to walk humbly with your God?"

"We who are gathered here today are humbled in the face of God's will," the parson said. "Let us remember that humility and not presume to judge."

Amen, Agnes said to herself. She knew what it was like to bear the brunt of an unjust accusation. She hoped Seth was guilty of nothing more than some ill manners. But what was that boy's comment about? She turned to Fanny. "Seth, dangerous? Who died? Was he involved?"

"Yes…and no…the truth is, Seth was in the wrong place at the wrong time," Fanny whispered with vehemence. "But he'd played with the devil in the past, and it caught up to him."

She heard Eunice walk up and let out a hard breath. "Certain men, not of this town, framed Seth," she said in a low voice. "They said he sold tainted, home-brewed spirits to a hobo passing through. The man died. Seth was charged with murder and thrown into jail."

Fanny opened her mouth to speak, but Eunice gave her a glance of warning. "Save the rest for later," Eunice murmured. "Our new teacher has had a trying day."

People shuffled about, and some glanced at Seth as though they wondered how and if to approach him.

"We hope this will be the first of many times you join in town life again, my son," Parson Pierce said.

"I mean no disrespect when I say I'm not here because of you or the town, Parson," Seth said. "I'm here because someone reminded me that it's fitting to pay respects to the departed, no matter what the arguments of the living." He spoke to the parson, but his gaze rested on Agnes. The man had actually listened to what she'd said at the mercantile. Her surprise must have shown because his lips almost curved into a smile of acknowledgment.

Fanny caught the exchange, said "my, my" under her breath, and squeezed Agnes's hand.

Seth walked off toward the outskirts of the crowd. Agnes watched as he sought and then started speaking to Clyde.

"Let's bring these flowers inside, shall we," said Eunice in her brisk, no-nonsense voice. Everyone seemed relieved at the diversion. It was time to stop the foolishness and get back to the sad business of the gathering.

* * *

Fanny, Eunice, and Agnes rearranged the flowers after they got inside. Agnes noted how much cooler the house was compared to the heavy dusk outdoors. The closed casket was propped on a door-board set across the backs of chairs in the parlor. The chairs that lined the wall were full. Some of the mourners cried, others sat in quiet reflection, others moved their lips in prayer. Even the children in the house were subdued. Agnes thought of Polly and her little orphanage charges so far away. How she longed to be with them.

She walked over and knelt beside the casket, made the Sign of the Cross, bowed her head, and said a Hail Mary and the Lord's Prayer for the soul of the beloved grandmother. She asked God to offer healing and mercy to the grieving family.

When she finished, she stood up and saw that Eunice had positioned a small table next to the casket. Fanny placed the bucket of flowers on the table. The three women stepped back together.

"I'd like to pay my condolences to Mrs. Bight," Agnes whispered. Fanny and Eunice nodded and guided her through a connecting door to the room behind the parlor. A young woman lay asleep, the picture of exhaustion.

"Everyone questions whether to wait until she awakens to do the service or to go ahead and do it and spare her more grief," Fanny whispered.

"Lay my grandmother's body to rest," the ghost on the bed said in a voice that was barely audible. "I can hear everything from here, but I need to stay abed."

They hurried to her bedside. Fanny replaced a cloth on the young woman's head with one that she dipped in the water in the washbasin on the bedside table. "Whatever you want, Miss Sarah," she said. Agnes impulsively took one of Sarah's hands in her own.

"I know you don't know me," Agnes said, "but I want you to know my prayers are with you and your family. Your grandmother is with God in heaven."

"Yes," said the woman, and tears trickled out of her closed eyes. "I know, but I can't help but wish God had seen fit to let her stay a little longer with us here on earth. She was such a wonderful.... You know, she raised me." She choked on her words.

Agnes's stomach churned. Maybe she shouldn't have said anything. The woman seemed one step from the grave herself. How long would it take her to learn the virtue of patience, of measuring her words before speaking? She was already twenty-five years old. Would she never learn?

Eunice brushed the girl's hair back on her forehead. "You get some more sleep now, Sarah," she said. The woman had indeed fallen asleep even as Eunice spoke to her.

Parson Pierce came to the doorway, Bible in hand. "I over-heard," he said. "Let's all gather in the parlor. I'll conduct the service inside, and then we'll move to the burial site out where Toby and the others prepared the grave."

People crowded into the parlor. It was close, and Agnes felt the sadness all around her. Her stomach remained unsettled, and she felt faint. The day's rigors, the lengthy travel, arrival in a strange place, heat, a jumble of new people, homesickness, the sorrow of a death in the community, all combined to take their toll. Perspiration dripped down her forehead, and the scarf suddenly seemed knotted too tightly. A headache attacked with a quick, sharp jab. The room started to spin, and pinpricks swirled in front of her vision. She felt jostled in the crowd. Just as her knees began to weaken, a firm hand propped up her elbow. Gratefully, she leaned back against a stalwart pillar that turned out to be Seth Taylor.

"I saw the signs of a heat spell coming on," he said as he steadied her.

She mouthed the word "thanks" at him. Her eyes felt heavy. She closed them and collected her wits. She wondered how he had shown up by her side at the moment of need but was too weary to give it much thought.

"Dearly beloved," Parson Pierce began. Then he read Romans 8:14, "For all who are led by the Spirit of God are children of God."

"God has embraced this good woman and called her home to him. She is a child of God, led by his Spirit, and it is not ours to question God's intent, but to put ourselves into his hands and accept his will. She lived a full life on earth and is now with our Lord and Savior."

Sarah's sad words echoed in Agnes's head as she listened to the parson recite the truths she believed. Still, it was difficult. She remembered how hard it was to lose little ones at St. Isidore's Home and to say goodbye to elderly sisters as they drew their last breaths on earth. But they had had the benefits of medical care and had received the sacrament of extreme unction. Would this woman have lived longer if a doctor had tended her? Did anyone give her last rites in the absence of a priest? Agnes didn't know if Phoebe was Catholic or not, but she knew from the service that she had accepted Jesus and that the community did the best it could to prepare her soul to meet the Lord. Agnes was learning a sudden, sharp lesson about the sacrifices necessary to create a new town out of a wilderness. She wasn't in a big city anymore, reading an advertising circular that offered glowing testimony about the land, soil, citrus, and community of Persimmon Hollow. This place truly was a frontier, and she was now part of it.

She thanked God for her blessings and reminded herself again that her mission in Persimmon Hollow was a straight path before her. One step at a time, she'd make it.

"Let us join hands," the parson said.

Fanny, who stood on one side of her, grasped her hand. Seth, on the other side of her, kept his hands clasped on his Stetson hat, firmly in front of him. On the far side of him stood Billy, who tugged on him, freed a hand off the hat, and linked his slightly smaller hand into Seth's larger one with a look of determination on his face.

Agnes was not so emboldened, but she didn't want to be the break in the chain of connection. *We are all brothers and sisters*, she thought as she steeled herself and tapped his arm. She gave him a questioning look, half raised her hand, and saw in response a muscle clench in his jaw. But he placed his Stetson under his arm and then reached for her hand. It felt strong and protective.

A girl who appeared a little older than Polly stepped to the center and led a chorus of "Nearer My God to Thee." Seth remained silent, but everyone else sang. Through their voices, Agnes sensed both the heartfelt emotions of people gathered in a tight circle of unity and God's protection against the harsh realities of the world.

Chapter Five

*H*ow come so many people gave us funny looks?" Billy asked as the small group trudged back to the Alloways' under a dark sky shining with stars. He slapped a mosquito on his arm. Agnes shooed one away from her face.

Agnes had questions aplenty, too, but was too bone-weary to ask them. The sadness of the funeral, the tensions that surfaced, Seth's story, and the heat all sapped her. Had she not forced herself to eat after the service, she was sure she would have buckled under by now. The zipper cream peas—so new to her—had had a meatiness that nourished. The sweet potatoes were hearty and flavorful. Even so, they were all she had managed to sample despite the array of food.

"I'm not sure, Billy," she said, and his small face tightened. "I don't fully understand it myself."

"Well, that man and those boys sure was mean about my uncle," Billy said. "Uncle Seth ain't dangerous, and he didn't kill nobody."

"*Were* mean, not *was*," Agnes said automatically, "*not* dangerous, and he didn't kill *anybody*." She prayed her words were true, beyond the corrected grammar.

Behind them, Eunice and Fanny remained silent. Clyde, who had stabled his tired horse earlier and walked back to meet them, held aloft a lighter-knot torch to show the way. He cleared his throat but also said nothing. Seth wasn't with them. He had left the Bights' immediately after the burial, even before the women had started to serve food and beverages.

"Uncle Seth is better'n any of them," Billy muttered.

"That's right. He's a good man, son," Clyde said. "Some folks don't know it."

"And you heard the parson warn others about passing judgment," Agnes added.

The scowl on Billy's face deepened in the shadows of the torchlight. "Yeah, I guess," he said.

They walked the rest of the way lost in their own thoughts.

"Bless her, Estelle stayed and kept a lantern lit for us," said Fanny as they approached the Alloway house. The dim glow that lit the front room of the darkened house was a welcome beacon. Within minutes, they were clustered in the parlor. Estelle came to greet them and bid them good night at the same time. Silence settled on the room in the wake of the door she closed. Shadows slanted off the sofa, sitting chairs, piano, and fireplace, and the kerosene lantern light on a side table flickered in the hint of a breeze that came through the open windows.

"Reckon I'll take my leave," Clyde said. He clutched his hat and stood awkwardly by an end table as the others collapsed into seats. The atmosphere was as gloomy as the shadowed room. "You ladies going to be all right?"

They nodded their thanks as he left. Billy's eyes closed, and his head started to nod.

"Billy, come, I'll show you to the sleeping porch upstairs," Eunice said, and he sat up straight, awakened. She took him by the hand. "This way, son."

Fanny and Agnes sat in quiet companionship as the hoots of owls, croaks of frogs, and other night sounds filled the silence. Agnes cast about for a way to ask the question that hung in the room more thickly than the tropical night air.

Her eyes had just started to flutter closed when Eunice returned. She and Fanny glanced at each other and then at Agnes. Fanny picked up a fan from the top of the piano and flipped it open.

"Oh, dear..." she fretted. "What shall we...my goodness, when I think about it, there's no good way...how shall we tell..."

"By getting right to the point," said Eunice. She began to pace back and forth between the piano in the corner and the sofa between the windows. Fanny alternately fanned herself and rubbed her hands together.

"Please," Agnes said. "If this is too difficult to discuss, perhaps it's best left for another time."

"No, you need to know, lest you hear more rumors and untruths from others," Eunice said.

"Seth Taylor has spoken more and shown his face more in town in the past several hours than in the past several years," Fanny said. "I believe that is due partly to your arrival. During Billy's previous visits, he stayed at the grove but ran around town without his uncle."

Eunice sat down in the rocking chair and scooted it forward in front of the sofa so that she faced Agnes. She sat tall and erect, with her hands clasped in her lap. Fanny, next to Agnes on the couch, fanned and fanned.

"Let me put this delicately but succinctly, Agnes," said Eunice. "Fanny and I have known Seth Taylor since the day we first stepped foot in what was to become Persimmon Hollow. Never once have we doubted his sincerity, his uprightness, his good heart, or his moral fiber."

But..., Agnes thought. There is always a "but." Better to find out now. She couldn't deny her interest in Seth. Was she attracted to him? Maybe. She wasn't sure she could describe exactly how she felt. She had had little interaction with men. She'd been with the Sisters of St. Francis since she was an infant. They said they'd found her in a basket on the orphanage doorstep. They had raised her and had taught her about Jesus and the Virgin Mary, St. Joseph, St. Francis, St. Clare, and all the other saints. They had taught her the *Catechism,* the Latin responses at Mass, and how to live in God's footsteps. But they hadn't taught her anything about men, except to never be alone with one until marriage.

Eunice drew in a breath. "The long and short of it is that Seth was accused of..."

"It all happened when we were back up North with our dear parents, God rest their souls, and so we weren't here when the actual event took place, but mercy me, it was not something I ever believed, not for one minute," Fanny interrupted, talking so fast Agnes almost couldn't keep pace.

Fanny leaned back with a huff. Eunice gave her a look of exasperation. "As I was saying, Agnes, Seth was accused of being the man who distilled and sold poisoned spirits to an unfortunate transient. The man had stumbled into town already under the influence and apparently demanded to be given spirits. The man, unfortunately, died after drinking this particular liquor."

Agnes gulped to swallow her shock.

"Such evils are hard to fathom," Agnes said, her lips dry. She couldn't quite fit the story she heard with the image of Seth she had already started to develop.

"It gets worse," Fanny whispered and leaned toward Agnes.

Eunice stood up again and paced. "It seems Seth was immediately accused, by a newcomer who claimed he was a witness. Seth was incarcerated in the next town until the circuit judge arrived. We have no jail or jailer in Persimmon Hollow—we've never had a need. The town with the jail is over an hour away by horse and buggy. While Seth was in jail, a fire broke out at his family's grove. It killed his brother and sister-in-law. Miraculously, Billy—who was only a toddler at the time—survived."

"How awful," Agnes cried and pressed her hands to her cheeks. *Dear Mary, pray for Seth, for Billy, for their entire family.* "It sounds like the trials of Job."

"Yes, and from the start we had our suspicions about the word of the man who accused Seth," Eunice said, frowning. "The man conveniently had the jail-town's marshal nearby, while our sheriff was on a hunting trip. The accuser, by the way, left town soon after the incident. Seth had been on the wrong path when he was much younger, but he had straightened up and was a responsible young man at the time the incident occurred. Not only were we suspicious about the charge, we also had questions about whether the fire was an accident."

"Yes," said Fanny, breathlessly. "Dear, how could a small child survive a fire that killed adults?"

"Unless someone interfered with or harmed the adults first," Eunice said.

Agnes's lips parted, but no words emerged. Eunice held up a hand to stop Fanny, who seemed ready to launch into more detail.

"We weren't here at the time," Eunice said. "We don't presume to know; we only have suppositions. There were certain unsavory elements in the settlement before it became Persimmon Hollow. Seth and his family's homestead claims predate our town. We also feel it prudent to note that his family is Catholic. There was an element of anti-Catholic prejudice against the Taylors and the Mexican family that settled with them on the property. We don't know if that played a role. We're relieved to be able to say such prejudices have no home in Persimmon Hollow."

What a nightmare, Agnes thought. *Could this story get any worse?* She wasn't sure she wanted to know. "What happened when the judge arrived?" she asked, while simultaneously putting up an internal wall of resistance. She knew she was somewhat naïve, but she understood enough to determine that spirits, suspicious deaths, jail, and a possible arson added up to someone she needed to keep her distance from. Furthermore, Seth had as much as disavowed his faith when he told her not to talk to him about God. Hadn't he also disparaged prayer, too? She decided Seth Taylor added up to nothing but trouble.

"The judge threw out the case, in part because of the absence of the accuser and in part because of testimony from Seth's Indian friend, Tustenuggee," Eunice said. "But not before most people in the area convicted Seth in their hearts by being quick to judge. Some were also upset the judge accepted the word of an Indian."

"Seth got his freedom back," added Fanny. "But his brother had been all the family he had left."

"It happened ten long years ago," Eunice said. "But Seth seems to remember it as though it were yesterday."

* * *

From what Agnes could see by the dim light of the candle, the Alloways had fixed her bedroom prettily. The covers were turned down on the bed, and the sheets smelled like fresh air and roses. All she wanted was sleep; all she could think of was the story about Seth. She slid the scarf off and shook her head to let her hair unwind down her back. She undressed, slipped on the light cotton nightgown the Alloways had placed on the back of a chair for her, knelt and said her prayers, and crawled into bed. Mosquito netting draped down over her from a thin bar suspended above the bed. So different, but not uncomfortable. Lying there, she felt like she was wrapped in a transparent cloud.

Despite her exhaustion, she tossed and turned, listening to the buzz and croak of night creatures. She was still awake when the grandfather clock chimed once. The day's many happenings ran through her mind, and Seth's story lingered.

Something hooted so close to the window that she sat up with a start. She hugged the nightgown to her throat until she heard a hoot in reply and realized what the first sound had been. After her eyesight adjusted to the night's darkness, she saw the silhouette of an owl in a branch of the tree just outside the window. Her heartbeat slowed. How silly to let an owl startle her so. But she was accustomed to hearing different sounds at night: the creak of buggy wheels on cobblestones, noises of rag pickers and night soil collectors as they went about their duties, distant shouts, and the clanging bells of police wagons.

Most of all, she was accustomed to the whispers and patter of little feet in the orphanage's girls' ward. She used to help the smallest say their prayers before bed. Her own tiny bedroom had been across the hall from them, and she'd always been nearby when nightmares or sleepwalking disrupted sleep. Here, it was quiet and still but for the noises of nature outside, and the creaks and sounds of the large house. The other guest rooms in the boarding house were empty. Agnes wished the winter visitors would arrive so she wouldn't feel so alone.

The words of Mother Superior came to her, as though she herself had suddenly arrived in Persimmon Hollow: "God is always with you. No one is alone who has Christ in her heart."

Agnes closed her eyes and eased herself down again. Sometimes God felt far away, and right now was one of those times. Everything had happened so fast. One day she was fine, the next in the middle of a real nightmare, and shortly after was on a train to the Florida frontier. She thought of Polly and the other little ones, of the sisters, chaplain Fr. Thomas Camps, the staff members, and the parish women who helped when needed. The sisters, especially, had taught Agnes right from wrong and sheltered her from the world's evils until darkness walked right into the orphanage. She sighed and rolled over. Still, sleep eluded her. The clock chimed two times.

She finally sat up again and hugged her knees to her chest. Mother Superior was correct. No one is ever alone who has Christ in her heart. Agnes searched her memory for Scripture passages she had come to savor through the years for the peace they brought and wisdom they contained. Galatians 5:22–23 came to mind: "The fruit of the Spirit is love, joy, peace, patience, kindness, generosity, faithfulness, gentleness, and self-control."

Kind, decent people had welcomed her to Persimmon Hollow with open arms. It was up to her to give back to them to her fullest capacity, as she had promised to do. Her loved ones at the orphanage were tucked in her heart. Love made hearts grow bigger, not smaller. "And now faith, hope, and love abide, these three; and the greatest of these is love." She whispered the words of First Corinthians 13:13 aloud and felt a warm breeze wash over her.

The moon had risen high, and moonlight spilled through the window. Its pale glow illuminated the plank floor, wood bedstead, washstand, cane-seat chair, dressing table, and fireplace surround and mantel. She stared as though seeing them for the first time. She appreciated the gentle touches that made the room seem homey: the lace-edged runner on the dressing table, flowers painted on the washstand pitcher and basin. Someone had devoted many hours to sew the star-patterned quilt she rested under.

Another breeze rippled through the lace curtains at the open windows, and Agnes smelled the rich, earthy scent of approaching rain. Soon, light raindrops tapped on the house's metal roof, the breeze grew brisk, and the temperature dropped. The raindrops beat a steady rhythm on the roof. The last thing she remembered was a tiny teardrop that slid down her cheek.

* * *

My Dearest Polly,

The Misses Alloway are the kindest, nicest ladies. I know they would take to you in a minute. They have spent the last few days giving me a tour into every corner of these strange new surroundings. There is so much new to me that it helps me forget my homesickness for you and everyone at St. Isidore's Home.

The people here come from New York, Kentucky, Michigan, the Carolinas, England, even the West Indies—you'd best look up West Indies in your geography primer. Everyone has what's called "orange fever." Even the most decrepit homestead has a stand of citrus trees, and the finer properties have acres upon acres of the glossy, globelike trees, all with dark- to light-green buttons of fruit hanging in the foliage. Some already show orange color. I'm told that most of the fruit ripens from October to March, and that all a person has to do for a sweet treat is walk outside the door and pluck a tangerine or an orange or a grapefruit off a tree. Imagine that! It's end of August now, so I won't have to wait too long to try.

Each homestead also has a large plot where vegetables grow, even now during the hot, hot weather of this region. It's hard to believe it's almost September. It seems more like it does at home on a hot July day. Close your eyes and imagine if each of the large apartment buildings in the city were to have its own vegetable garden full of the good foods that come from the soil. Imagine a few of the residents have milk cows, too, that live near the gardens.

I'm told that many tourists visit Persimmon Hollow in winter and early spring because the air is good for tubercular lungs. Right now the hotels and the Alloways' boarding house and other boarding houses are quiet, with only a few newcomers here to test the waters of a new life, like me.

Another new person is a young man about your age. He has returned to live here. His name is Billy, and you would like him very much. He is one of the students I will teach at the Academy.

Everyone here is friendly and hard-working. The entire town is about the size of our downtown shopping district.

There is an excitement here about the growth of a new town, but it is not an easy task. Hard work, neighborliness, and, above all, faith in God make up daily life here. Remember the brochure we looked at, the one that explained everything about Persimmon Hollow? Well, every word was true.

Town is still small, though, and there is no Catholic church. I don't know enough people yet to know how many share our faith—or if anyone here does.

She stopped writing and thought of what she'd learned about Seth's family. Yes, there were other Catholics here, or at least one other Catholic, even if he didn't practice. Best not to write about Seth. Best not to think about Seth. She dipped her pen in ink and continued the letter.

People of different beliefs gather together in the same meeting house to worship the Lord each week. No one group has enough money yet to build a church. Many ladies of different denominations bit by bit raise money for houses of worship, but money is hard to come by here.

I was surprised at first to see how well everyone gets along. The Alloways reminded me that the town was founded for faith and education. One of Miss Fanny Alloway's favorite sayings is that "all of you are one in Christ Jesus," from the book of Galatians chapter three verse twenty-eight.

These are not empty words here. I learned that a priest from Palatka—a town north of here—travels to all mission areas like this as often as he can. I will try to get word to him. Ministers of the Protestant faith ride large circuits to reach far-flung congregations. A rabbi occasionally visits from the northern Florida area. Miss Fanny told me that people of the Methodist, Baptist, and other Protestant persuasions are so curious about others' religions that they go to the services to see how their friends worship. Most Sundays, Parson Pierce, a local man of Baptist persuasion, leads townsfolk in a worship service of Bible readings and reflection. I attended a service, and everyone joined as one to thank God for our blessings. For as you know, everything we have is a blessing. But I do miss the sacred holiness of the Mass, and I sorely miss Holy Communion. I do morning and evening devotions at a small altar I set up on my dressing table. I started the first morning in my room, and it helped me feel closer to Jesus and all of you back home. In God's time, we will have a church here.

The town bustles despite being so small. We have a news-paper, school, and some businesses: a bank, livery stable, blacksmith shop, wagon factory, dry goods store, drugstore, feed store, mercantile, milliner, dress shop, and some others. The Alloways' house is near the dressmaker's shop, and they have been kind enough to outfit me in clothing more suited to the heat. All the store owners have orange fever, too. Even the stores' backyards have citrus trees.

You'll be happy to know I had a good look at the school-house and am very pleased. It is two stories with tall windows that let in the breezes. My classroom is on the first floor, and as soon as I have a minute's free time, I plan to start preparing it for the students. Classes begin in October. The Alloways said they plan to build Academy housing where students may reside in the future.

I have a new friend named Sarah Bight, who is sickly right now but mending. I visit her with the Alloways, and she grows stronger by the day. You can see I have landed in a place that treasures community, just like at St. Isidore's Home. The Alloways, Miss Sarah and her family, and the mercantile owner Clyde Williams treat me like family already. The Alloways and I are watching Billy until his uncle returns from a journey, and I am glad to hear a young voice in the house although it is not for long. Tomorrow, we all will ride out to his uncle's grove, as he is expected back in town late tonight. I will tell you about it in my next letter.

Well, this all sounds like busy times, does it not? My heart aches for you and the rest of my loved ones back home. Oh, that the distance weren't so great! Busyness helps keep me from sad thoughts. Dear Polly, no one will ever take your place in my heart. I send you love and hugs across the miles. I say a special prayer for you each day and ask Jesus to hold you in his heart even more tightly than usual. You will share every bit of my life through these letters.

I know I don't have to remind you to mind the sisters at the Home while I'm away. They know what's best for a young girl like you. Remember to help care for the little ones who are younger than you—especially the new residents who may have faced harsh lives before they found shelter at the Home. A kind word is long remembered. Remember the Bible passage we learned from Fr. Tom, the verse from Ephesians 4:32: "And be kind to one another, tenderhearted, forgiving one another, as God in Christ has forgiven you." I pray you take your daily Bible lessons to heart and that you realize the importance of your studies for the sacrament of First Communion.

Give hugs to all from me. Remember, should any suspicious visitors come to the Home seeking me, no one is to disclose my location. Send strangers immediately to Mother Superior or Sister Gertrude. I will do my work here and earn funds to help establish a home for me, you, and as many other children as we can fit in it, and to help St. Isidore's Home with its many expenses. I pray for God's blessing on my...

"Miss Agnes! Miss Agnes! Come quick!" Agnes jerked her hand, knocking over the ink bottle, as Billy's voice broke the quietness of early morning.

"What?! What is it!?" she called, jumping up. Within seconds, she had righted the ink bottle with one hand and pulled her wrapper around herself with the other. "I'm coming! I'm coming!" She ran toward the door just as there was a sharp *rap, rap, rap*, on the wooden panel.

"Yes, yes, what is it?" Agnes cried as she flung open the door. "Are you hurt? Is something wrong?" She already feared the worst in a frontier like this.

"No, I'm fine!" Billy said with a bright smile. His eyes widened. "Wow, your hair is puffy and long when not wrapped up on your head! Anyhow, I just want to show you how big this guy is." He pushed his hand toward her face. She was almost eye-to-eye with a giant bullfrog. It grunted. Agnes jumped and nearly let out a shriek before she covered her mouth. Heaven knows she didn't want to wake the Alloways over a frog.

"Billy! Get that outdoors this instant!" Agnes said as soon as she recovered her wits. She shooed him out of the room and hurried him down the stairs, following inches behind him.

Billy returned the bullfrog to a puddle of water near the birdbath, and it grunted before hopping away. Agnes closed her eyes and slowed down her breathing. Young men surely could be a handful.

Chapter Six

"Are we there yet?" Billy called from his perch at the back corner of the wagon, where he sat with Lumpy by his side.

"I can still see the bend in the road behind us, where you last asked," Agnes said. She leaned against the back of the wooden toolbox that separated the wagon bed from the front plank seat, where the Alloways and Clyde sat. "The Misses Alloway said it was two miles from town, not two feet."

"Aw, shucks," he said. "I can't wait to see Tustenuggee again. You know, he can speak Indian. I wanna learn how."

"Your uncle has quite a mix of people at his homestead, doesn't he?" Agnes said, as much a statement as a question. She liked how Seth welcomed an Indian and a Hispanic family to settle on his land. "I like when people of different backgrounds can bridge differences and be friends," she added. "We're all one in Jesus. He welcomed everyone."

"Uh-huh," said Billy, occupied elsewhere. He scrambled to help free a tiny anole lizard that clung to a coil of rope. The frog incident of the day before immediately hopped to Agnes's mind.

"And Jesus teaches us to respect all God's creatures, including the frog you carted through the house when it should have stayed outdoors in its puddle," she said.

Billy grinned. "I just wanted to show somebody, and there wasn't nobody else around. You was excited, too, I could tell."

He protected the lizard from Lumpy, who didn't even see it.

Agnes sighed. "You mean, 'there wasn't *anybody* else around,' and 'you *were* excited.' Yes, I am interested in nature's creatures. But next time, warn me about such treasures before they come my way. I thought you were injured when I heard you yelling. That kind of excitement I can do without."

"Okay, okay. Can I eat something?" Billy asked and stared at the wicker basket tucked by Agnes's side.

"I'm already guarding the basket from your buddy Lumpy," she said. "Don't tell me I have to guard it from you, too."

"No one will eat anytime soon unless your uncle invites us to stay, Billy," Eunice said from the front. She shifted in her seat so she could speak directly to Agnes and Billy in the back of the wagon. "Based on the note I had sent out, he expects us to bring you to the grove, but he doesn't know we planned a picnic."

"And a nice picnic it will be," added Fanny in her quick, breathless way. "Everyone will get along beautifully."

"One can hope," Eunice said, loud enough for Agnes to hear, but not Billy. "Seth's recent foray into neighborliness set so many tongues wagging, he might retreat to his hermitlike existence again just to avoid the chatter."

"Dear, dear Eunice, where is your heart?" Fanny chided her. "I believe Seth set eyes on our lovely Miss Foster and was smitten with Cupid's arrow, and that he decided to embrace neighborliness so he can court her."

Clyde snorted louder than a horse. "The world needs dreamers, Miss Fanny, but that's a bit much."

"Tsk, such sourness," Fanny said, as she fanned herself. "You mark my words. I'll remind everyone of them at the wedding."

Agnes busied herself with tidying the cloth covering the basket, but she was convinced the tips of her ears and cheeks had flushed bright red. Secretly, she looked forward to seeing Seth again, despite her questions about him. The Alloways thought highly of him, and their opinions counted.

The gentle roll of the hills that surrounded town started to flatten into a wide expanse dotted with massive oak trees. Beardlike wisps of growth hung from the branches and shrouded the trees, which were larger than any Agnes had ever seen. The gray growth was something new.

"What in the world is that?" she asked, pointing toward it.

"Spanish moss," said Clyde, Eunice, and Fanny all at the same time, and then everyone laughed.

"Ain't Spanish, ain't moss, but that's what the name is," said Clyde.

Agnes almost corrected his grammar but caught herself. It wouldn't be polite in front of the Alloways and especially in front of a youngster.

"I bet Uncle Seth knows all about it," Billy said. "He knows all kinds of stuff about animals and trees and stuff."

The wagon rounded a bend past a large, placid lake. Agnes was taken by the loveliness of the scene: the gentle slope of land, the magnificent trees, the dark blue waters against the lighter blue sky dotted with puffy white clouds. A bird soared overhead, then swooped down into a treetop, close enough for her to see it was a bald eagle. Her spirits soared with it. Just to be in such a beautiful, peaceful setting, with the warmth of good companionship, was a gift from God. She stopped fiddling with the picnic basket towel and closed her eyes. "The whole earth is full of his glory," she murmured Isaiah 6:3 in thanks for the people and beauty that surrounded her.

The lake was still visible behind her when Clyde turned off the road onto a narrower, rutted sandy trail. Citrus trees lined both sides of the trail, and they extended far back on either side. Soon they were in the midst of a grove that seemed to have no beginning and no end. Finally, the path curved and came to an end in front of a swept, fenced yard. Agnes's heart quickened when she saw Seth leaning on the fence. He looked handsome and at home, with one foot up on the rail, as though he'd known exactly when they'd arrive and had come out to welcome them.

He tipped his hat, but it was a slight gesture. "Morning," Clyde called as he halted the oxen. The rest of the group echoed the greeting. Billy jumped over the side of the wagon. "Hiya, Unc," he said and was gone in a flash toward the barn, Lumpy at his heels. Clyde got out and started to help Fanny and Eunice. When it became apparent Seth wasn't going to lend a hand, Agnes started to scramble out of the back of the wagon without waiting for Clyde.

"Let me," said Seth right over her shoulder.

She squeaked in surprise. "Seconds ago, you were on the other side of the fence," she said, but she allowed him to steady her as she stepped onto the sideboard and then down onto the ground. She used the reprieve to catch her breath and regain her dignity. She wasn't often caught unaware.

She saw Fanny nudge Eunice and then smile fondly in her and Seth's direction as the silence widened. Agnes fussed with smoothing her skirt. Seth cleared his throat. Agnes willed her heartbeat to slow down, to no avail.

"This appears to be a lovely ranch...uh, grove...you have..." She tried to say something more, anything, unfamiliar with her sudden inability to form words or engage in conversation.

"Billy better have behaved for you or...," Seth started to say at the same time. Agnes smiled but still couldn't utter a coherent sentence. Seth pushed his hat back on his head. The green of his eyes seemed more pronounced than the last time she'd seen them.

Clyde cleared his throat, loudly. "Taylor, can you get the basket out of the wagon since you're standing right there?" He called to Seth from the shade of a tree where he, Eunice, and Fanny, as if by silent agreement, had moved to put distance between themselves and Agnes and Seth. "We're fixin' to have a picnic, if you don't mind," Clyde added.

Seth seemed glad for the diversion, as was Agnes. "Shall we eat right away?" she called to Fanny and Eunice. She started to walk toward them, relieved to have a focus other than Seth. Agnes could always find something to say about food. She loved to cook and bake.

"Well, I assume that is all right with Mr. Taylor?" Eunice said. She scrutinized him with a level gaze behind her owlish glasses.

"This man never says no to a good meal," Seth said and almost grinned at Eunice. Her eyebrows arched in surprise.

"Wonderful!" Fanny said for her. "I just knew this would work out well.

"Now, where did Billy run off to? Minutes ago, he acted as though he was faint from hunger. Seth, is it all right for us to set up on that table next to the house?" She started almost before he nodded in agreement.

Fanny bustled about, directing Clyde to lay the tablecloth she'd carried in her lap from home, opening the basket, and starting to hand utensils and cups to Eunice.

"What can I do to help?" Agnes asked.

"Nothing, dear, you just catch up on business with Seth," Fanny cooed.

Agnes swallowed and glanced sideways at Seth, who looked as uncomfortable as she felt.

"Umm, I look forward to having Billy in my class at the Academy," she said.

A shadow of a disturbance passed over his eyes. "Maybe…but he may not be in class."

"Pardon me?"

"A picnic on my grove is one thing. Daily life in town is another. I've had my fill of people's small-minded ways, and I don't want my nephew infected with them."

"You don't understand," Agnes began, ever ready to discuss the importance of education.

"I understand plenty," he said. "You don't, not about me, anyway."

She prayed for patience, for the will to hold her tongue and not pry into his reasons. He didn't know she knew about his life and his troubles, and she sensed he wouldn't be happy to find out just how much she knew.

Agnes chose her words with care. "I do not allow narrow-mindedness in my classroom," she said. "I didn't up north, and I won't here. Trust me, it won't be as St. Paul feared he'd find the people of Corinth, full of slander and gossip."

"You believe that if you want," Seth said. "I'm not stupid. You can't change people."

"You can set a good example…and you can help guide youth," Agnes said. "That's one reason why it's important that young people receive good educations, to guide them through life, to reinforce morals, provide examples, and…"

Seth placed a hand on her arm, which surprised her so much she shut up.

"Miss Foster," he said, "I've seen all the examples I need to see. Thank you, but I'll keep Billy here. I'll teach him what I know, reinforce morals, provide examples, and bring in a tutor to do the rest."

"Yoooo-hooooo," Fanny chirped before Agnes had a chance to respond. "Lunch is ready. Come before the ants get here. Billy!… Billy!…Time to eat! Agnes! Seth!"

Agnes twirled away, so stunned by Seth's dismissal of the Academy that she was glad for a reason to walk away, else she might let her temper get the best of her. She clumped toward the table. She swallowed her annoyance and told herself Seth was just a stubborn man who thought he knew everything and who didn't know how to forgive. Well, let him be, then. She wouldn't let the situation rest long, though. Billy would benefit from interaction with the other children at school and from his lessons. They'd offset the time he spent running wild in the woods. He was a bright boy and deserved an education. Agnes would think of a way to get him into the classroom.

These thoughts swirled in her head as she walked too fast and paid little attention to where she stepped. She was still unaccustomed to the Florida heat and was doubly warmed by agitation.

Sweat glistened on her face almost immediately from the minor exertion of her rapid pace. A bead dripped into her eye and blurred her vision. She stumbled over a tree root protruding up from the ground and almost fell into the table. She reached out a hand to the table planks just in time to steady herself and avoid a full collision with the table's hard edges. A bite of fire coursed up her ankle.

She blinked hard and wiped the sweat from her eyes. As she cleared her sight and lifted her gaze, she stared straight into the face of a tall, strange man who, at that very moment, had rounded the corner of the house and stopped at the table. In one fast, surprised, shocked glance, Agnes took in deerskin leggings, a belted, colorful, knee-length tunic with a gun strap, and a turban. *Dear Mary, Mother of God, what now?* What was this strange apparition? Everything swirled in front of her, her breath grew labored, and her ankle throbbed. Not again, no, she told herself. She had almost fainted at the funeral. She willed herself to function, to not be a delicate weakling felled by the slightest exertion, rise in temperature, and encounter with the unfamiliar. She closed her eyes to gather strength but instead saw reddish colors, tiny pinpricks of stars, and then darkness.

* * *

Agnes wrinkled her nose at the sharp, tangy scent of vinegar and opened her eyes to see Fanny's concerned face. She hovered over Agnes and waved a vial of smelling salts near her nose.

"Oh, thank goodness, she's coming 'round," Fanny exclaimed. Groggy, Agnes tried to move and discovered strong arms carrying her. They held her close against what felt like a rock of stability. She angled her head to see who held her and why, but the slight movement made the trees, the house, a strangely dressed man, and Fanny's face spin out of control in her vision. She let her head lean back against the solidness of the body that supported her. She slipped in and out of consciousness and was grateful for the total support. Her arms and legs were too rubbery to move properly, and her ankle was raw with pain. Whoever held her smelled of a mixture of cotton, leather, and soap. In a haze, Agnes heard Fanny's voice, but she sounded far away and had an echo.

"The dear child laced her stays too tightly," Fanny said. "She's not used to this heat. Seth, bring her into the house. Eunice and I will attend to her."

"Is any of Billy's mother's clothing still here?" Eunice asked.

Agnes heard a male voice rumble, and just as it said, "Her things were never touched," the arms that held her gripped a little tighter.

Her fog lifted long enough for her to realize the voice came from the person who held her. A stranger. A male stranger. Who might have evil intentions. The last time she was this close to a man, her life had nearly been ruined. She'd had to travel a thousand miles away in an effort to recover her and the orphanage's reputation. It couldn't happen again. She had to stop him, to break free. She had to.

She slipped in and out of a woozy state but struggled to stay alert. She thrashed but every movement made her dizzier and made the man grip her even tighter. Fanny's face faded and reappeared and grew dark again. She dimly sensed another hand pat her arm and heard soothing words, only it wasn't Fanny's voice. Then she saw Eunice's face, but it too faded and reappeared. Only the vinegary smell of the salts kept Agnes from going fully under again. Jumbled voices urged her to keep still and told her repeatedly that all would be okay. But she knew otherwise.

Didn't they understand? He was taking her away, just like before, and this time there might be no escape. Her feeble attempts to disentangle herself were fruitless. She heard another man's voice say, "This way, I've got the door, and I've cleared the way inside." She knew the voice but couldn't place it. Then the man who held her spoke again. "Thanks," he said. Fear gripped Agnes. Two men were taking her somewhere. Why didn't the other women stop them?

Help me, she wanted to shout, but couldn't form the words aloud. Her breath caught in her chest, and she couldn't draw in enough air.

"Hurry!" Eunice ordered. Agnes felt another pat on her hand, and then everything went dark again.

* * *

Agnes awoke to a soft pillow and to crisp, clean sheets that smelled of fresh pine, a crinkly but soft mattress, and a light blanket. She felt wrapped in softness and safety, except for the steady throb of pain in her ankle. She opened her eyes and saw rough-hewn log walls with a fireplace in one wall and a window in another.

"Where am I?"

"In Seth's house," said Fanny, who sat in a chair pulled close to the side of the bed. Agnes turned her head toward her. Fanny leaned forward and patted Agnes's forehead and cheeks with a damp cloth. Eunice sat on a chair next to her.

"Mercy, child, you gave us quite a scare," Fanny said. "We thought it best to let you lie here awhile. Here, let me fan you." She pulled one of her ever-present hand fans from the wicker bag she'd carried for the day's outing. Eunice took the washcloth from her and patted Agnes's forehead again.

"It's unusual for anyone to remain faint for as long as you did," Eunice said. She dipped and wrung the compress cloth in a wash-basin on the bedside table. She again laid the compress on Agnes's forehead. It felt cool and relaxing.

"For a moment, you appeared to be on the verge of a seizure," Eunice continued. "You started to struggle and lose breath. Are you prone to seizures, Agnes?"

"No, ma'am," she said. Memory started to filter back, and she understood suddenly that she'd interwoven the past with the present.

"I...I...," she started to say, then stopped. How could she ever tell them what really happened? They might ask her to leave if they knew the whole story. Agnes couldn't leave. She needed the job and needed the time away from home.

"I had a...memory...of a frightening experience," she said. "For some reason, I thought the person who held me—who was that?—I thought he was someone who had harmed me in the past."

"Land sakes alive!" Fanny said. "Who would ever try to hurt you?" She fanned faster and turned it alternately on herself and Agnes. "Rest assured, you have nothing to fear in Persimmon Hollow. We are safe here. That was Seth who carried you."

"Do you wish to talk about your experience?" Eunice asked, and she watched Agnes with the close scrutiny of the school-teacher she was.

Intuition told Agnes she could share the whole story with the Alloways and that they wouldn't judge her. Others back home hadn't been as kind, especially the people who helped support St. Isidore's Home. They had threatened to withdraw donations because of Agnes's brush with sinister people and a house of ill repute. The patrons, well-fed and stout to a person, told Mother Superior that allowing Agnes to stay on the premises was a blot on the Home's reputation. Either Agnes went, or they'd with-hold their money. They'd told the bishop as much. Hadn't he said anything, they inquired? They were ever so polite.

Agnes closed her eyes lest the tears that threatened to spill started a flood as the memory grew stronger. Mother Superior had made a comment to the patrons about everyone being sinners and noted that Jesus welcomed all to the table. She explained that Agnes had been tricked. That Agnes would stay. And finally, that the bishop was in full understanding and agreement. But Agnes had eaves-dropped from the other side of the door. She knew, from the tenor, tone, and continued complaints from the vocal patrons, that they would withdraw financial support unless their demand was met and Agnes sent away. And she knew these patrons donated more than the diocese itself could afford to provide. After that ugly incident, Agnes insisted on leaving. She, Mother Superior, and Fr. Tom came up with the plan that led Agnes to Persimmon Hollow.

"Yes, I...I have something to explain," Agnes said to Eunice.

"Eunice, please! Let her rest," Fanny chided. "You tell us when you're ready to speak about it," she said to Agnes. "Right now, you need to get out of that corset and into less confining clothing. You'll soon learn you can't lace your stays for vanity here for any length of time. The climate will overtake you."

Eunice helped Agnes to a seated position while Fanny rustled through a cedar chest at the end of the bed. "Here, this day dress is perfect, and the color matches your eyes." She sniffed and raised the fabric to her face. "It smells a little musty. Not too bad, though. Cedar is such an asset in this humidity. And here is a chemise and a light polonaise jacket. It'll be a little warm, dear, but for modesty's sake you'll wish to wear it over the dress. We refuse to let you lace those stays again today."

Agnes revived after the women helped her unlace the corset they had already loosened before Agnes came out of her faint. What a difference a deep breath can make! She stood up to change and started to crumble as soon as she put weight on her ankle.

Fanny and Eunice rushed to help her sit down before she fell down. Eunice checked the ankle. "It's swollen but not discolored," she said. "It appears to be a sprain, not broken. But that's nuisance enough."

With their help and support, Agnes changed into the borrowed clothing. The garments were wonderfully loose and cool.

"This woman must have been slightly larger than me," she said. "Who was she?"

"Seth's late sister-in-law," Fanny said.

"The one who died in the fire?" Agnes asked.

"Yes," Eunice answered. "I believe the outfit you have on was one she wore when *enceinte*. That would explain why it's roomy, especially across the stomach area."

A poignant stab of pity coursed through Agnes. "Billy's mother," she said. Fanny and Eunice nodded, and the conversation fell silent. Agnes said a prayer for the soul of the woman, and then saw that Fanny had moved to the window and leaned out.

"Seth, Clyde, Billy, Tustenuggee, one of you...do you have anything here for treating a sprain?"

"Tustenuggee. That must be who that man was," Agnes said, as she deduced that the oddly dressed man was Seth's Indian friend. "I've never seen that type of clothing in Indian daguerreotypes I've seen up North."

"You've never seen an image of a Seminole, then," Eunice said. "Some folks in town don't cotton to having a Seminole Indian as part of the community, even though the man takes little interest in town life. I've heard that he has partial white parentage. If true, it might account for his decision to live here instead of with others of his clan. Some of them would consider his blood tainted."

Minutes later, they heard footsteps and a knock on the door. Seth entered, and Agnes scrambled to get under the sheets, suddenly shy about the lighter garments she wore. She pulled the sheet up to her chin. The scent of cotton, leather, and soap drifted in with him, and she knew who had carried her inside.

"Who's hurt?" he asked.

"Agnes," said Eunice. "Her ankle is sprained."

"How badly? Let me check," he said and approached the bed.

"No!" Agnes squeaked, and he stopped in mid-step.

"I mean no disrespect," he stuttered. "I just want to..."

"People on the frontier have no time for false modesty," Eunice said. "Seth has doctoring skills from his years of homesteading."

"Yes, he had gained quite a reputation for his skills before...oh, dear, I'm speaking out of turn," Fanny said, flustered, as the edges of Seth's already tight lips dipped downward.

"Before what?" Agnes blurted out seconds before she realized she should have kept her mouth shut. *Dear Lord, help me learn patience,* she prayed for what had to be the thousandth time.

Seth didn't answer.

"No matter," Agnes said. "People don't always understand, even when they know facts. Some things are best left unsaid."

A flash of appreciation and interest flickered across Seth's eyes.

"Through the years, Seth came to know many local plants and what they're used for," Fanny chattered. "It's a most remarkable skill. Don't you fret, Agnes. We'll stay by your side while he checks your ankle."

Eunice looked at Agnes with mingled compassion and amusement. "Just slide your ankle out from under the sheets," she suggested.

Agnes inched her foot out and almost pulled the covers over her head from embarrassment when Seth pulled up a chair and took her foot in his hand. Seth probed the ankle with the serious intent a farrier gave to a horse's foot when shoeing it. He was all business.

"Billy, get in here with that comfrey," Seth hollered out the window without getting up. He glanced at Fanny and Eunice. "It's not a bad sprain. A couple of weeks off her foot will take care of it." He didn't look at Agnes. In fact, he seemed unable to look at her. Which was just as well. His hands were large and firm but gentle, and she was too aware of his touch. And it had nothing to do with the sprain.

Billy burst into the room and set down a bucket by Seth. "Here you go," he said. "Tustenuggee checked and said it was the right const...con...sat..."

"Consistency," Seth supplied. Billy handed him the strips of cloth he carried in his other hand.

Agnes's curiosity overcame the awkwardness of the situation. She watched as Seth placed the poultice of wet, compressed leaves on her ankle. They felt wet and gushy.

"Ewww," she said, as Seth bound them loosely but firmly in place with the cloth.

"You can ewww all you want," Seth said, as he set her foot back on the bed and drew the cover over it. Only then did he look at her face. "Comfrey speeds healing. So get used to it." A glimmer of a smile lightened his eyes.

"Yes, it certainly will help, dear," said Fanny. "Now, Seth, if you would carry Agnes outside, perhaps we can all have a little something to eat. I'm starving!"

"I can walk," Agnes protested and started to get up.

"No you can't," the others said in unison. She looked from one to the other and flopped back on the bed. Any argument would be fruitless. Besides, they were right.

"You just let Seth help you out," Fanny said.

Agnes met his gaze and was glad that he appeared to feel as awkward as she did. Good. The last time he carried her, she was faint from heat and surprise. This time, she hoped she didn't get light-headed from the stir she felt in her heart.

Chapter Seven

I could get used to this," said Clyde, as he swung lazily in a hammock tied between two pine trees near the table. "You have the life out here, Taylor."

"Sure do," Seth said. He sat on a fallen log and chewed on a piece of cornbread. "Kind-hearted women bring me home-cooked meals every day, don't you know that?" He chuckled, and Fanny leaned over from the table and gave his hand a playful tap with her fan.

Agnes relaxed in the rocking chair Seth had placed next to the table. The afternoon air was soft and warm, and the sun broke through the dappled shade just enough to brighten without glare. Mockingbirds chattered and mimicked other birds. She'd already learned to recognize the active gray-and-white birds. She looked around at the gathering. Her heart warmed to the people who had welcomed her into their lives. Even Seth had let down his guard a bit. Tustenuggee no longer appeared intimidating. He'd bowed and kissed her hand when Seth introduced them. Agnes tried not to stare at his attire but did a poor job of hiding her curiosity. For his part, Billy clearly adored Tustenuggee. He sat by him and pestered him with questions about everything from the markings of a woolly bear caterpillar to why Tustenuggee wore a turban.

Row after row of neatly spaced citrus trees surrounded the clearing as far as Agnes could see. Tall, stately pine trees with thick, straight trunks ringed the house and dotted the open area. She saw similar treetops far in the distance, where the grove ended. The sky was a sharp, bright blue that was mirrored by the lake in the distance.

The only shadow over the day was the throb of her ankle. "As soon as this sprain gets better, I'd like to walk down to that lake," she said, thinking aloud, then gulped at the forwardness of inviting herself to stroll around someone else's property.

Fanny nudged Eunice and smiled as Seth said he thought a future stroll to the lake was a great idea. The Alloways thought Agnes didn't notice the exchange between the two of them, seated at the table with heads lowered toward each other. Tustenuggee saw that Agnes saw and cleared his throat loudly.

Fanny glanced up. "I declare, I've done most of the talking here this afternoon," she said to him. "Are you still hungry, Tustenuggee? Would you like some more cornbread? Chicken? Oh, get away, flies," she said and waved her fan at a pair of flies that flew in and hovered over the food she and Eunice had covered with cloths.

"That pair of pests reminds me I haven't yet spoken of two other pests," Tustenuggee said as he looked at the flies. "Seth, the reason I came up to the house today was not to scare your lady friend, but to alert you. Strangers have been on your land."

"What strangers?" asked Seth. He leaned forward, and his smile faded. "When?"

"Two of them, judging by their tracks. Last night. Amateurs in the wilderness. They tried to cover their tracks but did a poor job."

"That's good," Seth said. "It'll help us flush them out. What did you figure out?"

"They traveled the fence-line, along the lay of the land where the railroad will run its tracks."

"That says a lot, a whole lot," said Seth. "It says the railroad is behind it. I hope they don't send in some fast-talker again to try and buy the land. We need to fence the property, and fast."

He got up and started to pace, and every step sent a jolt of tension into the afternoon's tranquility.

"Oh, dear," Fanny said. "And here I was about to ask Seth if he'd like to come to dinner in town tomorrow. Have you considered becoming more friendly with townsfolk now that Billy is with you again?"

"Not to mention that townsfolk will help you fight off any problems out here," Eunice added.

"No, Misses Alloway," Seth said. "I've got all the help I need right here. I've already told your new schoolmarm that Billy stays here. He'll get schooling enough—and I'll bring in a tutor to cover any gaps. I've got work for Billy to do, and he can fit the lessons around it. I need him here right now. We've got to get that fence up. The railroad has been after my land before, and it looks like they're after it again. I don't plan to let them have it."

"Can you be sure the people on your land were from the railroad?" Agnes asked, using her good foot to slow down the rocker.

"I'm close to certain," Seth said. "The South Line's main office has already made two offers on my place. They weren't happy when I told them to stop wasting their time because the land ain't for sale."

"Isn't," she murmured out of habit and glanced up to see that Seth had caught the remark and cast her a look of challenge. Well, good. She liked a challenge. After all, he'd used the word more than once, and she *was* the schoolmarm, as he put it.

"I just thought I'd, oh, note that little grammatical slip-up in case, well, you did say Billy would be taught here, and of course you want to teach him proper English," Agnes said in a low voice, just loud enough for him to hear. She kept her tone serious but glanced at him with a smile in her eyes. She stretched back in the rocker, tapped her fingertips on the armrests, and stared at him with her best air of deliberate innocence.

He walked over and stood in front of her, arms crossed in front of his chest, and gave her a long, deliberate look. Then he slipped his hands into his back pockets, without breaking the gaze.

"Is that so? Miss Foster, I'm not in the habit of having women correct me about anything," he said. He did his best to sound stern, but his eyes betrayed a glimmer and an expression of interest.

"No need for concern," Agnes said lightly, with a flick of her wrist, as though she just brushed an errant hair out of the way. "Only God is perfect. That makes all humans imperfect. Therefore, at times, we all need to be corrected." She used her best teacher voice. "Done with the best of intentions, you understand."

He pulled his hands out of his back pockets and gestured upward with a shrug of surrender. "I give up," he said. "How can I answer a comment like that?"

Clyde guffawed. "You can't. I don't mess with God-fearing women, Taylor. They're always right. Ain't you learned your lesson yet?"

Seth tilted his head as he looked at Agnes. "He said 'ain't'? Why don't you correct him?" he asked.

"He hasn't offered to oversee Billy's schooling," she said.

Seth drew his brows together. "You're a stubborn one. I'll think about it."

"About what?"

"Billy's schooling."

"You won't regret sending him to the Academy," she said and leaned forward in the chair. "Trust me, you won't. You've heard Proverbs chapter nine, verse nine: 'Give instruction to the wise, and they will become wiser still; teach the righteous and they will gain in learning.'"

"Uh, sure," he said, but his face didn't reflect recognition. "I'll think about the school thing. That's the best I can offer. Right now, I need to get that fence up. After that, we've got a store to build. Billy's a good hand at both."

"A store?!" Fanny and Eunice said in surprised unison.

Seth turned, and Agnes glanced toward the Alloways, startled. She'd almost forgotten anyone else was here with them, and he seemed to have done the same. The world had drawn close around the two of them.

"I rounded up a lot of information up in St. Augustine," Seth said. "The owner of the Ponce de Leon Hotel, Henry Flagler, wants to open a new hotel somewhere across from my land, on the other side of where the tracks will run. The railroad plans to add a station house and sell homesteads there, too. They've already got the land on that side of the track line. Now they want mine. Nothing doing. I'm going to capitalize on the progress. My plan is to add a store and use my grove as a place where tourists can visit, tour a grove, and buy and ship citrus and other things back to their homes."

"What a wonderful idea," Agnes said. "You could sell jellies and marmalades and candied peel and... Gosh, we could make all kinds of things." Her mind raced through memories of the sweets the girls and she had made each holiday at the orphanage. Oranges were a rare treat, and they'd made the most of them. Nothing was wasted, not even the peel.

Everyone's attention was on Agnes.

"I hadn't mentioned a partnership," Seth said. "Thought you were a teacher."

But her ideas had caught his attention, she could tell. Meanwhile, she started to calculate how much extra money could be generated for St. Isidore's Home if she supplied—no, if she sold— homemade products to the store. Every extra dollar earned meant extra money for the orphanage and for Polly. And every extra dollar meant one less day Agnes would have to stay in Persimmon Hollow, nice though it was becoming for her.

*   *   *

The next afternoon, Agnes's ankle throbbed worse than the day before. She sat in a wicker chair on the Alloways' front porch and tried to keep her attention on the balsam flowers she was embroidering on a muslin apron for Polly's Christmas gift. Her foot was propped on an ottoman, and the throb claimed most of her senses. But it wasn't the only thing that intruded on her thoughts.

Fanny bustled out with a tray of tea and slices of pound cake. "Estelle makes the best pound cake I ever tasted," she said and placed the tray on the wicker set's table. "Try some." In the next breath, her conversation lighted on the one thing even the pain in Agnes's ankle couldn't push out of her mind. "I wonder if Seth will change his mind about our dinner offer," Fanny said, unconsciously putting a finger to her cheek as she pondered the idea.

Darn. Agnes would never get him out of her thoughts now. Worse, she hoped he would show up for dinner. What had come over her? She didn't plan to stay in Persimmon Hollow. Why get involved with a man whose roots in the region were deeper than the gnarled cedar trees in the Alloways' backyard? Agnes's tidy dreams of a husband and a home full of children were neatly wrapped in a steeple-church neighborhood in a city up North. The plan had no room for a non-churchgoing, unsociable man in the tropics of Florida, no matter how much of a good, decent man lay underneath the tough exterior. Even if the thought of him did make her heart beat faster.

"He certainly has taken a liking to you," Fanny said as she sat down in a chair that was a twin of Agnes's and poured each of them a cup of the amber liquid. "And I believe I sense the same response in you."

"Ouch!" Agnes yelped as she accidentally stuck herself with the needle on a messy stitch. "I'm not interested in courting," she mumbled and peered at the crooked stitches of yellow thread. They bore little resemblance to a flower petal.

"Do you think I should add a touch of red thread to this yellow flower?" she asked and held up the apron to show Fanny. "Polly loves bright colors."

"Mercy! All young women are interested in courting," Fanny said. "I certainly was when I was your age. I allow that I was a bit of a belle, even. I don't understand your reluctance about Seth. Has his past colored your feelings? I hope not. Yes, I think a touch of red would be lovely."

She handed Agnes a slice of cake on a small plate. Agnes laid her sewing in her lap to savor the treat. It was as good as Fanny had said.

"No, that's not it," Agnes said between bites. "I mean, well, he certainly wasn't friendly that first day, but even then he showed his integrity. Since then, I've seen his human side and his good heart. I've learned the hard way that rumors aren't always true, so that's not it either. He has fallen away from the church, which bothers me greatly, but I have hope he will find his way back. It's just that...well..."

"What, dear? We don't insist that our teachers remain unmarried here, like other places do. Is that what you're fretting about? I know you mentioned you'd be sending wages back to your loved ones in the North. Seth would think that is a good notion, I assure you. Of course, if things progress the way I foresee, you'd step down from teaching when you become in the family way. Oh, dear, but listen to me play matchmaker! And Eunice has her heart set on a teacher who will stay for a few years and help guide the Academy without the responsibility of husband and children. Indeed, I do get ahead of myself."

Fanny chuckled, oblivious to the strain Agnes struggled to keep out of her expression. "But there's no harm in courting, dear, don't you think?" Fanny continued. "It's simply..."

"Miss Alloway!" Agnes blurted and set down her teacup hard enough for the saucer to rattle.

"Please, I beg of you," Agnes continued. "I'm not ready to court or have a beau. Right now, my duty is to my teaching. True, I plan to send my wages back to St. Isidore's Home, and eventually to return to the Home. There is so much need there. And...

well…if you must know, I have what some people think are funny notions about marriage. I believe it is a partnership between two people the Lord brings together, as it says in St. Paul's Letter to the Corinthians. He says that…"

"Of course, dear," Fanny interrupted as she reached over to fluff the pillow underneath Agnes's ankle. "Everything happens in God's good time. I just try to help by planting the seed when the season is right and…oh, we have company! A caller. How nice."

She stood to greet a young woman who came up the walkway, but not before Agnes saw concern darken Fanny's eyes, despite the smile that curved her lips.

"Adelaide Land!" Fanny said. "What a surprise. We didn't expect you to ever return to Persimmon Hollow. Are you enjoying your stay?"

"It's so wooooooonderful, Miss Fanny, and it is sooooooo good to see you," sang Adelaide. She was slender and elegant, with smooth, dark hair that stood out against her pale face. Instinctively, Agnes patted her thick, unruly, wavy locks that routinely slid out from the bun she had taken to wearing. Adelaide wore a hat more fashionable than any Agnes had seen since her last encounter with the orphanage's most wealthy patrons.

"Oh, you must be Agnes Foster," Adelaide cooed with bright eyes and a wide smile as her gaze took in Agnes's simple frock and bandaged ankle. "I stopped at the mercantile for some ribbon— of course the selection is quite poor, such a backwater this town is—and who was there but Miss Eunice chatting with the store- keeper. I overheard so much about you. I just couldn't wait to meet you. Are you truly from New York City? I confess I had hoped to glimpse the latest in fashion on anyone from New York.

My! Where are my manners?! How forward of me to ask such questions!"

Fanny called inside the house for another cup for tea then turned back toward them. "Adelaide spent last season with her parents at the Land Inn after they bought it, but our country life didn't suit her, and she returned rather quickly to Chicago," Fanny explained to Agnes.

"Thank you, Estelle," Fanny said as Estelle opened the screen door, handed out a teacup, saucer, and spoon, and gave Adelaide a tight-lipped look before going back inside.

"Here, Adelaide, have a seat and some tea," Fanny invited. "What brings you back to Persimmon Hollow?"

"I visited relatives in St. Augustine and thought I'd journey here to visit with Mama and Papa before going back to Chicago," Adelaide said.

"Alone?" asked Fanny, surprised.

"Oh, no. I would never travel alone. My maid has been my constant companion."

The conversation faded.

"St. Augustine. Is that the place Seth visited?" Agnes asked when the silence became too lengthy. How odd for Fanny to fall silent at such a time. Agnes couldn't fathom why.

"Do you refer to Mr. Seth Taylor?" Adelaide asked, too eagerly. When Agnes nodded yes, she lowered her voice to a conspiratorial whisper. "I must tell you. I heard you have been keeping company with him. I wanted to get here without delay to warn you, before your reputation suffers!"

Fanny picked up one of her fans from a side table and snapped it open. "You heard what? And how did it travel to Chicago?"

"Miss Fanny, Agnes, hear me out, I beg of you," Adelaide said, her eyes wide with an innocence that struck Agnes as forced. "I am in constant communication with family and servants during the months they spend in Florida each fall and winter. What I have heard about Mr. Taylor has spread as far as St. Augustine. Yes, word is even in that town."

Fanny stood up as though preparing to go inside.

"Do stay," Adelaide said to Fanny, who complied, but unwillingly. Pinched lips replaced the bubbly warmth that was so much a part of her.

Agnes picked up her embroidery, smoothed the fabric, and started to unravel the crooked stitches. "I'm compelled to tell you I'm no fan of gossip or rumor," she said to Adelaide.

"What are you, a Quaker?" Adelaide asked, then tittered and covered her mouth with her gloved hand.

"No, I'm Catholic. But I met some Friends once, when they visited the orphanage where I was raised. They seemed to be kind, decent people."

"Catholic? You are a Papist?" Adelaide looked horrified before she smoothed her expression. "And an orphan! My, how original. But my news is a luscious tidbit. I guarantee you will want to hear it. You simply must stop that sewing for a moment and pay attention."

She scooted her chair closer to Agnes and placed a gloved hand over hers in a gesture of forced intimacy.

"I heard, on the best authority, that Seth Taylor is a criminal outlaw," Adelaide began. She lowered her voice. "He's a ruffian, not to be trusted. He was in jail for an unspeakable deed, and he escaped. The reason he won't mix with polite society is because he fears he'll be recognized and sent back to jail. For your safety, please distance yourself from him. I even question whether we should alert authorities about him."

Her behavior left a bad taste in Agnes's mouth. She drew back her hand.

"Adelaide!" Fanny reprimanded her. "He didn't commit any 'unspeakable' deed. Yes, he broke out of jail, but it was because he was falsely imprisoned and because he saw smoke billowing on the horizon from a fire in the direction of his homestead. If anything unspeakable is going on, it's the falsehoods and poison you spread."

"I understand many people in town didn't exactly welcome him back," Agnes added. "That could account for the way he keeps his distance."

"Ah, aren't you both such small-town do-gooders, happy to ruin a juicy morsel with snippets of truth," said Adelaide. She waved a hand in airy dismissal at Fanny and Agnes. "I'm only here to tell you because one can never be too careful about people, or about one's reputation. I, for one, wouldn't want to meet Mr. Taylor alone."

Agnes returned to her embroidery and jabbed the apron so hard with the needle it pricked her hand underneath, again.

The conversation thudded to a halt. Agnes couldn't imagine someone with whom she had less in common. There certainly wasn't anything she wished to discuss with Adelaide. Who ever dreamed up the formalities involved when receiving callers in polite society? Agnes wanted nothing more than to tell this gossiper to go away. But even Fanny held her tongue.

"I, uh, appreciate your concern," Agnes finally said.

"Did I mention the moonshine?" Adelaide asked in dramatic whisper. A thin smile played over her face, as she waited for Agnes's reaction. "Mr. Taylor was in the illegal liquor trade," she continued. "I know this for a fact. Ooooooh, it makes me want to keep my distance from such a dangerous man. I wanted to make sure I shared this with you. When I heard Mama say you all had actually visited him, I said to myself, 'You simply must call on the Alloways, even though you are still exhausted from traveling.'"

Fanny rose. "I forgot how fast word travels in a small town," she said. Adelaide took her cue and rose as though by private accord.

"Well, I'm off to go see Sarah Bight," Adelaide said. "You know she just lost her grandmother? I hear she is...well...not right, in the head, you know, from grief. I hear she has been..."

That did it. Agnes stood up, and her embroidery ring and fabric slid to the floor. "Good day, thank you for coming," she said, before even Fanny could speak. The pain in Agnes's ankle screamed at her to sit back down, but she ignored it.

The sound of horse hooves broke the tension and provided a needed diversion. Agnes plopped back down as Seth cantered up, with Billy on the horse behind him, and stopped in front of the house. Billy leapt off and ran over to the mercantile, while Seth got down, pulled something out of a pack, and headed up the walk.

"It's him!" Adelaide said in a high, dramatic whisper. She grabbed Fanny's arm with one hand and started patting her hair with the other. "Can you believe he has the nerve to just gad about?! I simply cannot stay anywhere in the near vicinity. His presence in town does not bode well for the reputation of

Persimmon Hollow. Wait until Mama and Papa hear about this!"

Agnes had her own ideas about whose presence was a blight on the town's good face but struggled not to judge. Who knew what made Adelaide act the way she did. But Agnes could pray for her. Or try to, at least.

Adelaide started down the front step at the same time Seth put his booted foot on the bottom step. Adelaide scooted past him, holding her skirts flat against herself to avoid contact with him. She gave him a haughty glance as she trotted past him as fast as fashionably allowed.

Fanny was almost speechless. "Whatever has gotten into that child?! She wasn't quite so malicious last year. Perhaps her city cousins are a bad influence. I'll add them to my prayer list."

Agnes pressed her lips tight to keep from saying anything uncharitable. "Yes, I will pray for her, too," she said.

Seth tipped his hat. "My arrival caused a stir, huh? Now you know why I keep my distance from town. Came in to bring some more comfrey for that ankle."

"You could say I'm beginning to understand your reluctance," Agnes said, as she watched the retreating figure. "My thanks are double-fold. You brought comfrey and caused her"—she pointed to Adelaide—"to leave."

"Glad to hear it, and you're welcome," Seth said as he set down the packet on the table. "Yours?" he asked, nodding toward the floor. He squatted and picked up the embroidery ring and handed it to Agnes.

Their hands touched in the exchange, and Agnes felt as though a spark had leapt out of a cooking fire at the brush of his hand against hers.

"Ankle doing all right?" Seth asked as he withdrew his hand and stepped back quickly.

"Oh, yes, yes, thank you," she said, ignoring the intensified throb caused by her earlier attempt to stand. She bent her head over the embroidery but stayed fully aware of everything going on around her.

"The dinner offer still stands," Fanny said. She busied herself with the tea tray. "Some tea?"

"No and no," Seth said.

Agnes was both relieved and saddened at his answers.

"Consider the dinner offer an open invitation," Fanny said as Seth adjusted his hat and headed toward the steps.

"Oh, Seth," Fanny called as he started down the front steps. "I forgot to tell you about the town painting day to whitewash the meeting hall where we worship. I believe it is scheduled for next Monday. Every hand is needed and welcome. There will be a town meeting about it after services Sunday."

"Put me on the list for laying pine straw on the roads next time that project comes up," Seth said, beginning to walk toward his horse. "Keep me off the church list."

"Tsk, tsk," Fanny said under her breath.

Agnes's breath collapsed inward. She was troubled at the way Seth pushed God away. At the same time, she wished he had stayed a little longer with them on the porch.

"I expect to see Billy in my classroom bright and early when school starts," she called. "If he's not, I forewarn you I will come look for him."

Seth turned and looked at Agnes with an open amusement that made her bristle.

"You do that," he said.

She sniffed. "I believe I will."

Fanny turned away with a half-hidden smile on her face and started to pick up the tea tray.

"Miss Agnes!" Billy hollered from across the street as he burst out of the mercantile. The screen door slammed behind him. He ran toward the Alloway porch in full speed, waving a piece of paper in his hand. "Telegram! You got a telegram! It's stamped 'Urgent'!"

Fanny put down the tea tray. Agnes stood and hobbled to the porch railing and leaned against it to take the weight off her sprained ankle. Seth stopped in mid-step. Eunice and Clyde had followed Billy out the mercantile door and walked toward the house with concerned expressions. Adelaide emerged from behind a screen of wax myrtle bushes on the adjoining homestead and watched with sharp-faced interest.

Nobody at St. Isidore's Home had pennies to waste on telegrams unless the news was dire. Agnes couldn't think of anyone else who would send her a telegram. A black cloud of dread passed over her. "Lord, give me strength," she murmured as Fanny put an arm around her waist. Tears pricked the corners of Fanny's eyes as she read the look on her sister's face.

Chapter Eight

$\mathcal{A}$gnes's hand trembled so much she could hardly scan the words on the paper. She turned away from the small crowd now gathered on the porch. "Please," she whispered to Fanny and limped alone to the end of the porch and sat down on the top step.

Almost afraid to focus on the words, she closed her eyes for a moment to gather herself. What if Polly were sick or dead? Or one of the other orphans or the sisters?

She steeled myself and started to read.

RUFUS WANTS POLLY. STOP. THINKS SHE'S YOUR SISTER AND CLAIMS KINSHIP. STOP. THREATENS FORCE IF LAWS WON'T HELP. STOP. MUST SEND POLLY TO YOU FOR SAFETY. STOP. WIRE FARE IMMEDIATELY. STOP. NO MONEY HERE. STOP. PRAY FOR US. STOP. YOURS IN CHRIST.

Polly? He wanted dear, precious Polly? *Over my dead body*, Agnes thought. The telegram fluttered to the ground as she started to push herself up, and she plopped back down as soon as her ankle protested. Her sorry circumstances whirled through her mind. Polly was in danger, and here she sat with no home but a borrowed room, no possessions but a few changes of clothing, a Bible, a few other books, and some trinkets, and no money to wire up North. *Think, Agnes, think.*

Please, God, give me guidance, she prayed.

Fear, worry, and homesickness jumbled together inside, and she fought the urge to cry. She thought of St. Frances de Sales and his counsel to never give in to anxiety. She thought about how Jesus said in the Scripture not to worry. These reminders were distant buoys that helped but couldn't keep her totally afloat, not at this moment. Her shoulders shook from the tears she suddenly couldn't hold back.

"Agnes, dear, what is it?!" Eunice's voice was close by her side. "Is there anything we can do? Tell us, how can we help?"

"Oh, yes, do tell, what is the news?" Adelaide chirped.

"Agnes, honey." Fanny's voice was now near, and Agnes felt her hand on her shoulder. "Has there been a death in the family?" she asked softly.

Agnes willed myself to stop sobbing and hiccupped as she turned toward them. "N-n-n-n-o death," she stuttered, then inhaled and tried again. "I...I have to leave," she said, without any kind of clear thought in her head and no plan beyond getting back to save Polly. "Today. Right now. I must go home immediately."

"What?! But why?" Fanny exclaimed. "Dear child, that is impossible!"

"You just got here," Eunice added.

"Whatever for?" Adelaide asked with too much enthusiasm.

"Train's already passed through today," Clyde said. "And it's getting late in the day for a run out to the river landing to try and flag down a steamboat."

Only Seth remained quiet, and out of the corner of her eye, Agnes saw him watch her with a thoughtful look on his face.

"I'll read you the telegram," she said, but the telegram wasn't in her lap, or by her side on the step, or on the porch floor proper. She looked in the folds of her skirt.

"Under the steps," Seth said and nodded in the direction of the fallen telegram. He retrieved the paper and handed it to Agnes.

She grabbed it from him with such force that it ripped in two.

"Everything will be okay," he said as he handed her the other half. He stepped back but commanded her with his gaze. She saw strength and assurance there. She looked down at the two halves of the telegram as though new information might appear.

"We lean on one another here, honey," Fanny said. "Let us help."

Silence stretched when Agnes couldn't bring myself to read the words aloud. How could she ever explain Rufus to them?

"I think it's time everyone left," Eunice said and started to shoo Adelaide, Seth, Billy, and Clyde off the porch. "The afternoon's waning, and nothing can be done today in any case. Clyde, in a bit Fanny or I will be over with a reply to be telegrammed back."

"Everyone pray for a solution to the problem that has caused Agnes such distress," Fanny said.

Agnes barely heard the commotion. She hadn't even started work at the Academy yet and had hardly a penny to her name. Could she get a loan? Doubtful. She had never even been inside a bank. She would move mountains and anything else to protect Polly and find a way to go home, get her, and bring her safely to Persimmon Hollow.

She glanced at the kind-hearted Alloways as they kept people away from her. The time had come to tell them the entire story of why she left everything behind to start a new life. They'd either throw her out or would understand her plight. Would they understand it enough to offer help and shelter for Polly? Was it too much to ask? Agnes stood a good chance of losing the fragile thread of community she'd started to sense and treasure here.

She sat up straighter and squared her shoulders. Her only choice was to share her tale and seek a loan. Polly and St. Isidore's Home needed her.

"Trust in him, and he will help you; make your ways straight, and hope in him." The phrase from Sirach 2:6 repeated itself in Agnes's mind, like a beacon. She also knew the additional meaning of the words, the truth they'd lived by at the Home: God helps those who help themselves. He would protect and guide. Agnes had to take action and save Polly.

* * *

Seth hung back as the others left and Eunice went inside. Agnes saw him as she brought her wandering thoughts back to the scene in front of her. Their glances met. He stood at the bottom of the steps with one foot on the first step and one hand on the railing. He radiated such a quiet assurance that she wanted to lean on him. His silent offer of help affected her more than the spoken ones had, and a fresh round of tears slipped down her cheeks.

"Let me help you up," he said and offered his hand. "It'll be okay."

"Bring her here," Fanny said, plumping the cushions on the porch swing and pulling the ottoman forward. "She can rest her foot here."

Eunice returned with a brisk step as Seth and Fanny helped Agnes get settled.

Eunice set down a thin dark bottle and a juice glass and poured a small amount of a dark liquid into the glass. She handed it to Agnes. The liquid smelled atrocious, like old shoes.

"We keep this on hand for medicinal purposes," Eunice said. "Try to ignore the unpleasant aroma. The taste isn't as bad as the smell, and I sweetened it with honey to make it more palatable."

Agnes took the glass with a shaky hand. "What is it?"

"Probably valerian," Seth said from where he had again retreated to the steps. "I can smell it over here."

She held the glass of vile-smelling liquid away from her and wrinkled her nose. It was the most disgusting thing she'd ever smelled.

Eunice brooked no nonsense. "Yes, it's valerian, Agnes, an herb with a disagreeable odor, but an herb that is proven to help relax nerves with a gentle touch."

Agnes wet her lips with the liquid and was surprised. It indeed tasted better than it smelled, but she couldn't go so far as to think it pleasant. She drank it, coughed, set down the empty glass, and took a glass of water from Fanny's outstretched hand. "From our artesian well, dear," she said.

"For a minute there, I thought you brought out spirits," Seth said.

"We do not allow spirits in this house, young man," Fanny admonished him, in a tone that was sharp for her. "Watch your tongue. Remarks like that are how rumors get started. You should know better."

Seth fell somber, and the porch was quiet except for the sound of Fanny's rocking chair as it squeaked against the wooden floor.

Tiredness started to steal over Agnes as her muscles released some of the tension that knotted her neck and shoulders. Rumors. How well she knew about rumors. How weary she was of running from them, hiding from them. No more. She had to face them, for Polly's sake.

"I need to...we have to..." She lifted her hands in dismay. "There are some important things I have to talk to you about."

"Mercy me, of course, you poor dear!" Fanny said, and Eunice nodded in agreement. "But first you must rest. Now put your head back and close your eyes for a few minutes."

"No!" Agnes said. "Polly needs me. I must go." Panic rose in her despite the subtle effects the valerian had started to have.

"Going back at the snap of a finger is not possible, child," Eunice said, not unkindly. "You are many miles from home. Rest for a bit, just fifteen minutes or so, to gather your thoughts. Give your agitation time to calm. Panic serves no one. It muddles thought."

"If you insist," Agnes said aloud, but inwardly every bit of her screamed just the opposite. "But I am determined to speak. I must. In ten minutes. I'll rest for ten minutes only. This can't be delayed."

"Do you need some help getting upstairs?" Seth offered.

"No," Agnes said. "I'll stay right here."

"Fine," Eunice said. "You stay wherever you wish. No permission required. Treat this house as though it's your own."

"It *is* your home," Fanny echoed. She leaned toward Agnes, adjusted the pillows again behind her on the porch swing, and smoothed her hair before standing up. "You rest. We'll be back out here in no time at all." She picked up a Bible from the side table, pressed it into Agnes's hands, and then turned toward Seth. Despite her unsettled state, Agnes was very aware of how closely he watched her.

"Miss Agnes may not need your assistance to get upstairs, but I need your help for something else," Fanny said to him. "If you don't mind, please take a look at the smokehouse door. It doesn't seem to be closing properly. Only if you have time, mind you. It likely may take a few hours to repair."

Seth shifted his gaze away from Agnes to respond to Fanny. "At your service," he said and tipped his hat to her.

"Of course we'll feed you dinner as a thank-you," Fanny said and went inside before Seth could answer. "Agnes, I'll be right back out to sit with you," she called as the screen door closed behind her. Eunice picked up the bottle and glass and followed her sister inside. "Call if you need anything," she said to Agnes.

An awkward silence fell. "Well, I'll be getting on," Seth said. "Miss Fanny has set me to work."

"How do you hold your head up when people spread untruths about you?" Agnes asked, out of the blue and with a suddenness that surprised even her. But Seth, of all people, might have advice to share about how she could return to the orphanage without causing distress to all concerned.

Then she remembered. Seth didn't know that she knew about his background. She wished she'd kept her mouth shut.

"The reason for that question is what?" he said in a level, careful tone.

"The Alloways told me—I mean, I asked about you and they mentioned...um...some hardships...," she started to say. His expression tightened, and his jaw line clenched.

There was no going back now. "I had to come here, many miles from home, because of an untruth told of me," she added.

Seth stepped closer, and his look of wariness changed to one of guarded concern.

"Bad?" he asked.

Agnes mouthed yes but didn't elaborate. "I owe an explanation to the Alloways first," she said. He nodded and didn't press her for more.

"Things tend to work themselves out," he said. Agnes nodded but was at a loss for words.

"I'll be getting to work on that smokehouse now," he finally said. He started down the steps but looked back as he reached the ground. "Always hold your head up, no matter what, no matter who," he said then headed toward the smokehouse in the far corner of the yard.

Agnes felt drained, worried, and unsure how to explain herself to the Alloways. She had started to care about the people in Persimmon Hollow and didn't want to hurt them or keep secrets from them. Truth be told, she didn't want them to hurt her with a rejection after they knew the truth. She prayed that wouldn't happen.

"Don't worry, Polly," she murmured aloud. "I'll rescue you. Somehow. I'll rescue you. These kind people will help me help you, even if they judge me. God will give us strength."

She rifled the pages of the Bible until it opened onto Psalm 46. She felt as though God had just spoken:

> God is our refuge and strength,
> a very present help in trouble.
> Therefore we will not fear, though the earth should change,

though the mountains shake in the heart of the sea;

though its waters roar and foam,

though the mountains tremble with its tumult.

She closed her eyes and absorbed the calming words.

The next thing she knew a mosquito buzzed in her ear. She awakened fully and saw the darkness of night all around her. She sat up straight as everything flooded back. The creak of the porch swing brought Fanny, Eunice, and Seth outside within seconds.

"We let you sleep," Fanny said. "We didn't want to wake you, even for dinner. We've just now finished, and we've got a plate warming on the stove in the kitchen. Are you hungry?"

Agnes had no appetite and shook her head no. "Please," she said. "I need help."

"We're here, child," Eunice said.

She gathered the courage to speak. The croak of tree frogs and buzzing of cicadas grew louder in the silence. In the distance, an owl hoot-hooted, and another, even more distant, responded.

"Owls are the voices of wisdom," Fanny said softly.

Agnes prayed for the wisdom to tell her story in a way that could be understood without judgment.

"I'll get right to the point," she said finally. "No, please stay," she said to Seth, who, upon hearing her start to talk, had put on his hat and turned toward the steps to leave. "You have a right to hear this. Your nephew is one of the people I'm charged with setting a moral example for. That's what teachers do, not just teach reading and writing."

Seth sat down on the top step and turned sideways to lean against the railing with one knee up and his arm resting atop it.

Fanny, seated across from Agnes, took her hand. Eunice lit and adjusted the wick of the kerosene lantern on a small table so that a low pool of light shimmered.

"Take your time," Fanny said and patted her hand.

"Got all night, if you need it," Seth said. "Billy's over with Clyde; he's safe."

She gave a small smile at his remembrance of her concerns about always knowing Billy's whereabouts.

"The child didn't even want to come over for dinner, he was having so much fun playing storekeeper," Fanny said with false brightness.

It was now or never, Agnes thought, and took a deep breath.

"I came here after I escaped from a house of ill repute," she blurted, then hurried on. "Now I have to return to the orphanage because a child I love is threatened with the same fate. I must save her before it's too late."

Chapter Nine

*F*anny's mouth formed into a perfect O. Her eyes were opened wide.

Eunice pressed her lips together into a thin line. Her nostrils looked pinched.

Seth let out a low whistle. "You? In a brothel?" he said. "Now that has to be a mistake."

"It was," Agnes said. "But it ruined my reputation. And now the person responsible is trying to ruin a child I love, a child I hope to formally adopt. Her name is Polly."

"What about St. Isidore's Home?" Eunice asked. "Does it exist? Or was it a ruse to get us to hire you?"

"No!" Agnes exclaimed. "I mean no it's not fiction. St. Isidore's Home is a real place that is dear to my heart. Every word I've said about the Home is true. I didn't try to trick you. I'm guilty, though, of not telling the whole truth. For that, I apologize."

"Go on," said Eunice, unsmiling.

"Powerful patrons threatened to withdraw funding when they learned the sisters had taken me back when I fled to the orphanage for safe haven after escaping the...the...," Agnes took a deep breath.

"The brothel?" Seth supplied the word.

"Yes," she said and winced. "The patrons are wealthy supporters whose donations are essential to keep the Home open. The Church is generous—our bishop is beyond generous to us— but the sisters don't turn away any child in need, and the need is great. Some of the patrons didn't believe I had been the victim of a kidnapping. They complained that…"

"Dear child, you consider it kidnapping?!" Fanny leaned forward in her chair.

"Yes," Agnes said. "But these patrons seemed to have pre-judged me and decided the worst. They…"

"How Christian of them," Seth muttered just loud enough for Agnes to hear.

"They said I should have gone to the 'Fallen Woman Home.' They said my presence was a bad influence for the young wards. They really seemed convinced I was…something I wasn't. One man even said he would report the Home to the authorities, because the city pays the orphanage for wards it sends to the sisters. The government money comes with rules about how the shelter must operate."

Agnes could still remember hearing the shouting and loud words coming through the thin walls of the Home.

"Mother Superior reminded the patrons, more than once, that everyone is a child of God and that I was one of their own and a help to them. The patrons insisted the orphanage is for children only, that it should be run as they—the patrons—saw fit. Mother Superior thanked them for their dedication and told them I was a good teacher who contributed greatly to the Home. She said I had been welcomed back as a member of the family. She spoke of the Home's Gospel mission."

Agnes felt her words tumble out so quickly her tongue stumbled over them.

"The patrons assumed I was a fallen woman," she said. "My virtue is intact. God in his mercy protected me." She made the Sign of the Cross.

"Did he get any help on that?" Seth asked.

"One of the house's…uh…residents helped me escape before anything happened," Agnes said. "God helped her help me."

Seth shifted his position, drew up his knees and linked his arms around them. "Whatever you say," he said.

Fanny and Eunice remained silent. Agnes read sympathy in Fanny's eyes and skepticism in Eunice's.

"Would you pray with me?" Agnes asked, speaking to them all but gazing at Seth. He stood up with an abrupt quickness and shifted his weight from foot to foot. "I need to check the smoke-house door to make sure it's holding," he said. Before he took a step, Eunice reached out, took hold of his hand, and tugged him toward the porch chairs near Fanny and Agnes.

Fanny leaned from her chair to the porch swing and squeezed Agnes's hand. "All will be well," she whispered.

Seth plopped down next to Agnes on the swing, which creaked as he got settled. Eunice released his hand and pulled up a rocker. The foursome made a small circle of togetherness in the middle of a dark night.

Seth didn't look happy.

Agnes didn't care.

She took his hand and clasped it tightly. Eunice took his other hand and reached across to Fanny. Agnes prayed aloud from the Gospel of John:

"In the beginning was the Word, and the Word was with God, and the Word was God....The light shines in the darkness...."

"In the name of the Father, the Son, and the Holy Ghost," Agnes said, slipping her hand out of Seth's and making the Sign of the Cross. She was flustered by the touch of his hand on hers, something she shouldn't even have noticed while praying. She nearly choked in surprise when Seth followed her lead and also made the Sign of the Cross—and did it as though he were familiar with the gesture. *Yes, that's right*, she thought. The Alloways had said his family was Catholic. He had obviously fallen away from the church and religion, but she was warmed that they shared a beautiful faith. If only he would return.

Agnes struggled to shift her focus to her prayers and away from the figure by her side. She clasped her hands together, deliberately avoiding Seth's. "Please help us find our way through the darkness," she prayed aloud. "Please guide us as we protect Polly and keep her from harm. We thank you for the blessings you bestow upon us. We bow to your will today and forever. Amen."

"Amen," said Fanny in a fluttery whisper.

"Amen," said Eunice in a loud, firm voice.

Seth kept silent.

"Let us sing 'Amazing Grace,'" Eunice said.

"Let us not," said Seth. He stood up and clomped to the porch stairs. The sacred moment was broken.

Agnes looked up. "Why are you so afraid of prayer?" she asked. "I'm desperate to help Polly. I'm a thousand miles away from her and not sure which way to turn to assist her. Yet I know I can always turn to God. He's always there. No matter how bad life gets."

"You believe what you want," Seth said, a testy edge to his voice. "God never showed up when I needed him. I ain't exactly fond of praying to him."

"You can't bargain with God," Agnes said. It was as though Fanny and Eunice were no longer there and she and Seth were alone in a tug of war that pulled them in opposite directions even while keeping them connected.

"Life and faith aren't games," Agnes continued, as she gave in to her penchant for preachiness. "Life is hard. It doesn't always go the way we want. Bad things sometimes happen to good, faithful people. Look what happened to Jesus."

Seth let out a puff of exasperation and clamped his lips as though trying to stifle unpleasant words.

"Have faith, Seth," Agnes said, in a lower, softer tone. "That faith helps us survive the hard times and drink in the joy of good times. I have faith that Polly...I must have faith that Polly will be all right and that..."

She heard her words growing tremulous and clenched her fists in an attempt to hold back tears that threatened to spring. She turned to the Alloways.

"I beg you to let me bring Polly here, if even for a short while." She held up her hand when she saw Fanny open her mouth as if to speak.

"I know, I know, it's an imposition," Agnes continued. "But, please. She can stay in my room. She'll help with chores. She's a good little worker. She'll be no trouble. She'll..."

"Of course she can stay with us," Eunice said.

"We have a large house that's usually empty except for the winter season," Fanny said. "A child will brighten our days, even when the house fills—especially when the house fills."

Agnes continued her nervous talk without comprehending their words. "I know it'll be a tight fit in the room. We'll make it fit. It's so very important. The man who tried to ruin me is now after Polly." Her voice rose to a higher pitch. "He..."

"Dear, we said yes, bring Polly here," Fanny interrupted her.

"Oh! Oh, thank you, thank you, thank you," Agnes let out a breath she didn't realize she'd been holding. "You've no idea what a relief that will be and what it means."

"Tell us," Eunice said.

"The man who kidnapped me did it legally, or so we thought," Agnes explained. "He claimed kinship to me. In my innocence, and my and the sisters' belief in the goodness of all people, we accepted his paperwork that showed he was a long-lost uncle. We had no reason to doubt him. Orphans have come and gone with the discovery of relatives. We learned too late that his papers were forged. He told me and the sisters that he wanted to see me safe and settled in an arranged marriage. I tell you, I wasn't happy about the idea of an arranged marriage, but it has long been a custom of my people. I felt I had to show respect and at least meet my intended and perhaps start courting, rather than immediately protest to this long-lost uncle that we are in America now, not the Old Country. I had no intention of going through with the marriage if I had objections after I met the man."

Agnes took a shaky breath.

"We arranged for me to meet my groom and his parents at a special dinner. The sisters, Polly, and several other orphans helped me dress in my Sunday best and arranged my hair. They were giddy with my good fortune. I admit, I was curious about what was to come.

"The man claiming to be my uncle came to escort me, and we left with everyone's good wishes echoing. Well, we were no sooner down the block and into a waiting carriage than his demeanor changed from humble deference to harsh control. There was no trip to meet a groom and his parents. The man abducted me. He kept a tight grip on me and directed the driver to Four Points. That's when I knew something was horribly wrong. Four Points is the harshest slum in the city. I tried to get away, but he hit me so hard it left a bruise by my eye. He kept an iron grip on me until the carriage rolled to a stop before a house of...the place that is..."

"...a house of ill repute." Seth filled in again. He began to pace. "Would I like to get my hands on this guy."

Agnes took a shaky breath.

"Mercy! How long were you there?" Fanny asked.

"Overnight—I left early the next morning."

"Overnight!" Eunice and Fanny exclaimed together.

"What was it like?" Fanny asked, and Eunice tut-tutted her.

"Horrible," Agnes said. "Except for the kindness of some of the women. When they heard my story, they sheltered me for the night in an empty room on the third floor and told the man I was sick and couldn't do 'business' for a few days. His curses carried through the building. I started to quake when I heard him coming up the stairs, but some of the women distracted him. I didn't sleep at all that night, from fear and from the noise—the shouting, piano-playing, singing, laughing, crying. It went on and on.

"The next morning, two of the women dressed me in servant's clothes and rushed me out the back door with the two washer-women who came to pick up the laundry. I was in a part of the city I didn't know, and I stumbled about for a few blocks until I found a street name I recognized. I ran as fast as I could back to the Home, fearful that my abductor was right behind me. Everyone at the Home was in a stir when they saw me and heard what happened. Fr. Tom came from the rectory right away to hear my confession and to offer Mass for the women at the…the place.

"You know," Agnes continued, "those ladies of the night told me they were happy with their lives, but…I don't think they told the truth, or admitted it to themselves. I felt for them. They smiled and laughed, but not a one of them had a light in her eyes. Their eyes were dull, and their gazes weary. I prayed for them as well as myself as I huddled in the corner of the room for that long night. I was so glad I had my rosary in my skirt pocket, like I always do."

"Did that man harm you in any way?" asked Seth.

"No," Agnes said. "Nothing happened to me, but my reputation was in tatters. I sought a position far from home in order to put distance between myself and the orphanage, to salvage my reputation and to protect the name of St. Isidore's Home."

Agnes took another deep breath. "That same man has now learned—somehow—of my closeness with Polly. He thinks we're sisters. We're not. I helped raise her from the day she was brought to the orphanage as an infant. We are closer than sisters, and she awaits my return so I can adopt her. The man…this Rufus…he says he can prove Polly is my sister and that he is kin. I'm sure he has papers to prove it legally. They're forged, of course. But he wouldn't try such a stunt without having documents. He doesn't know the sisters know what happened with me. That buys me some time, for the sisters will stall him. But he's smart and has money to bribe authorities. I must get to Polly."

She started to get up and try her weight on her unsteady foot.

"Not so fast," Seth said.

"What he means is he has something to tell you," Eunice said and gave Seth a knowing look before she continued. "Seth came inside after doing the smokehouse repairs, just as Fanny and I were talking about offering you an advance on wages to cover expenses of Polly's journey. He insisted on taking immediate action."

Agnes sat back down. Seth took off his Stetson hat and inspected it as though it were a new and interesting thing. Then he looked at Agnes.

"I walked over the mercantile and arranged to have fare money wired to St. Isidore's Home," he said. "Polly will be here as soon as they can get her on the train."

Agnes gave a small shriek of joy. She reached over and grabbed Seth's arm to steady herself. In her happiness, she pulled him toward her and turned her face upward. He looked down, a question on his face, and she gave him an impulsive kiss on the cheek.

"Bless you and thank you, Mr. Taylor." Then, as she felt her cheeks grow warm, she released him and pressed her hands to her face. "Oh, gosh, my enthusiasm ran ahead of my good sense."

"Fine with me," Seth said and grinned.

She twirled in her seat and grabbed Fanny and Eunice's hands. "And thank you, both of you, thank you. You won't regret letting her stay. I promise you won't. She won't make a peep. She's the best little girl in the world. Oh, I miss her so much."

As the enormity of what Seth had done settled on her, she turned back toward him. "How did you know?" she asked. "Why did you send money before I even had a chance to explain what had happened?"

"I didn't know the full story," Seth said. "When I picked up the torn telegram from the ground I saw enough to realize a child was in trouble and that a place named St. Isidore's Home needed train fare for the child. I sent money with a telegram letting them know more information would be forthcoming."

"That was a truly thoughtful action, Seth," said Agnes, but then she frowned. "I'm touched. But I can't accept a monetary gift like that from you. It's not proper."

"Since when is helping a child not proper?" Seth asked. "I understand, Agnes, what it's like to have guardianship over a child. I'd wrestle the devil himself if I had to, to protect Billy. If it makes you feel better, the money isn't a gift. It's a loan. I expect it paid back."

Agnes watched him with wary eyes. The women at St. Isidore's Home had warned her about men who make gifts, especially monetary gifts, on the pretext of helping. Then they asked for payment. They often wanted something unsavory or immoral. She inched a little closer to Fanny and Eunice. She tried to figure Seth out. She intuited that his intentions were honorable. Nevertheless, no man was ever going to be in a position to take advantage of her ever again.

"You will have payment each month when I receive my pay," she said. "Every penny, until the fare is paid. The Alloways are my witnesses. As is God."

"I have a better plan," Seth said. "I like that idea you had about making items for the depot store. I'm fixing to open in time for the winter season. You can pay me back by making whatever kind of foodstuff you ladies make out of citrus. If it sells at the store and I need more stock, you could be earning more than that teacher's paycheck."

"Smart idea," Eunice nodded her approval.

"Marvelous," Fanny clapped her hands. "Agnes, the earliest citrus is on the verge of ripening. Once harvest season begins next month, we positively bathe in citrus, there is so much of it. This is marvelous!"

"The Satsumas will be ready in less than a month," Seth said. "Then the mid-season varieties kick in, and finally the late-season oranges. Enough to keep you busy for at least five months."

"By then, the season starts to wane," Eunice said. "Most guests start arriving in November, but a number come earlier, in October and even September. By April and May, most go back up North. Business should be brisk until then."

Agnes tried to take it all in. It seemed too good to be true. She'd have Polly with her, she'd earn her livelihood as a teacher, and she'd make extra money to send to St. Isidore's Home. Her conscience probed her to admit the rest of the truth. She'd be able to spend time near Seth. Maybe she'd even be able to convince him to grow closer to God and the Church. Surely, he remembered how merciful God's grace is and how the Church's sacraments, rituals, and counsel help a person grow in their relationship with God.

She had some tough jobs ahead of her, she knew. With God by her side, she'd be ready for the challenge.

* * *

Agnes's heart overflowed as she sang and prayed in worship at the settlement service. *Thank you, Lord, for leading me to this shelter of Persimmon Hollow and thank you for the special people who make this their home.* The only thing that could make it better would be a visiting priest to say Mass. Her mind whirred ahead, as usual. If the citrus venture proved successful and the orphanage received the funds it needed, there might be enough money left over to start a collection for a Persimmon Hollow Catholic Church.

Parson Pierce closed his Bible with a soft thud and ended the service. Agnes waved the Alloways ahead and waited until the aisle cleared before she started to step-hop from the pew-bench toward the door with the aid of her crutches. As she neared the exit, she saw Sarah Bight, pale and wan, standing with four of her little ones next to her in stair-step order and her youngest in her arms.

"So good to see you out!" Agnes stopped and exclaimed.

Sarah nodded. "It's good to be here. And I see we're both in stages of recuperation."

Agnes smiled and swept her gaze over the children. "And I'm certain all of you are on best behavior while your mother regains her strength. Aren't you?" Four heads nodded in vigorous unison. She spoke to the oldest, who appeared to be a miniature Sarah. "My daught...my almost-daughter looks to be about your age. She'll be here soon. Maybe you can be friends."

"This is Pansy," Sarah said and put her arm around the girl. "She's eleven."

"That's how old my daughter is!" Agnes said. "Her name is Polly."

Adelaide, who had been standing in the doorway, whirled around.

"Why, Agnes Foster. You told me you were raised in an orphanage," she accused. "How can you have a daughter? And you're not even married." She glanced at Agnes's ringless third finger.

"Just why is this your concern, Adelaide?" Agnes asked, in no mood for this woman who seemed to dislike her for no reason she could imagine.

Adelaide ignored the question and raised her voice slightly. "Oh, Misses Alloway, we know you mean well, as my mother tells me, but perhaps you should screen your guests more carefully," she said. "The propriety of guests is of the utmost sensitivity for those of us engaged in lifting the mien of this town beyond wood sidewalks and sandy streets where hogs and chickens run loose."

That did it. Agnes succumbed to her twin nemeses, impatience and unsolicited preachiness. "Goodness of heart is better than false piety," she blurted to Adelaide and tried to nudge her aside with her crutch.

"Ladies, please," Fanny interrupted as she hurried back in from the front steps. "Polly is Agnes's *adopted* daughter. And what has come over you, Adelaide?"

Adelaide sputtered. "Well, why, nothing but what I said. You can't be certain about people from orphanages, you know, and now this news of a sort-of daughter, and, of course, the nonsense of Seth Taylor coming around to see her."

Fanny arched an eyebrow. "Ah. And perhaps you would rather he came to see you, despite your recent protestations about his character."

Adelaide's face flushed, and she strode out without another word. Agnes stared after her. Of all the things! Jealousy was what she had least expected, especially from a woman who seemed to have so many privileges.

"Come, dear," Fanny said to Agnes. "You, too." She beckoned to Sarah and the children. Together, they made their way to a shaded section of the yard where Eunice and other women were gathered. As they passed the men, they heard them discussing particulars of how to organize the whitewashing of the meeting hall.

"I hope you don't mind if we come to call sometime," Sarah said to Agnes. "I know Pansy would love to meet your Polly. And any daughter of yours is welcome in my house, too."

"When is she gonna get here?" Pansy piped up.

"Soon, honey, within a couple of weeks, I hope," Agnes said and smiled down at the girl. "And we'd love for you to call."

"You two keep company while Eunice and I help set out the food," Fanny said to Agnes and Sarah and brushed away their immediate protestations. "What can you do with a sore ankle, Agnes, and you with all those children to look after, Sarah?" she said to the two of them.

"She's impossible to argue with when she's in a mood," Eunice added with uncharacteristic teasing to her voice. But her voice went flat as she beckoned Adelaide to go with her to the rest of the women.

The voice of the parson broke into everyone's conversations.

"We need a few more men than the Good Lord has sent us today if we're going to get the job done," the parson bellowed.

"Mercy, I've never heard Parson Pierce speak so loudly in any day I've been here," Fanny said to Eunice as they hurried off toward the plank tables set up in the shade of the building.

Parson Pierce stood in the sparse shade of a palm tree and wiped sweat off his brow with his handkerchief. "With enough men, we could be finished in a morning. Ladies, you always serve us plentiful, tasty fare, but perhaps you could outdo yourselves on a special picnic. Gentlemen," he paused and looked over the men who milled in front of him, as though counting each one and memorizing their faces. "Do I have the assurance of volunteer help from each of you in the near future? We need to get this done before the Academy opens for classes so they can use the building for assemblies."

Every man and the older boys stepped forward with decisive action. Agnes looked around for Seth and felt a flush of disappointment at his absence, followed by impatience at her own expectations. Had she really expected him to mend his ways simply because he'd prayed with her once?

"Something the matter?" Sarah asked, peering at Agnes's face.

"I'm just sorry that Seth isn't here, is all," Agnes said as she shifted her stance to grab more of the dappled shade thrown off by a cluster of longleaf pines.

"You can't push a man too fast or too hard," Sarah said. She moved the baby to her other shoulder and patted his tiny back. "Even a good man like Seth."

"How old is he?" Agnes asked Sarah about the baby, to change the subject. She didn't want to think she was pushing Seth Taylor to do anything.

"Six months now," Sarah said and lifted the child's arm so that he appeared to be waving at Agnes. The baby gurgled a happy laugh. Agnes waved and smiled in return but watched the baby with wistful longing, remembering all the orphans and wishing they were near.

The heat was making Agnes's ankle throb, her hands felt clammy on the awkward crutches, and her reliance on them prevented her from using a fan.

"Give Seth some time, Agnes," said Sarah in a soft voice.

"The Alloways keep telling me he's good," Agnes said. "But how good can a man be if he refuses to attend service and doesn't step forward to volunteer for the good of the town?"

"I'm sure he has his reasons," Sarah said, but she frowned. Her husband Toby had been one of the first men to step forward to help paint. "For everything there is a season, and a time for every matter under heaven," Sarah said, quoting Ecclesiastes 3:1. "Seth's time hasn't yet arrived."

"Yes, Fanny and Eunice say similar things, too, and in my heart I feel it's the truth," Agnes said, but in her heart she also felt despair. Was she falling for a man who had no faith? Why else would she care whether he was here or whether he was acting as she thought a man should act?

"Seth has always been kind to us the few times we've encountered him," Sarah said. "Once, he sold Toby an acre's worth of young seedling citrus and then canceled the debt when a hard freeze wiped out every last plant. That freeze nearly destroyed our little settlement. The Alloways' father went bankrupt and died of a heart attack after repaying settlers for what they'd lost."

"How sad!" Agnes exclaimed. "The Alloways never said a word about it to me."

"That's why they take boarders now. Their father had guaranteed settlers' investments. And he stayed true to his word. A lot of settlers left and went back to the states they had come from, to Kentucky, the Carolinas, New York, Ohio, and other such places. The ones who stayed are a hardy lot...and not all of them are always as kind-hearted as they could be," Sarah said. "They judged Seth harshly over that incident with the moonshine and the death, and they don't all approve of his living out at the grove with an Indian friend and a Mexican family. The family is, I believe, Catholic, as Seth's family was. Not everyone is happy about that either."

"I'm Catholic," said Agnes quietly.

Sarah blinked. "I'm Baptist," she said. "I don't know much about your faith, but I can tell a woman of character when I see one. My offer still stands."

"Thanks," Agnes said. "I appreciate it. I know little about Baptists, but I, too, can tell a woman of character." They both laughed in a warm moment of sharing.

A pair of horsemen thundered up to the yard, kicking up the dusty sand. For the briefest of seconds, Agnes hoped it would be Seth, but it turned out to be strangers. One was thin, with a long, dark handlebar mustache. The other was as round as he was tall and reminded her of a barrel.

The thin one dismounted and swaggered up to the men while the round one hurried to keep up with him.

"Little bird told us you folks need some menfolk for painting," the thin one said, and Agnes saw him wink at Adelaide. "My friend and I are just passing through for a few days, but we'd be glad to do some of the Lord's work. Plus, it allows us to stay a little longer at Land Inn and enjoy the vittles."

A wave of unease flitted over Agnes. Something about the thin, slippery-looking man reminded her so much of Rufus she felt bile rise in her throat.

The parson scratched his head and looked like he wondered whether or not to take these men at their word. "I could use the hands," he began.

"Our word is as good as gold," the thin man said.

Agnes gasped as memories flooded over her. Rufus had used the exact same words. She had glossed over her experience in the brothel when telling the story to the Alloways. She had come much closer to ruin than she cared to remember. Rufus had run up the stairs, pushed his way through, and attempted to force himself on her before the other women made him leave her alone.

She shuddered. "Are you all right?" Sarah asked.

"I feel a little unwell," Agnes said. "Please tell the Alloways I returned to the house."

"Are you sure you're all right? Do you want me and the children to go with you?" Sarah asked anxiously. "You look pale."

"No, it's just my ankle," Agnes said, stretching the truth. She felt shaky and ill at ease. Her intuition was sending out warning signals. She had learned the hard way never to ignore her intuition. It was always correct. She thanked her guardian angel for that.

"Please be careful," she said to Sarah. "Keep your girls close and away from strangers."

Sarah smiled. "There are no strangers in Persimmon Hollow, Agnes." She patted Agnes's back. "Go get some rest."

Agnes turned and felt a chill as the thin man made bold enough to catch her glance. He then spoke loudly. "And my friend and I are wondering if you have any ladies we can court while we're staying here," he said, finally looking away from Agnes and instead at the parson.

Agnes started to hobble away, thankful that the Alloways' house was near the meeting hall. She couldn't get there fast enough. She heard the man's thin laugh ring out.

Chapter Ten

*S*till unnerved, Agnes eased herself into a chair in the blessedly quiet Alloway parlor. How she wished for the sanctuary of the Adoration Chapel, with its reassuring presence of the Holy Eucharist and its sense of peace. Quiet prayer and reflection would help her untangle the day's anxieties. But there was no chapel in dusty Persimmon Hollow. There wasn't even a real church.

Why had those two men disturbed her so much? Evil wormed its way everywhere. Even the harmony of a Persimmon Hollow religious gathering wasn't exempt. She gingerly propped her foot on the ottoman and leaned back against the plushness of the cushions. Distance hadn't soothed all her fears over the nightmarish brothel episode. She wondered if she'd ever overcome the hurtful effects. Would shadows and slander follow her wherever she went and taint good people who tried to help her? Would she forevermore be suspicious of strangers?

If she couldn't manage herself and her emotions, she certainly couldn't take responsibility for Polly. Agnes sighed. The world outside the shelter of the orphanage had been one surprise after another, not all of them good.

The grandfather clock ticked a soothing rhythm in the shadowed parlor. The drapes drawn against the afternoon sun and heat muffled even the cicadas. A family Bible lay open on the end table near her seat, as though waiting for her. *Have faith, Agnes,* she told herself. *Remember the gifts of the Holy Ghost.* Could she? She leaned forward, picked up the gilt-edged Bible, and rested it in her lap while she brought the seven gifts to mind: Understanding. Fortitude. Wisdom. Counsel. Purity. Knowledge. Fear of the Lord. Yes, fortitude especially would help her. Gently, she thumbed through the Bible's slender pages, so thin they were almost translucent. *Have faith in the goodness of Persimmon Hollow and in the Spirit working through people like the Alloways, Clyde, Sarah, little Billy and even his uncle Seth. Good always triumphs over evil. Sometimes it just takes a long while.*

She stopped at the psalms. Mother Superior always spoke about the comfort of the psalms. Agnes loved to listen to the sisters chant them. There were so many of them, though...more than a hundred. Agnes could never hope to keep them straight. Her gaze lingered on words and stanzas here and there as she paged through, until it landed on a phrase in Psalm 130 that spoke to her wounded heart: "Out of the depths I cry to you, O Lord. Lord, hear my voice! Let your ears be attentive to the voice of my supplications!" She murmured the words once, twice, and then a third time, pleading with God to hear. She closed her eyes and listened to the silence, sensing God's nearness.

He seemed closer than she expected, actually. As though the Lord's presence swept up from the pages and into her soul, Agnes sat up taller, suddenly alert, opened her eyes, and focused on the unbidden thought circling her mind. It was a thought she knew well: *God helps those who help themselves.* Of course. Hadn't she, Agnes, said that to others more than once? Yes. And furthermore, turning to vigorous work always uplifted her spirits no matter how low they might be sinking. She had found that it was especially true if the work helped others.

With renewed energy, Agnes looked through the pages of the Bible, searching. She knew many of the verses well, thanks to the sisters, but the one she sought right now eluded her. Was it in Timothy or Thessalonians? First or Second? Oh, there it was! First Timothy 6:18–19. Smoothing her hand over the page, she read aloud:

> They are to do good, to be rich in good works, generous, and ready to share, thus storing up for themselves the treasure of a good foundation for the future, so that they may take hold of the life that really is life.

Oh, how true, she thought. What perfect words. She could best help everyone—including herself—by taking up Seth on his offer instead of wondering about the propriety of working with him or being too near. And she could start right now, by making some of her favorites and having them ready as treats for everyone who came back to the Alloways' house. *Even Seth?* a small voice inside her asked. She took a deep breath, grabbed her crutches, and hobbled into the kitchen. Yes, even Seth. Especially Seth. One way to a man's heart was through his stomach. Maybe that was the way to approach helping him rediscover his faith. She so wanted him to find it again. For his sake and, she admitted, for her sake, too.

* * *

Several days later, Agnes was sitting on a low stool in the back yard in the shade of late afternoon, filling a pine basket with sprigs of rosemary and lavender clipped from the herb bed, when

Seth arrived. He carried what had become his near daily delivery of fresh comfrey for her ankle. Agnes smiled and waved hello. Fanny straightened from weeding the zipper cream pea patch in the adjacent kitchen garden. She brushed her hands on her apron and gave Seth a cheerful smile as she opened the gate separating the side walkway from the fenced backyard.

"Afternoon, ladies," Seth said with a tip of his hat as he neared. "I brought some more...wow, is that sweet potato pie?" He sniffed as though inhaling perfume, left the comfrey in a pile on the back porch step, and made haste toward the kitchen window. Just inside the window stood a pie safe. Two plump pies, still warm from the oven, were tucked neatly inside the pie safe. Their aroma scented the yard.

"Yes, Agnes made them," Fanny said. "The breeze has been blowing that heavenly scent our way for more than half an hour. Makes my mouth water! It's one of my favorite ways to eat sweet potatoes, and you know the crop is heavy this year."

"Mmm...mmmm," said Seth, walking back toward Agnes and Fanny. "I don't guess you're fixing on cutting into one of them anytime soon, are you?" he asked, stopping beside Agnes.

"Why, that's an excellent idea!" said Fanny. "I think we..."

"...should wait and serve it after the meeting hall is white-washed," said Agnes. "I understand the parson hopes to get the job finished and out of the way soon, maybe even tomorrow. That's what you said, right, Fanny? Yes, that was it," she answered herself. Agnes tilted her head toward the herb basket, so that her hat shaded her lips and Seth couldn't see her smile.

"That's blackmail," said Seth, in a tone that told Agnes he was not amused.

"Nothing of the kind," said Agnes, looking up at him and biting her lip to stifle a laugh. "I made those pies as a reward for the hard workers who paint."

Seth scowled. "You don't give up, do you?"

"Not when I believe in something," she said.

Fanny joined in. "The parson really needs extra hands. Even if you're...um...busy, perhaps Billy can help?"

"If he finishes his chores, he can," Seth said.

"I'd rather see you and Billy than those unsavory gentlemen who showed up at the meeting hall yard when the parson called for volunteers," Agnes said.

"What 'unsavory gentlemen'?" Seth asked frowning.

"Two men who made me nervous," Agnes said. "One was skinny, with a nasal voice and a long mustache, and the other was round like a barrel."

Seth's frown settled into a slash. "I've got a long score to settle with a man who's skinny, has a long mustache, and a nasal voice," he said. "Did he give his name?"

"He didn't say," Agnes said, "at least not while I was there. Something about him reminded me of the man who abducted me. So much so that I left and came home."

Home. She'd just called the Alloways' house her home. Warmth flooded through her.

"He introduced himself soon after you left," Fanny said. "Said his name was Lester Little."

"You're sure?" Seth asked, taking a step toward Fanny and Agnes then stopping abruptly. He started pacing. The mellow humor of a man trying to sweet-talk a slice of pie had evaporated.

"Why, yes," said Fanny. "Seth, are you all right?

He stopped and pushed his hat back. His face was tense. "Lester Little is the name of the man who framed me in the moonshine incident," he said. "Because of his accusation, some lawman—a friend of his, I suspect—hauled me to jail down in Lemon City. Illegally, it turned out. Meanwhile, my house was burning down and…" He stopped talking, but his pacing increased. Agnes and Fanny exchanged glances. Neither needed to hear anything more. The anger and grief etched on Seth's face and in the stomp of his heels said more than words could.

"Been waiting a long time," said Seth. His green eyes had a dark hue. "A showdown is overdue. What time does the whitewashing begin?"

Agnes hoped her glance at Fanny conveyed the worry building in her.

"What time?" Seth asked again. He had stopped pacing. He was alert and tense, like a man poised to meet an enemy.

"As soon as the dew dries in the morning," Fanny said. "Seth, perhaps you'd do well to reconsider whatever it is you plan to do. Revenge never pays."

"Yes, it does," Seth said.

"No," Agnes jumped in. "Forgiveness is better. Seth, please try to find forgiveness in your heart. You can do…"

"Forgive?" Seth was incredulous. "Did you forgive the fool who harmed you?"

"No…no, not yet…I'm trying, but it's too soon…I haven't yet been able to."

"Then don't preach to me," Seth said. He bowed stiffly. "Good day, ladies. Perhaps we'll see each other tomorrow." He jammed his hat on and started to leave.

He paused, his fist squeezing the top of the garden gate as he closed it behind him.

"Better bring both pies," he said. "Anger makes a man hungry."

"Oh, Fanny, this is dire," Agnes said as soon as he was gone. "What should we do? I meant for the pies to draw him to the whitewashing, not to feed bloodshed. I almost wish I hadn't baked them. See what I get for meddling." She leaned on Fanny's arm as she rose.

"You're not meddling," Fanny soothed her. "Seth would have been here, pies or not. He's come into town more in the past few weeks than in the past few years. It's because of you, honey."

She shooed Agnes to the garden bench that edged the vegetable plot and brought over the clippers and laden herb basket as she joined Agnes. "Stop trying to do too much," she chided. "Your sprain will never heal."

"Let's sit here a moment and savor this beautiful day," she suggested to Agnes.

Their viewpoint opened onto the roadway, where the dust kicked up from Silver's hooves still hung in the air.

Fanny let out a warm sigh as the trails of dust faded. "When the Lord sends love, Agnes, circumstances aren't always convenient. Maybe our Lord sent you here because you are meant to try and help Seth find his faith again."

Agnes coughed. And coughed again. "I don't think so!" she said, then had a coughing fit. "It must be that dust," she croaked, gesturing to the now-empty road where the sand lay quiet. Fanny's raised eyebrows suggested otherwise. "All right," Agnes said. "Perhaps you're right. I guess we never really know what we're supposed to do or meant to do."

"The Lord gives us pretty good ideas," chirped Fanny. A cherubic smile plumped her cheeks.

"You're such a matchmaker," said Agnes. She toyed with the herb sprigs and inhaled the distinctive scents.

"Who, me?" asked Fanny, all innocence. She grew absorbed with the day's harvest. "What are you doing with the herbs?"

"Making sachets and day pillows to sell in Seth's store," Agnes said. "Oh, darn. I forgot to ask him today what he thinks of the idea."

"Well, I think it's wonderful!" Fanny said. "But it is his store. You'll just have to ask him tomorrow when you offer some pie." She beamed at Agnes.

"A matchmaker and a romantic!" Agnes said, laughing. "Perhaps the food and friendship will sway Seth off his path of revenge."

"I detect a romantic in you, too, under those layers of practicality and responsibility," Fanny said. "Life is hard, and life's work is demanding and wearying, but even Eunice agrees we can't let the harsher realities overshadow the beauty in our worlds. We always give blessings for what we have."

Agnes smiled and nodded, Fanny stopped talking, and the two of them sat and admired the landscaping. The tidy shrubs, the neat little courtyard with jasmine-covered arbors at each end, the tangerine, orange, and lemon trees, the kitchen garden, and the patch of herbs enveloped Agnes in warmth and goodness. She thought of Seth's special delivery of comfrey for her ankle, of the support of the Alloways, of the anticipation of seeing Polly much sooner than she'd ever have imagined. A bumblebee hummed over the spotted horsemint, and Agnes grew drowsy in the sun and heat.

Pop. Pop.

"Mother of Mercy, gunshots!" Fanny shrieked and sprang from the bench. She crouched down on the brick pavers and pulled Agnes down with her. "Get down! Cover your head!"

Panic flooded Agnes. *See. See what happens when you let down your guard for even a few moments,* she thought. She trembled at the shrieks, yells, and rapid thudding of horse hooves thumping along the sand road. She heard footsteps from all directions, and she wished Seth hadn't been so quick to leave.

"Fanny! Agnes!" The two peered around the edges of the bench and started to rise. Eunice ran into the courtyard with Clyde behind her, guarding her back and scoping the surroundings. "Come quickly!" Eunice said. "There's been a shooting at Land Inn."

Eunice, Fanny, and Clyde hurried to the front path, and Agnes hobbled behind them. The three elders stopped in unison at the clump of the crutches.

"No, dear," Fanny said, and she turned and gestured toward Agnes's ankle. "You stay here."

"No, I will not stay here," Agnes said. "Everyone's help might be needed. You go ahead." She motioned for the three of them to go. "I'll catch up."

"No, no, you mustn't...," Fanny said, as Eunice shook her head no. Clyde's thin mouth was set in a disapproving line.

Shouts and commotion from Land Inn increased in intensity. "Go!" Agnes said, shooing them away before they could think of a better reason to detain her.

"If the walk becomes too difficult, I promise I'll turn right around and return," Agnes called after them.

She was determined to do no such thing, no matter how much her ankle protested.

She inched her way along the walkway as Fanny, Eunice, and Clyde strode down the street. Horse hooves galloped in the distance. They drew closer as she reached the street, and within moments Seth rounded the corner on Silver. He slowed the horse, which stepped and pranced.

"You heard the gunshots?" Agnes asked.

"Couldn't miss them," he said, his brows drawn together as he stared at the crutches. "What are you doing out here? You planning on wielding those things as weapons?"

"No" she said and scowled at him. "Clyde and Eunice said the shots were at Land Inn. I'm walking down there to see if I can be of any help. They went ahead with Fanny. They told me to stay here, but I'd rather not."

"You are a stubborn woman," he said, and in a flash he had dismounted Silver. He grabbed one crutch and tried to take the second before Agnes gathered her wits.

"What are you doing?" she demanded. "Give that back."

"Lean on me and give me the other crutch," Seth said. He tied the one he had to his saddlebag.

Favoring her sprained ankle, Agnes leaned off-center but tightened her grip as he reached for the remaining crutch.

"Let me have it," Seth said. "I'm only going to tie it next to the other one. It's obvious you won't stay here despite the good counsel of the Alloways. At least I can make sure you don't walk the whole way."

Agnes was too smart to let pride get in the way of acceptance. She handed up the crutch and put a hand on Silver's bridle to steady herself.

Seth tied the last knot and then turned to Agnes. Before she had time to determine the propriety of what he proposed, he put his hands on her waist and hoisted her onto the horse as if she weighed less than a sack of feed.

He put his foot in the stirrup and swung his other leg up, seating himself behind her.

"Lean back a bit," he said. "I can't see through your head."

Gingerly, she did so, uncomfortable at such closeness without a chaperone or youngsters or anyone else nearby. "Uh, I can't do this," she said, as her muscles tightened. "Let me down, and I'll walk."

"If you insist," said Seth, "but it's a short distance, and it's an emergency." He held Silver in check, but the horse was frisky.

"All right," Agnes finally agreed. "This truly will get me there faster."

He signaled Silver forward. "Like I heard Eunice tell you, we've got…"

"…no room for false modesty on the frontier," Agnes spoke the words in unison with him. Still, she held herself stiff, alert, and willing to risk a fall from the horse if the need arose.

"You have my word as a gentleman that I mean no disrespect," Seth said as he kept Silver at a slower, steady pace that she suspected was for her.

Agnes remembered the falsity of similar words spoken by Rufus, words she had believed in her innocence. Not again. She would never be fooled again.

"You do know by now that I'm not the same cut of man as your abductor," Seth said, as if he understood her reticence.

"You're sure that's what I'm thinking?" she asked.

"Something like that," Seth said. "Your whole body tensed the minute I swung into the saddle behind you, and you haven't relaxed since."

"A woman can never be too careful," she said.

"But she can learn to trust the right man," he said.

Land Inn nestled in the middle of a small orange grove. A few men lay stretched on the ground, and Agnes couldn't tell if they were dead or alive until she heard moaning. People scurried to and fro amid debris from a scuffle that appeared to have started indoors and moved out. The front door hung half off its hinges. Seth dismounted and prepared to help Agnes, but Clyde and Eunice came hurrying forward from the crowd.

"Here, Agnes, let me assist you," Clyde said.

"No need to call attention to that closeness we saw as you rode in," Eunice added. "There's enough of a mess here already, and we don't want to give people anything else to gossip about."

Agnes was perplexed. Eunice had just contradicted her familiar stance against false modesty. Whatever for? Agnes leaned on Eunice and used Clyde's arm to steady herself as she slid off Silver and assessed the surroundings and situation. Seth handed the crutches to her. Adelaide watched her every move from the porch, with a sharp look on her face. Agnes had a feeling she knew why Eunice had suddenly became concerned about propriety.

"What's happened?" Agnes asked. Seth was already helping with cleanup, picking up splintered chair legs from the ground and spindles that had wedged in orange branches. "Were those men shot?" she asked about the injured.

"No, and the injuries aren't life-threatening, thank God," Eunice said. "One has a broken nose, another has sore ribs, and the third has either a broken leg or ankle. Apparently there was an argument and fight involving the two strangers who showed up at the churchyard, the ones who troubled you. One of them, the round man, shot off two rounds in the air. Then both of them took off for who knows where."

"I don't know how such ruffians ended up in our town," said Fanny, who came hurrying out of the building. "They certainly don't embody the spirit of Persimmon Hollow. We'll breathe easier now that they're gone."

"If they're gone," said Eunice, and Agnes thought of the looming showdown that might occur in the morning if the two men showed up for the whitewashing. She prayed God would send some guidance to all involved and resolved to say an extra decade of the rosary before bed.

Eunice and a few other women tended to the injured men, while Agnes and Fanny went inside to soothe Adelaide's mother, who was near hysteria. Seth and Clyde worked on repairing the front door, and other men finished clearing away pieces of wood and straightened overturned tables and chairs.

Fanny walked Mrs. Land to her room upstairs and helped her into bed. She tucked a quilt around her and prayed and talked with her until her nerves settled. She soon slipped into a restless sleep, and Fanny tiptoed out of the room, closing the door gently behind her.

"Mrs. Land is resting upstairs," Fanny said when she rejoined Agnes and the activity on the main floor. "She wishes to feed everyone for their help and regrets that she sent the servants home when the fighting broke out. Adelaide, would you please act in your mother's place and start preparations? We'll help if you direct us to your foodstuffs and utensils."

"I don't cook," Adelaide huffed, as if half-astonished at the assumption and half-annoyed. She flounced away.

Chapter Eleven

Using the pine table as her workspace, Agnes kneaded dough for biscuits, rolled it out, and cut circular disks. Fanny and Sarah tended the fire in the wood stove, made coffee, and fried ham slices. As soon as the first batch of biscuits came out of the oven, Agnes had another tray ready for baking. Fanny and Sarah scrambled a few dozen eggs and made a pot of grits, and all three scurried to dish out the meals.

The men clustered around tables pushed together in the hotel dining room. The three injured men insisted on eating before being moved to one of the hotel rooms, but all three were pale and in danger of sliding off their chairs. Eunice bustled back and forth between the kitchen and dining room. She delivered meals, helped spoon-feed the injured, and checked their bandages and temperatures. She directed youngsters, abuzz with energy over the day's events, to wave large palmetto woven fans near the tables to keep flies away. Sarah kept the coffee flowing. Fanny lit tabletop lanterns as afternoon shadows started to lengthen. The doorways of the kitchen and dining room, which faced each other across a breezeway, were propped open because of all the cross-activity. Every so often, Agnes looked up and saw Seth watching her from the breezeway. She blushed and lowered her head to her tasks.

Amid the clatter of cutlery, thud of boots, and scraping of chairs being pushed back, the crowd jabbered questions and speculation.

"Who were those men? Can anybody here vouch for them?"

"Where did they go?"

"Did you see what happened? Did anyone?"

"How long have they been in town?"

"I tell you, I had a bad feeling when they showed up at the churchyard."

"Why did Land Inn allow them to board?"

"I heard Mrs. Land mention that they are from her hometown, that's why."

"So you say. I heard they are acquaintances of Miss Adelaide."

"This sure ain't the type of place Persimmon Hollow is meant to be."

"The sheriff will get to the bottom of this. He ought to be due back from the river camp any time now. Fishing must have been good."

Around and around the questions went, with few satisfactory answers. Agnes was glad Polly hadn't yet arrived. This was all too unsavory, and nothing in this frontier town ever seemed to be withheld from youngsters even when the topic was inappropriate. They were well aware of all that happened in Persimmon Hollow.

"I'm going to help Eunice tend the sick men," Fanny said, going out just as Sarah entered the kitchen. Sarah set aside the coffee pot and moved to the table where Agnes worked, sitting down beside her. "We're blessed that the injuries aren't more serious," Sarah said. "That's the good news."

She helped Agnes pat the biscuits into shape. "I heard plenty as I poured coffee," Sarah continued. "The two men are from

Chicago, but they have no references, and nobody knows why they are here or why they got into a fight. Clyde said they claimed to be surveyors interested in buying land and moving their families here. But with no references...and considering their recent behavior... no one seems convinced they are truthful or trustworthy."

Agnes hesitated to share her instinctive reaction to the two strangers. She disliked speaking ill of anyone. Her guardian angel nudged her conscience and her intuition, and Agnes assessed the situation from all sides. Did she have an obligation to speak up, for the safety of everyone? Two of Sarah's little ones, a boy and a girl with cherub cheeks and blond curls, toddled over and hugged their mother's waist through the folds of her dress. Sarah leaned over and gave each a kiss atop their head.

That was as clear a signal as Agnes needed.

"My guardian angel is prompting me to speak up," Agnes said.

Sarah straightened and stared at her. "Your *what*?"

"Oh, my guardian angel," Agnes said. "They are personal guardians, heavenly guardians, who steer us from danger."

"They talk to you? You see them?" Sarah looked at Agnes quizzically and somewhat apprehensively. "I've never heard of such a thing."

"I guess you could say they communicate without words. No, I don't see them. I have a sense of them when a thought springs unbidden into my conscience or my intuition causes me to be wary of something that on the surface appears perfectly normal."

For the first time in her life, Agnes really understood what it meant when people held different faith beliefs. "Guardian angels are important to me," she said. "They are part of me."

"You have more than one?"

"I don't really know. Everybody has a particular one, but…I'm not sure." She wished, not for the first time, that a priest lived close enough to provide spiritual guidance and answer the deeper religious questions.

"What is your angel telling you to say?" Sarah asked.

"They don't give you word-for-word messages," Agnes said. "My conscience, my intuition, and the guidance of the Holy Ghost—through prayer—made me wary of those men before today's troubles."

Sarah nodded in understanding.

"Please, Sarah, keep your children clear of them until we know more. Keep yourself clear of them."

Sarah frowned. "Persimmon Hollow has always been a place of open doors and friendliness," she said.

"Progress and growth bring the bad along with the good," Agnes said. "I pray God helps us discern the good from the evil."

Neither Eunice nor Fanny had returned for more food, so Agnes piled a platter full for Sarah to carry into the dining room.

"Thank you for having our interests at heart," Sarah said as Agnes accompanied her slowly across the breezeway and through the dining room doorway. "You be careful, too, y'hear?"

Before Agnes could answer, a shadow loomed over the two of them. She glanced up and met Seth's gaze.

"I'm heading back home for a fresh horse," he said, twirling his hat in his hand. "We men will keep watch here tonight. Can I carry you back?"

The babble of talk around them quieted, and Agnes became uncomfortably aware that she and Seth were the new item of interest. Everyone had talked out the morsels of knowledge about the shooting, and the sheriff hadn't yet returned from the river. His arrival would give them the opportunity to repeat everything they'd just said. While they waited, something new—such as Seth and Agnes—became a welcome topic of interest.

"Why, how sweet!" cried Adelaide in a falsetto as soon as Seth asked his question. *Where did she come from?* Agnes had no idea she'd returned after flouncing away from kitchen duty.

"You two didn't tell us you were betrothed!" Adelaide exclaimed. "Isn't that nice, everyone? Agnes and Seth are betrothed!"

For the few seconds before he thrust his hat on and lowered the brim, Seth looked like a deer caught in the glare of blazing torchlight. Agnes, for once, was speechless. Oohs and aaahs erupted. Eunice and Sarah appeared puzzled, and Fanny had a hurt look on her face.

"I guessed it the minute I saw them ride up here alone together, cuddled with each other on the horse," said Adelaide, smiling, although her eyes looked like sharp arrows to Agnes. "I said to myself, 'Of course! No respectable woman allows a man such close physical liberty unless she were spoken for by him. Surely not!'" She smirked at Agnes.

Agnes couldn't force her lips to form words, much less command a sound to come out of her throat. She carefully leaned her crutches against the nearest table and reached into the pocket of her skirt to grip her rosary while she prayed for wisdom.

Seth recovered his composure first. "We're fixin' to tie the knot as soon as Agnes's adopted daughter arrives," he said in a strong, steady voice. "It's a family matter. Which is why we didn't feel obliged to tell you."

Agnes fought to keep her surprise from showing, and her crutches slid to the floor. Her hands become clammy. Adelaide narrowed her eyes at Agnes and Seth, pursed her lips and looked as though she'd swallowed a frog.

"Well, I'll be sure to mention it to the school superintendent the next time he visits," Adelaide said. "Our schoolteachers have to be above reproach."

"Agnes, I didn't know. How wonderful," Sarah said, touching her arm. She lowered her voice to a whisper. "I knew you'd see the good man underneath the tough exterior."

"Yes, it is so wonderful, but to think you felt a need to keep the secret even from us!" Fanny said, as tears welled.

"But...but...," Agnes stuttered, still unable to say anything coherent. Part of her wanted to protest and proclaim the truth. But she couldn't afford even the tiniest blemish on her reputation, not if she wanted to protect Polly. Adelaide had set Agnes up for blame, and Agnes saw no way out of it. She also didn't understand the venom in Adelaide.

"Now if you'll excuse us, I'll see that my fiancée gets home and tends to her sprained ankle," Seth said. He adjusted his hat and swooped down and scooped Agnes into his arms to carry her out.

"I'll get the crutches," Fanny said and moved as fast as her plump feet would let her. "We'll help," Eunice and Clyde said at the same time. "I'll finish here," Sarah said, nodding as the five of them left.

The crowd behind them was aflutter with talk. Night had fallen, cloaking them from the people who stared from the yard and peered through the windows, their faces illuminated by the dim glow of the lanterns indoors. Seth set Agnes down when they reached the horses.

"We'll sort everything out tomorrow and make the proper announcements," Fanny said. "Everyone is distraught right now and not thinking properly. Oh, look, Clyde, bless you, when did you find time to go back and get the wagon?" Not waiting for an answer, she took Agnes's hand and patted it. "Agnes, dear, come with us. No one is in any condition for walking, and you and Seth shouldn't compromise yourselves by being together on the horse again."

"I gather this betrothal is as much a surprise to the two of you as it is to me, Fanny, Clyde, and everyone in that hotel, including Miss Adelaide?" Eunice asked, giving Agnes and Seth her level gaze as Clyde fussed with the wagon hitch.

"Nobody's more surprised than me," Seth said as he helped Agnes into the wagon. He hollered for Billy, who came running from the barn.

"I am," Agnes squeaked. "And I'm not ready to get married."

"Well, land's sake," said Fanny, raising her hands up in exasperation. "This isn't at all the way I planned this match."

"Well, you can thank our friend Adelaide," Eunice said. "I've watched the ways of people for many a year. Agnes, you either have something or are something that makes her envious or threatens her."

"Me? What do I have that Adelaide doesn't?"

"A heart," said Seth. "And a God you believe in."

* * *

The moon rose, and the stars cast a brilliant light as Clyde guided the team of horses toward the Alloways' house. No one spoke, and the gentle clip-clop from the team's and Silver's hooves were the only sounds that broke the steady hum of cicadas and crickets, frog croaks, and owl hoots.

Agnes was confused and uncertain how to react to Seth's declaration of betrothal. She slid a glance at him, riding beside the wagon. Her emotions jumbled and grew warm despite her efforts not to react. Surely he had been playacting, to ease the tension in the Land Inn and avoid harming her reputation. Yet, a part of her wanted, yes—she had to be honest—wanted his words to be true even though he hadn't yet overcome his indifference to God and religion.

Despite the short time they'd been acquainted, Agnes had determined Seth wasn't the type of man to spin falsehoods. She gulped. She couldn't deny her attraction to Seth. It was clearer every time she was near him.

"Are you all right, dear?" Eunice asked from the wagon's front seat. "I think so," said Agnes. A sleeping Billy snuggled beside her. He'd fallen asleep within minutes after climbing into the wagon. Even Fanny's head nodded.

They both woke as the horses slowed and came to a stop at the Alloways' gate.

"I'll put these horses up, saddle my mare, and head back," Clyde said to Seth, who had halted Silver but didn't dismount.

Seth nodded. "I'll take Billy to the grove and change horses. If you don't mind waiting until I return, we can ride as a team." Clyde gave a terse nod and nudged the horses toward his yard. In unison, Fanny and Agnes insisted Billy stay with them for the night. Billy waited only for Seth's nod before racing up the walkway and into the house, his energy restored by the quick nap.

They fell silent and stood huddled as though unsure what to say or do next.

"Well," said Fanny, finally, as she stifled a yawn. "Perhaps we had best spend at least a minute or two figuring out what's going on."

"Tomorrow," said Seth and started turning his horse back toward the road.

"One minute, young man," Eunice said. "For one thing, this young lady hasn't accepted the offer you haven't made. I'd say we have a lot to talk about, starting right now."

Agnes felt overwrought by the day's events. She craved sleep, even if it meant this state of confusion lasted a little longer. It would give her more time to sort out her feelings.

"I...I'm greatly fatigued," she said. "If it's not an imposition, could we wait until morning?"

Seth was off the horse almost before she finished talking. "Let me carry you in," he said and lifted her from the wagon. "Fanny or Eunice, would you mind getting her crutches?"

"There's really no need," Agnes said. But truth be told, her ankle pained her greatly from the short time she had spent standing and preparing food at Land Inn, so she added, "I do appreciate the offer."

Eunice held the door open, and Fanny went in first. She plumped some pillows on the settee before Seth set Agnes down as carefully as he would place a fragile glass object onto a rough-edged plank bench.

"We expect you for breakfast," Fanny said. "And Clyde and anyone else who needs a hot meal."

"Thank you," Seth said as he covered Agnes with the crocheted afghan from the back of the settee and made sure she was settled amid the pillows.

"About that comment…" he started to say, in a low voice only she could hear.

"Oh, there's nothing to say," Agnes said in a rush. "Thank you for thinking so quickly and pretending the way you did. It avoided causing me any scandal."

Their gazes locked, and Agnes's heart pounded so rapidly she was sure he could hear the thump or see the rise and fall of her chest.

"I wasn't pretending," he said.

"I…I don't know what to say," she stammered.

His lips grew tight. A dull, heavy feeling settled over Agnes. She yearned to cry out that yes, she accepted, if only he would have faith, if only he would agree to give God's grace a chance to heal him.

A surge of courage swelled inside her.

"I think you are a fine man who any woman would be proud to have as a husband," she said. The room around them was quiet except for the ticking of the grandfather clock and the sounds of Billy's footsteps in his bedroom above them. She was keenly aware that Eunice and Fanny had left the room.

"But not you," he said. He jammed his hands in his pockets and took a step backward.

This wasn't going well at all. It was, in fact, horrible.

"No!" she said and leaned forward and stretched out her arm toward him. "I mean yes! Oh, I mean, Mr. Seth Taylor, that I can't consider any man who doesn't hold Jesus in his heart, who won't return to the Church or seek confession and take the sacraments."

He kept his steady gaze on her but said nothing.

"No matter how much I wish I could," she added. Sorrow weighed on her. "And Seth," she added, "I truly wish I could."

"It's going to be a mighty long betrothal period, then," he said and frowned. He twirled his hat with his hands. A flicker of hope stirred in Agnes.

"Open your heart," she whispered. "Let God in."

"I'll think about it," he said. "That's the best I can say right now. I've got to get back to the Land Inn. Get some rest."

"I'll take that kind of an honest answer over a false promise, any day," she said and gave him a smile that spoke of her heart. He grinned, put on his hat, and stood awkwardly for a few moments.

"I'll be getting on, then," he said.

"Stay safe," she called as he took his leave. "You and all the other men."

Joy and hope filled her. He hadn't outrightly refused or chided her for interfering in his business or preaching about matters of faith. He hadn't slammed the door to his heart. He left it open a tiny crack. She had hope. Yes, she had hope. She recalled the words of Romans 5:5: "And hope does not disappoint us, because God's love has been poured into our hearts through the Holy Spirit that has been given to us."

Chapter Twelve

*A*gnes slipped out of the house into the dewy fog of dawn, managing not to slam the door as she maneuvered through on her crutches. Mockingbirds, great-crested flycatchers, hawks, and cardinals greeted the morning, but otherwise town was quiet as she made her way to the meeting hall. Inside, she knelt and prayed for guidance. Her carefully crafted plan was fraying at an alarming rate. Her world hung on a simple dream: a return to St. Isidore's Home until marriage and then continued care for the orphans while living nearby with her own family. How distant it all seemed. Each day seemed to draw her further away, and the more she tried to bend to what apparently was God's will, the more resistance she encountered.

A most unsuitable man had not only claimed an increasing chunk of her thoughts and feelings, but now appeared serious in asking for her hand.

"God did you place him in my path?" she whispered, not expecting an answer. God didn't supply explanations. Still, so many pieces didn't fit. Seth was in need of salvation. Not only that, he'd made it clear the day of the picnic that city life didn't suit him. She remembered the conversation. They had chatted about hometowns. Agnes couldn't imagine life anywhere but in a city. Seth couldn't imagine life in one.

Nevertheless, Seth had offered marriage to protect her reputation. It was such an unselfish action, and it warmed her toward him all the more. And he had left open the door to reclaiming his relationship with Church and faith.

She blessed herself and leaned on a bench while rising and positioning her crutches. Her foot and ankle improved daily. She was sure she'd be able to set aside the crutches for good in a matter of days. Definitely before the start of school.

The door opened as she headed toward it. "I thought I'd find you here," said Fanny with a beaming smile. "Breakfast is ready. You'd better hurry, or two hungry fellows might gobble everything up. Make that three, if we add in Billy. Sometimes I think he eats more than two grown men."

Agnes smiled because the Alloways and their cook Estelle always made enough to feed half the town. One of them brought food daily to neighbors they knew needed a hand and always made it appear the recipients were doing the Alloways a favor by making sure food didn't go to waste.

"How's your sprain?" Fanny asked.

"Much better. I should be off these crutches before classes begin."

"I can't believe how close we are to the start of school."

Agnes nodded her agreement. "And I'm glad Billy enjoys spending time in town with us. That may help us convince Seth to let him stay in town for lessons."

Silence grew at the mention of Seth's name.

"Honey, do you want to talk about it?" Fanny asked as she kept a light but firm hand on Agnes's elbow and helped her out the door and down the steps. The early sun was burning off the haze. Bluejay and squirrel chatter mingled with the growing din of insects. A bright blue dragonfly with lacelike wings hovered and settled atop one of Agnes's crutches long enough for her to admire the intricacy and brilliance of the slender insect.

"I'm not sure what to do," said Agnes frowning. "You know my reasons for not being ready for marriage. And surely Seth was just being gentlemanly. He'll see things from a different perspective today." She didn't mention his assurance of his intentions. They had been whispered at the end of a very trying, wearying day.

"You know what my plans are," Agnes insisted. She hated deviating from a good plan.

"Yes, dear, I do," Fanny said gently. "I also know that the Lord sometimes has other plans for us. It's as plain to me as the sun in the sky that Seth never lost his good heart, kind ways, and the path of righteous living, even after he started believing God abandoned him. Your piety is making an impression on him. Honey, he thinks you are an angel."

"Well, I'm certainly not," said Agnes.

"Maybe the Lord sent you to Seth to help him find his way."

"I'm only going to be here for the school year, remember?" Agnes said. "Possibly two years, but that's it. There's work for me to do at St. Isidore's Home."

"Yes, dear, I know," Fanny said, patting her arm as they neared the back door of the Alloway house. "But you can't do it now. As you said, Polly needs to be far from the reaches of that evildoer who bothered you, the orphanage, and now Polly. You may end up here a bit longer than expected. You and Polly." She smiled. "We would all be blessed if you did."

Agnes looked at her with gratitude. Yet something nagged at her. Something didn't fit together properly in the truths Fanny spoke, but Agnes couldn't pinpoint the jagged edge.

"God's love works in wondrous ways," Fanny said as they entered the kitchen. The aromas of sizzling bacon, warm biscuits, and strong coffee enveloped them with a feeling of comfort and abundance.

"Here, sit by me!" Billy called. He waved and scooted over on the bench seat without missing a mouthful of grits. Seth stood at the stove, pouring himself a cup of coffee. Agnes suddenly felt shy. He turned toward her and nodded as he put down the pot. "Morning," he said. "Good coffee," he added, holding up his cup. "And good food," he said, nodding at his full plate next to Billy's. Eunice and Clyde sat on the other side of the table. Both shared good-mornings.

"Plenty more where that came from," Fanny said. "Eat up."

A wistful twinge tugged at Agnes. This could be a happy family scene. *Her* happy family scene. Mother, father, child, grandparents, kin... Fanny was like a grandmother and Eunice like a great-aunt. Clyde could easily be a grandfather. Estelle was essentially a member of the family. It was all so perfect, so filled with love, goodness, and abundance. Agnes imagined Seth placing his cup on the table, walking over to her and perhaps giving her a kiss or a hug and sharing the joy of such a beautiful morning. Their love would be a strong bond between them, and their home a haven, and...

It was a dream. And its beauty made Agnes realize what left her uneasy with Fanny's version of the way events had unfolded. And what made her uncomfortable about accepting Seth's honorable offer, an offer that she suspected any other woman would jump up and seize. Seth didn't love her. How could he? They hardly knew each other. He offered the protection of his name and his partnership because it was the right thing to do. Not because he loved her and wished to spend his life with her and raise a family together. His reasons weren't the reasons God joined men and women in holy matrimony.

A heavy, sinking feeling weighed on her, and she suddenly was tired, more tired than since she arrived or when she sprained her ankle. She knew what she had to do, and the knowledge stuck at her like the sharp spine of a palmetto leaf. Seth had done the honorable thing. Now it was her turn to do the same. She had to release him from his pledge.

"Here you go, sweetie," said Estelle as she set a plate of steaming food and a mug of coffee in front of Agnes, who had sat down heavily. "Gotta get some meat on those bones."

"I think they look mighty fine, if you don't mind me saying so," Seth said, and everyone chuckled. Seth's and Agnes's gazes met. His reflected strength, compassion, warmth, care...everything except love.

If God were answering her prayer for a home and family, this certainly wasn't the answer she had expected.

The conversation circled around the previous day's turmoil, until reaching the point they all wanted to discuss. Nobody said a thing. Voices faded, and the ringing of cutlery on plates filled the void.

"Why'd we leave in such a hurry?" Billy piped up. "Me and the guys were in the middle of a game of marbles, and then all of sudden folks were riled up about you," he looked at Seth, "and

Miss Agnes getting hitched, and then we had to leave in a hurry. What's up?"

Agnes looked at Fanny who looked at Eunice who looked at Clyde who looked at Seth.

"Your uncle can best explain that," Clyde said.

Seth straightened.

"I stand by the word I spoke last night, if Miss Agnes will have me."

"So what's the big deal then?" Billy asked, more interested in the new pile of grits Estelle had heaped on his plate. He shoveled them into his mouth.

Seth wiped his brow with his napkin. "I know it's sudden. I just ask that Agnes consider my proposal…for as long as she needs," he said. "I, too, have some thinking to do." He looked at her as he spoke.

An ant's footsteps would have sounded loud.

"With God's guidance, I will consider your offer," Agnes whispered, her face solemn. Fanny's smile faded. Eunice's eyebrows arched in surprise. Agnes looked at them, trying to wordlessly convey the doubts and misgivings she'd had after she and Seth spoke privately the night before. She held that encounter close to her heart.

The faces around her reflected puzzlement. What might have been a happy betrothal morning ended shrouded in silence.

Seth perched back in his chair, raising the front legs off the floor. His face was impassive. "I'm going up to St. Augustine to see if I can uncover anything at railroad headquarters about our two troublesome town visitors," he said, as though the group had merely been discussing the weather seconds before. "I've got some friends there and a gut feeling that Lester Little is the one trying to get my land again."

"Good idea," Clyde said. "Last night the pastor postponed the whitewashing. Wants to get to the bottom of these strange goings-on in town first. You may turn up something that will help us all."

"If you ladies are agreeable, Billy will stay here so he can start classes if I'm not back in time," Seth said, but he spoke formally and wouldn't look at Agnes.

"*O give thanks to the Lord, call on his name…*" Agnes thought of First Chronicles 16:8. Seth had actually reconsidered his refusal to let Billy attend school in town.

"Thank you," she said quietly to Seth, as Fanny beamed her enthusiastic approval at allowing Billy to join them. She wasn't sure Seth heard her. He acted as though he hadn't.

Seth rose and reached for his hat on a peg on the wall. "Take some slices of pie for the ride," Agnes offered.

He accepted, but it was stiff and formal, and he left before Estelle had time to draw a pie from the pie safe.

* * *

Town talk quieted over the next few weeks as the nearness of the new school year and the coming citrus harvest became the focus of attention. Agnes's excitement about the approaching first day of school helped mitigate her constant worries about Polly and St. Isidore's Home. Both were ever-present in her thoughts.

A few days before classes began, Eunice, Fanny, and Agnes walked the four short blocks to school on a breezy morning to make sure all was in order and to test the strength of Agnes's ankle. Persimmon Hollow Academy impressed Agnes from the minute she saw it up close, and her admiration grew as they strolled up the front walkway and climbed the three steps to the double wood doors protected by a small, square porch.

Before they went inside, Agnes halted and looked at the surrounding countryside. The Academy stood atop a knell high enough to offer panoramic views of the gently rolling hills of pine country. The wind whispered in the tops of the thick-trunked long-leaf pines that surrounded the two-story Academy and provided dappled shade in a tranquil setting.

"Your father certainly chose the perfect spot for his school," Agnes said.

"He certainly did," said Eunice. "Opening the Academy was a dream close to his heart. He thought ahead. At four acres, we have room to grow. We're considering adding a building to house students and teachers. That way, students from greater distances could attend."

"Come on, we'll show you your classroom," Fanny said as she opened the doors. Inside, the central, paneled hallway smelled of wood and polish. Large classrooms opened up onto the hall from either side. "Two more are upstairs," said Eunice, pointing up the stairway nestled against one side of the hall. Behind the stairs, an opening led to another, narrower hallway.

"That hall leads to the library and the music room, which doubles as our auditorium," Fanny said.

"We also have an office back there," Eunice added. "I generally head there for morning paperwork after I ring the bell." She checked the watch hanging from a chain around her neck, as if ready for a school day to begin.

"Agnes, you will teach right here," said Fanny, pointing to the first classroom on the building's south side. "I'll be right across the hall, within calling distance should you need assistance." She opened the door to Agnes's classroom. The bright, tidy room was flooded with sunlight from two pairs of large, almost floor-to-ceiling windows positioned on the south and west walls. Eunice raised the lower halves of the double-hung frames, and a cross-breeze flowed through, bringing with it a hint of fresh pine. A clean chalkboard behind the wooden teacher's desk stretched the length of the opposite side of the room. Wood floors, wainscoting, and a green fern-patterned wallpaper gave the room a finished touch.

Agnes's heart warmed to the neat coziness of the space. "I hope my teaching skills do this room and you justice," she said to Fanny and Eunice.

Fanny took both Agnes's hands in her own. "My dear, we haven't the slightest doubt."

* * *

But Agnes did. She awoke early the first day of school with a mixture of apprehension and enthusiasm. Her first real teaching job. *God, give me strength,* she prayed silently as Clyde's horses ambled up the sloping hill in the clean morning sunlight, pulling the Alloways' barouche with her, the Alloways, and Billy inside.

It seemed as though all of Persimmon Hollow had the same intention. As they neared the Academy, Agnes watched students arrive on foot and in wagons, buggies, and on horseback, from all four directions.

"See ya in a few," Billy yelled and hopped out of the carriage before Clyde halted the horses to a full stop. He sprinted off to meet friends waving at him from the far side of the building.

"You best listen for that bell, young man," Fanny called after him.

"Only five minutes," Agnes said, checking her watch. She hurried inside the building, and within minutes the chimes signaled the start of the new semester.

Pupils whom Agnes judged to be anywhere from four to fourteen milled around in boisterous clumps until she helped line them up and usher them into the building. She organized her own class of fifteen into seats, showed them where to tuck luncheon pails and buckets, and passed out McGuffey Readers to each. She assessed her charges as they settled down. They were a varied lot, everything from a precocious sprite who appeared to be about seven to a hulking adolescent who could almost pass for an adult. Many of the girls wore new starched and ruffled gowns and had hair plaited and held back with big bows. Others wore patched pinafores. A few of the boys were barefoot. One was in a suit, starched collar, and shiny shoes. The rest of the class, boys and girls both, were like Billy—neatly dressed in clean clothing neither new nor old. They all watched her silently as though with one pair of eyes. Even Billy behaved.

"You the Yankee teacher?" a boy in overalls asked.

"I'm Miss Foster," Agnes said. "Yes, I am from the northern states. But this is my home now, and a wonderful place it is. I'm honored to be here."

"We're glad you're here, too!" Billy piped up. She couldn't resist a smile.

"Miss Foster boards with the Misses Alloway," Billy informed his classmates. "She makes really good pie. And you should see…"

"That's enough, class," Agnes interrupted in a stern voice, although she was laughing inside. "Let's open our readers to page one. We'll go around the room, and I want each of you to intro-duce yourself to me and then read a few paragraphs."

Panic appeared on more than a few faces. "Don't worry about how well you can or cannot read," she said. "You're here to learn." Some of the stressed looks subsided. "The exercise will help me determine your reading level and decide how to place you in groups for future work. This exercise will not be graded, so relax and do your best. Ready?"

Her pupils nodded.

"We'll start here," she said and pointed to the girl in the first seat in the row closest to the door. "Tell the class your name, young lady."

"Pansy Bight."

Agnes deliberately chose to start the exercise with Pansy. She knew Sarah taught all her children to read at a young age.

"Thank you, Miss Bight. Let's begin, shall we?"

The morning vanished quickly, and Agnes was surprised to hear the lunch bell ring. She dismissed class and sank down in her desk chair. The shrieks, chatter, and sounds of rustling paper and banging pails outside contrasted with the sudden stillness surrounding her.

"Everything go okay?" Fanny peered around the corner into the open classroom door.

"I think so," Agnes said. "Their abilities vary greatly. The stronger ones are already helping the others with reading and geography, though. This afternoon, we tackle mathematics."

By the end of the school day, Agnes was tired but happy with the day's progress. "Bye, Miss Foster," the students said, one after another, as they departed. "See you tomorrow." The hours had been exhausting but productive, and Agnes expected each day would fall into a pattern as she grew to know her pupils better. She neatened the addition and subtraction papers on her desk and started organizing the crate she brought in to use as her file cabinet. The sounds of youngsters going home grew dimmer.

Knock, knock.

"The door's open," she called, her back to the door, but she didn't stop placing dividers into the crate. She reached around and up to grab the math papers, gave a startled jump, and knocked the papers across the floor. Seth stood in front of the desk, an orange in his outstretched hand.

"I don't have an apple for the teacher, but this orange is just as good," he said. He placed it on the desk and bent down to help her collect the sheets of paper.

"My goodness," Agnes said. "How do you manage to move so quietly? I heard nothing after the knock on the door." She took the papers from him and placed them in her crate. "Thanks. And thanks for the orange. When did you get back into town?"

"This morning," Seth said. "The stealth is from years of practice. I didn't intend to startle you. I stopped by to ask if you're interested in a ride to see the groves. Almost harvest time."

"I'd...I'd like that, but...well, are Fanny and Eunice joining us?" she faltered. He'd strolled in as if nothing were amiss, as if he didn't remember the tense way they last parted. Was he planning to bring up the matter once they reached the grove? She wasn't ready to discuss anything. She'd hardly been able to think straight about what had happened that night. She had, in fact, kept pushing away the thought of his offer. And though the thought kept pushing back, she'd kept it successfully buried under school preparations and teaching.

"No. When they saw me arrive, they said to tell you they were leaving." He picked up the orange and tossed it from hand to hand.

"We'd be going alone, then?" She hated the high note that just squeaked out of her.

"No, Billy's going with us," he said. "But we're betrothed, remember?"

"That isn't something to take lightly," Agnes said as she stiffened. Had it become a joke?

"I'm serious," he answered and put down the orange. He put a finger under her chin and tilted her face toward his. "Are you afraid to be with me or to be seen with me?" The question was as much in his eyes as in his words.

"No, no, that's not it," she said and took a step back. His touch had felt intimate, too close. He instantly lowered his hand. Confusion roiled inside her. She had missed him, more than she cared to admit.

"Truth be told, Seth, it's good to see you," Agnes said. "And I owe you a thanks for allowing Billy to attend classes. But I'm not ready to pick up the conversation where we left off the night of the shooting."

"Then we won't. But you could show your appreciation about Billy by granting me the honor of your company for an afternoon ride." He bowed, and when he straightened, there was a glimmer of humor in his eyes. Agnes finally relaxed.

"Especially because I wasn't able to show it with a sweet potato pie," she said, her lips curving upward.

"I could be persuaded to try a slice, if there's any left," he said.

"Oh, gosh, no," she said. "After the pastor canceled the

whitewashing, we carried the pies over to Clyde's where he sold slices for a penny a piece. They were gone in no time at all. But I'm always baking. It's how I relax. You can rest assured there will be more pies on hand the day of the church meeting hall whitewashing."

"Still determined to get me closer to God?" Seth asked as he escorted Agnes out and helped her into his wagon. There was no bitterness or defensiveness in his voice.

"Oh no, God does that," Agnes said. "I'm just the messenger."

As they started out on the drive, a woman called and waved.

"Yoo-hoo," she said and pulled her wagon alongside Seth's. Three towheaded children sat in the back, including two of Agnes's pupils.

"Hello there," she said, with a hearty wave. They responded with shy smiles and waves.

"I just want to say congratulations," said the woman, without introducing herself. "We're new settlers—been here only two weeks—and of course one of the first things we heard tell is that the new schoolteacher is betrothed. That's right nice. Folks like a good love story, especially when times are tough." She laughed. "I mean I like a good love story when times are tough. Living on this frontier is what I call rough and tough, let me tell you. Never saw so many insects and critters in all my life up in Kentucky where I'm from." But she smiled as she spoke and waved again, and before Seth or Agnes could reply, she yelled giddy-up to her horses and was gone.

"Does the entire town know?" Agnes asked as she watched the wagon roll away.

"I reckon," said Seth, and he urged his team forward.

"Hey, drop me off at the crossroads," Billy interrupted from the back of the cart. "I wanna go run with Lumpy. He's waitin' on me. I been cooped up all day in that classroom."

"He's *waiting* for me, not waitin'," Agnes corrected. Seth gave a nod of approval to Billy. "Oh, boy, thanks," he said and jumped out as they reached the main crossroads.

Agnes and Seth watched Billy run toward Clyde's mercantile yard. The silence grew more obvious the farther away Billy ran. Seth started the cart rolling again, in silence.

Agnes sighed. "We can't continue to ignore this, Seth. But I'm not sure what to say, where to start, or how to proceed."

"I do," Seth said. "What do you want for your future?"

"Well, you know I want to give Polly a good home," Agnes said. "That's the most important thing. I plan to return North after the gossips' tongues quiet down up there and..." *And what, Agnes?* she asked herself. Leave Seth, when she was more drawn to him every day?

"And?" Seth prompted.

Neither of them spoke as the wagon rolled beyond the tidy homesteads and toward the gently sloping hills and the lake and grove beyond.

"Can you see yourself as mistress of the Taylor Grove homestead in Persimmon Hollow?"

Agnes inhaled and hesitated, searching for words. What she already felt for Seth could grow into love the minute she opened her heart. Could he open his, though? Not just to her, but to God? Could she love him enough to stay?

"Mistress of a grove owned by a man of faith?" he asked.

She gripped her hands on the plank seat and stifled a cry of surprise. Had he been touched by the grace of the Holy Ghost?

"If that man had truly been touched by grace and wasn't pretending," she answered carefully.

Seth pulled on the reins, circled the horses around, and stopped atop a gentle knoll near his citrus processing buildings. The town stretched out below them as a neat, tidy, sheltering collection of homes and people. Ahead was a long, slight, gradual slope toward the lake. Row after neat row of citrus trees laden with fruit reached toward the horizon. The acres of rounded trees evoked a sense of order and plenty.

"I gave this some hard thought," he said. "I'm serious. But I reckon I need some help getting there from here. If you'd be willing." He spoke the last sentence so low she had to lean in to hear him.

"Seth Taylor, do you really mean it?" She placed a hand on his arm. "You're not just saying it?"

"I'll give it a try. I ain't promising anything. Like I said before, God threw some boulders at me over the years. Big ones. Nobody's got to tell me life's not fair, but somewhere a man's got to draw a line. God had no time for me."

Agnes scooted over next to him. "Seth, times of trouble are when you have to rely on your faith the most, not push it aside. You turned away from God almost as if you wanted to punish him. That's not how it works. We're too small to test God."

"Ever had a loved one die on you, Agnes, because you couldn't save them?" he asked, his voice low and ragged.

Agnes drew in a breath. "I have seen others die at St. Isidore's Home," she said. "My own family I never knew. They died in an earthquake in Italy. Some of the survivors left for America and took me with them. I was just a baby. They left me on the orphanage's doorstep with a note pinned to my blanket."

Seth placed a hand over Agnes's where it rested on his arm. "No wonder you are so protective of the orphanage," he said.

"It means the world to me," she said.

"My family was my world," Seth said. "Losing my brother and his wife made me bitter. Bitter and angry. I was supposed to protect them. I failed in my duty." His other hand clenched into a fist on his thigh. "Stuck in jail on false charges and, boom, they're gone before I can get there."

"I wish I had answers, or something soothing to say," Agnes whispered, placing her other hand atop his. "No one has all the answers, or even some of them. That's why we have to have faith, have to know that God is always there for us, no matter what happens. We have to trust."

"I was raised with religion," Seth said. "Same as you. Same religion." Agnes's heart did a little skip of joy.

"For a long time, there's been no place in my life for God," Seth continued. "Until..." he fell silent.

"Until what?" Agnes asked.

"Until you," he said in a low voice. "Your example. Your conviction."

Thank you, Lord, Agnes prayed inwardly. The idea that she might have been helping someone find their way back to God made her heart soar. That it was Seth filled her with joy.

"Would you like to pray with me?" she asked and slipped her hands out of his and held them open toward him.

He shook his head no.

"Not yet," he said. He turned toward her, and she searched his eyes. There was no sign of deceit or trickery. If anything, he seemed tired and unsure.

"Soon, dear Agnes," he said. "Soon. In the meantime, pray for me."

"I already do," she said. Then, to lighten the mood, she playfully punched his arm. "Give me some warning when you're ready to go to church, all right? So I can bake you some sweet potato pies."

He smiled and nodded, and she laughed, and Seth picked up the reins again. They rode at a slow pace through the heart of the grove, surrounded by dark emerald-colored leaves in which nestled bright globes of orange fruits.

"This is a magical place," Agnes said, inhaling the citrusy spice of the trees and fruit.

"Most of the time," Seth agreed. They made a loop and started back toward town. Seth helped Agnes out when they reached the Alloway house and escorted her up the walkway.

"Thank you for the ride, Seth, and I thank God, too, for you, the ride, the beautiful day, the abundant harvest, the..."

"...beautiful women who bake delicious desserts," he finished the sentence. "Hmmm, do I smell sweet potato pie?"

"No," she said and laughed. "Nice try, though."

A rustling in the overgrown wooded area next to the house caught their attention.

"Even the birds stir at the mention of pie," Agnes said.

"Smart birds," joked Seth as they reached the porch and went inside.

* * *

"You hear that, boss? Sweet potato pie. My stomach's hungry already," said Barrel, rubbing his rotund abdomen as they backed up through the undergrowth. "That was a close call, huh, a close call," he continued his nervous patter. "I was almost out of the woods and into the clearing when that wagon rolled up."

"Pipe down, Barrel, while I think," said Lester. "Man can't even get a bite to eat in this town ever since you started that stupid fight and shot off your gun. This slinking around's getting real tiresome to me."

"I had to shoot," Barrel squeaked. "He was questioning me like I was a liar or something. Ain't no man gonna second-guess Barrel and make like I'm a fool."

"What else did you hear them two lovebirds say just now? Getting mighty chummy, those two. Complicating the picture."

"Nothing interesting that I could figure," Barrel said. "She was preachy. God talk."

"Great," said Lester. "A do-gooder. And here I thought this was going to be an easy job. I might up my price. Railroad's got deep pockets. Oughta make them pay."

"One thing I can't figure," said Barrel. "How we supposed to get him to sell his land, huh? He done said no to the railroad and no to you way back when, right? You said you started some fire out at his grove and even that didn't work?"

Lester turned on him. "Don't you ever say nothing about no fire, you hear?"

"Didn't some folks die in it?" Barrel asked, scratching his head.

"There wasn't supposed to be no folks there that day!" Lester hissed as he mopped sweat from his face. "It weren't my fault. Didn't go in there fixing to knock anybody off. It was an accident. You say a word about it ever, and you might die mysteriously, too."

"Okay, okay," Barrel squeaked. "So how you going get him to give up his land? He don't look like he scares easy."

"Maybe at the end of a shotgun," grunted Lester. "Maybe by

messing with the woman and kid. I dunno yet. I'll think of something. Right now I'm hungry, and I see a garden we can raid soon
as the sun goes down."

Chapter Thirteen

*F*inally! Today was the day. Agnes had thought it would never arrive. She could hardly keep still as she waited for the train to pull in to the station. Within minutes, she'd be reunited with Polly. She smiled at Seth, Billy, Fanny, Eunice, Clyde, and Sarah and her children. The Polly Welcoming Committee. Oh, what a beautiful day!

"What's she look like, huh, Miss Agnes?" Billy asked as he played fetch with Lumpy, who'd also come along for the ride.

"She's a little bit shorter than you and has brown hair that curls and bounces when she walks. She has light brown eyes and freckles on her nose."

"Is she a girly-girl, or does she like dogs and stuff and playing marbles, that kinda thing?"

"Well, she hasn't ever lived in the country," Agnes said. "She's being raised to be a proper young lady, if that's what you're asking."

Billy shrugged, threw a fallen pine branch, and ran with Lumpy after it.

"What he's really asking is whether Polly will be agreeable to getting into mischief with him, is my suspicion," said Fanny. She fanned herself in the unseasonably warm weather.

"Here she comes!" Billy hollered as the distant toot of the train's steam whistle broke the heavy air. He guided Lumpy back to the wagon for safety.

Agnes smoothed her skirt and tucked a curl under the scarf she wore for everyday work. Her heart quickened. Her dear Polly! Finally here! She glanced toward the others to share her joy. Seth watched her from where he leaned against the side of Clyde's wagon. Without warning, she imagined Seth as Polly's adoptive father. The picture fit. He waved at her and tipped his hat in acknowledgment of the moment's significance. She waved back, smiling, but her innermost self churned with more than excitement over Polly's arrival. She had to give him an answer, and soon. It wasn't fair to let things linger. She had to decide. But not today. She was still confused about Seth Taylor. She'd think about it later. This day belonged to Polly.

The train rumbled into the station and screeched to a halt. Agnes stepped forward, then waited, unsure which car held Polly. The train door opened, and the conductor helped a lone passenger disembark. The small girl gripped a valise and looked around with a worried expression as the conductor patted her shoulder, said a "How do?" to Agnes, nodded at the others, and headed back up the steps. The girl peered to see who the conductor spoke to, and with her hand, shaded her eyes against the sun. She gave a little squeal, dropped the valise, stretched out both her arms, and ran to Agnes.

"Miss Agnes, I missed you so much, I'm so glad to see you, I didn't understand why you left, what happened, why are we here?" She stopped her tumble of words long enough to draw in a hiccupping breath, throw herself into Agnes's arms, and plant a big kiss on Agnes's cheek. Then her little face contorted into tears as she hugged Agnes and hid her face. Agnes drew her tightly into an embrace.

"All is well, sweetie, my dear, sweet Polly," Agnes said. She alternately kissed and hugged Polly close and held her out so she could see her face. Soon they both were crying. "You have no idea how happy I am to see you, to know you are safe. I missed you, honey. More than you'll ever know. Stand back, now, let me get a good look at you. How you've grown in such a short time! Almost a young woman!"

Polly blushed and smiled and wiped away the tears. "Yes, I'm almost an inch taller since you left."

"Soon you'll be taller than me," Agnes said and hugged her again. "Come, I want you to meet our new Persimmon Hollow family and friends. They're anxious to get acquainted."

She led Polly to the welcoming shade of a live oak, where everyone had gathered. "How do you do?" Polly said politely at each introduction, masking her curiosity with courtesy and a pretty curtsy. The worry etched on Billy's face grew more acute as he watched each formal introduction with the Alloways, Bights, Seth, and Clyde.

When they reached him, he jumped up from the farthest branches of the oak's spreading trunk. "Hi, I'm Billy, you must be Polly," he said, worming his way between Polly and Agnes before Agnes had a chance to say anything. He stuck out his hand in an awkward, formal handshake gesture.

"Did your Uncle Seth teach you that?" Agnes asked.

"He sure did," Billy said. "Last night. Made me practice till my arm got sore."

Agnes leaned down and whispered into his ear some ideas for greeting a pretty young lady. His ears became as red as the radishes in the Alloways' kitchen garden.

"Shucks, Miss Agnes, do I have to?"

"It's the gentlemanly thing to do," she said.

Seth drew closer, curious, but Agnes gave him a quick, wordless nod, and he remained silent.

Billy hemmed and hawed, scuffled his shoe in the sand, and then, with one quick gesture, grabbed Polly's gloved hand and pecked a kiss on it. He let go of her hand and stepped back so fast he bumped into Seth, who put a hand on his shoulder.

"Nice job, young man," he said as his gaze caught Agnes's. More than the heat of the day passed between them.

Polly curtsied, and Billy's ears grew redder.

"You like dogs?" he asked.

"Oh, yes, I love animals," said Polly, clapping her hands.

"Come on and meet Lumpy," he said, and she followed with eagerness to the wagon. Within seconds, Lumpy had slobbered kisses onto her. Polly giggled with childish delight and hugged the friendly dog. Billy appeared visibly relieved that a real person existed under the gloves, hat, travel attire, and stiff formality.

"I say we have a natural Floridian on our hands," Clyde said.

"Looks that way," Seth said and picked up the valise Polly had dropped.

Joy coursed through Agnes. Maybe this was a magical land after all, and God had guided her to it with a sureness of purpose.

*   *   *

"You arrived at an exciting time, Polly," Agnes said the next morning as they greeted the day with fresh squeezed orange juice, eggs, ham and biscuits, hot coffee for Agnes, and fresh cow's milk for Polly.

"Think this'll be enough?" Fanny came bustling through the room before Agnes had time to explain. Fanny carried a plate stacked so high with ham biscuits they could hardly see her face peering out from behind it.

"Mmmmmm, they smell yummy," said Polly, who ate as though she hadn't seen food before.

"I predict they'll be gone before the men even pick up a paint-brush," said Agnes.

"What's going on?" Polly asked, wide-eyed. "Who's painting?"

"That's what I started to tell you. You arrived at an exciting time. Most everyone in town is coming together to whitewash the meeting hall building we all use as a worship space," Agnes explained.

"Like I told you in my letter," Agnes said, "Persimmon Hollow is still a small settlement, so we all share one building for services."

Polly crinkled her nose. "Yes, but do you mean a preacher talks in one corner while a priest says Mass in another and...?"

"No, honey, we take turns," Agnes said. "Each week a different denomination has a service, and everyone else is welcome to attend—no matter what form of worship they practice. We are all united in our love for Jesus."

"That's weird," Polly said. "Isn't it a sin?"

"No, honey, it's God's way of telling us that people follow different paths to praise Jesus and hear the Lord's words. I felt like you did at first. Then after going to different services, I saw that everyone is as serious in their worship of the Lord as we are at Mass. God hears prayers that are heartfelt. But I understand what you are saying. And certainly, if we had a church in town you and I would attend Mass only there. I would so love to see a Catholic church, our very own church, in Persimmon Hollow."

"Then Fr. Tom could say Mass and tell us stories about Jesus like he does at St. Isidore's Home," Polly said, nodding in agreement. "And give us Communion. I just received my first Holy Communion last month!"

"How wonderful!" Agnes said, tilting her head down so Polly couldn't see her dismay at how rarely the sacrament was offered in Persimmon Hollow. At most, the priest from Palatka was able to get to town once a month. Just a week ago, he had said Mass for her and the few others who traveled with him.

Polly tilted her head and looked pensive. "Maybe we could build a church," she said.

"Maybe we could," agreed Agnes.

Eunice had been listening without comment. "In a small, new settlement like ours, it's important that everyone work together so that the settlement survives and prospers," she said. "I agree with Agnes that the Lord orchestrated our building arrangement so that we'd have to come together and work together instead of being suspicious of one another. As money is raised, we'll see that those churches are built."

Fanny had put down her plate and rearranged the biscuits. She laid a clean kitchen cloth atop the savory pile. "That's right. As town grows and more people move here, faith communities will have the means to build and sustain churches," she said. "It'll be so lovely to hear church bells."

"I love the sound of church bells," Polly agreed with vigor.

Eunice checked her watch. "We won't hear any bells if we don't get over there and help," she said.

"Huh?" said Polly. "I mean, excuse me, what did you say?"

"There's a bell in the yard of the meeting hall," Agnes said as they rose from the table. "It's rung for all occasions: as a call to service or to a community meal, to mark the school day hours, to announce a wedding or funeral, and for emergencies so everyone drops what they're doing and runs to help solve whatever the problem is."

"Oh, I understand now. What do we do at the whitewashing?" Polly asked as Agnes fixed the bow at the back of her dress.

"We'll help set up the food tables and serve the meals. We'll also make sure the painters have something to drink as they're working."

"Oh," she said, but the tone was less one of understanding than of disappointment.

With little enthusiasm, Polly helped Agnes gather plates, place pies in a picnic basket, and tuck in a tablecloth and napkins.

"We'll have to guard these pies," Agnes said. "Some people have talked of eating dessert before the meal." She anticipated Seth's appreciation at the sight of sweet potato pie.

Estelle helped them pack another basket with the biscuit sandwiches, plates, cups, and utensils. "I'll carry these separately," said Eunice, and she hoisted two pitchers of fresh-squeezed orange juice.

Agnes, Fanny, Eunice, and Polly set out for the churchyard. "Look, everyone is coming from all directions," Agnes said to Polly across the basket they carried and nodded her head toward other settlers on foot, in wagons, and on horseback, each carrying food or project materials.

"Good thing we don't have far to go," Fanny said, lugging one of the baskets. "Where is Clyde?" Agnes and Polly exchanged a glance of understanding. Polly let go of Agnes's basket handle and grabbed one of the handles of Fanny's to help her. Agnes shifted the weight of her basket to better carry it alone, and Eunice balanced her pitchers, one in each hand.

"Clyde said he'd be at the hall at dawn to get an early start," Eunice said.

When they arrived, scaffolding had already been erected around two sides of the building. A makeshift assortment of tables was lined up nearby, each made of planks of wood atop wooden horses or tree stumps. People milled around, setting up food, pouring refreshments, mixing whitewash, laying down dropcloths. Some of the men were already washing the building.

"This is the most people I've seen gathered in one spot since I got here," Agnes said. "Even more than at the Academy on the first day of school or the funeral my first day in town."

"We help one another and work together in this town," Eunice said, standing tall and nodding with approval at a nearby group of young men unrolling drop cloths.

"Not everyone is so lucky," Fanny said. "Some new settlements are ghost towns already because of people fighting one another over this or that."

Agnes searched for Seth and was disappointed when she didn't see him. *Well, it's early yet,* she thought.

A few minutes later, the parson called the crowd to silence. "Bow your heads in prayer, and let us thank the Lord for this beautiful day, this solid building, the ability to do service in his honor, and for this wonderful group of people called to respond to his needs."

A ripple of assents and amens ran through the group, and the parson then led them through the Lord's Prayer. Agnes felt a spirit of kinship. They were as one family.

"Amen," said Parson Pierce, and the resounding amen was loud, firm, and warm.

"Let this day of work in honor of the Lord's house begin!" said the parson, and the group broke apart, and people set out toward different tasks.

"Who's cleaning off the roof?" Clyde asked a group of men.

"Whitewashers, over here," another man called and gestured toward where he stood with pails of whitewash.

"Where are the brushes?" another asked.

Polly watched, her mouth open in fascination at the orchestrated movements. "Come, honey, we need to cut the pies," Agnes said. She put her hand on Polly's shoulder and led her to the tables where the women arranged the food in groupings of savory and sweet.

"Are you feeling well?" she asked, bending down to check that Polly wasn't feverish. "You seem listless."

Polly shrugged. "I'm okay," she said, but clearly she wasn't.

A noticeable hush fell over the crowd. Seth, with Billy behind him on the horse, had just arrived.

"Ha'nt seen that man in a year or more," Agnes overheard a woman, a stranger, whisper to a friend. "Looks familiar to me, but I can't place him. You know him?"

Her companion nodded, her lips in a pressed line. "He's that one whose family died while he was liquored up and in jail. Least that's what folks say. Can't believe he's come here to a house of God."

Agnes strained to hear the rest of the conversation.

"Well, ah declare," said the first woman. "I remember now. What was he in jail for?"

"Something about a tramp's death. Some hobo died. Some folks said he didn't do it, some said he did."

"Well, did he?"

"Can't rightly say. Was a long time ago. I thought he left town. Heard he was going out West."

"Hmph. Maybe he should still go. We don't need his kind here."

Agnes bit her lip to prevent herself from retorting to their judgmental intolerance. Once and for all, she needed to ask Seth for the whole story from his mouth, in his words. She'd come close, the day of their ride to the grove. The moment hadn't been right. Clyde, Fanny, Eunice, and Sarah's support of Seth spoke volumes to her. His deceased sister-in-law's family's willingness to put Billy in his care said even more. The information from the Alloways and the little bit Seth had already volunteered told a story different from the one gossips spread. She wanted to hear his version. How could she not? She was thinking of spending the rest of her life with him. She had to know all the pieces. The people she relied on the most in Persimmon Hollow trusted him. Fully. And called him friend. She already trusted him. And loved him.

The silence among the gathering persisted. Some of the men looked uncomfortable, a few muttered, some shuffled and looked down toward their feet. No one did a lick of work.

Clyde stepped forward. "Glad you could make it, Taylor. I need another man on the roof. Billy can help the men preparing the building."

Clyde walked to a central spot and looked around. "I reckon that's okay with everyone," he asked, but it wasn't really a question.

The parson walked up and stood by his side. "We welcome everyone to this sacred ground. God loves us all. Saint and sinner."

The tension diffused somewhat, but some faces remained hard. Seth tipped his hat to Agnes as he made his way toward the roofing crew, but his face was grim. She and Polly waved hello with enough gusto for Agnes's nearby gossips to notice. Fanny called out to him. "When you fellows are done with the roof, we got some fresh sweet potato pie waiting." Seth glanced again at Agnes, and a grin replaced the grimness. Agnes felt a rush of a warm joy, almost as though Cupid hovered over her.

Billy ran over to them. "Hey, Polly, come work with me on scrubbing the building clean. We get to climb on the ladder!"

Polly brightened as though the sun shone rays directly on her. "Oh, boy, what fun!"

"Polly, honey, that's a job for the men," Agnes protested. "We have plenty to do to get the food ready."

"Oh, please, please," Polly begged, showing the animation that had drained from her earlier in the morning. "I'll help here later, just let me do it for a little while. Please? I've never been on a ladder. I want to see how things look from up there."

"The Bight girls are helping. See?" Billy pointed, and Agnes watched Pansy Bight and her twin sisters looking like they were having the time of their lives. They scrambled up and down the ladder, carrying rags and tools to and from the men, who were handling the harsh, hard-washing chores.

"Women do things on a frontier they may not do in city life," Eunice noted.

"Well, I guess, for a little while," Agnes said, "although it's not a very ladylike task. Polly, I expect you back here as soon as I gesture to you, in about a half an hour. We'll need your help to serve food."

"Okay, thank you, I will," Polly said. And she and Billy ran off.

* * *

A few hours later, when the sun was high above them all, Agnes was busy cutting slices of pie when Seth strolled over, carrying a plate piled high with food.

"Heard there was sweet potato pie over here," he said.

"You heard correctly," Agnes said, smiling. "You men must have been hungry. You finished the whitewashing in record time."

"Funny how fast a hungry man can work when he knows good food's waiting at the end of the job," Seth said.

Grateful that the settlement had abundant food to share, she sliced him an extra-large piece of pie and slid it onto a plate. Their hands brushed when she handed the plate to him, and their gazes met. She was both bashful and happy at the same time.

Seth set down his plate of roast pig, preserves, sliced tomatoes, corn, and biscuits and dug into the pie. "Mmmmmm," he said, taking another bite.

"I'm trying to interest Polly in pie-making," Agnes said. "She hasn't taken to it yet."

"She did a good job with Billy on the prep work," he said.

"I know," Agnes sighed. "It doesn't seem proper for Polly to favor such unladylike work. Look at her now. She's over there with Billy and the Bight children feeding squirrels. She nodded to the far side of the yard, where the youngsters tossed peanuts to the little animals and laughed at their antics as they grabbed peanuts and raced back up into the trees.

"Let her be," Seth said. "Folks don't always fit where they're expected to be. This place is new and different to her, and she's looking for a way to fit in. Better than her being homesick."

"True," Agnes said. She sliced and distributed pie to other hungry workers who lined up behind Seth. He stepped to one side to make room for them, but he didn't leave.

"With a mother who can bake like you, she's sure to pick up the skill," Seth said and with another two bites finished his pie. He held out his plate. "Another, please."

"Don't you think you should eat your lunch first?" she said, but she turned away from the others in order to give him an extra piece.

"Hey, no cutting in line," Clyde called from a few men back. His blue eyes sparkled with mirth.

"Don't know why we got lowlifes like him here," muttered someone else in a sour voice. The voice was lost in the crowd, but the smile left Seth's face and was replaced by a hard line.

"Let it be. Anything else ain't worth it, son," Clyde stepped forward and said in a low voice, just loud enough to reach Seth and Agnes.

"Here you go!" Agnes said brightly and slid the second slice onto Seth's plate. His war within himself played out on his handsome face. His fist clenched his fork. *Guide him, Lord,* she whispered in her heart. *Help him overcome the bitterness and ignore the hurtful comments of the ignorant.* After a few long moments, the tensed muscles in his face relaxed. *Thank you, Lord,* she murmured under her breath. Seth took the offered pie with a nod of thanks.

"Amazing what a good piece of pie can do for a man," Clyde joked.

"And what God can do for us all," Agnes said.

"Amen," said Clyde.

Seth said nothing. The day's brightness dimmed just a little for Agnes, but her hope and faith remained buoyant. *All in good time,* she said to herself.

The parson strolled over. "Any good food left over here?" he asked, maneuvering so that he stood by Seth, who had stepped back a few paces from the crowd. "I'd like to thank you for your help today, Seth. We couldn't have done it without people like you willing to share in the Lord's work. Look at that building!"

Seth assessed the parson as though trying to determine if false gratitude lay behind the statement. Agnes held her breath. It was so obvious the parson's words were from the heart.

Seth nodded a curt thank-you. "Glad I could help," he said.

"We're glad you're here," the parson said, giving him a firm handshake. "Don't wait so long to come back again."

Seth didn't respond to the invitation. Agnes wanted to run over and shake some sense into him. Instead, she inhaled, set down her serving spoon, and walked over to where Sarah was ladling molasses syrup atop shortcakes.

"Why does he push away people who have his interests at heart? Why?" Agnes murmured to Sarah. "People are extending welcomes, and he ignores them."

Sarah nodded. "I've been watching," she said. "Give him time. What you have to understand, Agnes, is that certain—ignorant—people in town were set against Seth during that time of trouble.

They were harsh in their judgment. Just the very idea of his joining the group today is heaven-sent to me and to many others. He's here partly because of you, Agnes. You're drawing him back into community life."

"That's what Fanny says," Agnes said and glanced back to where Seth had stepped away with the parson and Clyde.

"I want to ask him to tell me what happened, but I don't know how," she said to Sarah. "I don't want to pry. But sometimes if a person talks about what happened, it can help them heal any bitterness," she said. "I've seen that happen, more than once, with some of the girls who hadn't been treated well before they came to the orphanage."

"Well, you two are supposed to be betrothed, aren't you?" Sarah said. "You have every right to ask."

"Oh, Sarah, I have such mixed feelings," she said.

Fanny bustled up. "It's so busy over here. Let me help."

Agnes was glad for the extra hands. She was already too distracted.

"My feelings for Seth are growing," she said as she helped Sarah plate shortcakes and cornbread and set them in rows for Fanny to hand out. "He knows how I feel about my faith and how important it is that the man I marry share the same deep beliefs."

"And what did he say?" Sarah asked in a gentle voice.

"He said he'd try. I do believe he is starting to open his heart."

"Maybe he is," Sarah said. "Maybe it isn't happening as fast as you'd like it to happen. God moves in his own time, Agnes. I counsel patience."

Agnes sighed. "That is a virtue to which I need to devote a lot of practice."

"Seth has made tremendous strides in reaching out to people since you've arrived," Sarah said.

"That is what I keep telling her," Fanny said. "It's as plain to me as that sun shining on us that he is in love with her and has been from the day they met."

Agnes felt a blush heat up her face. "Fanny, you are such a romantic!"

"Well, I'm glad she is," Sarah said. "The world needs love and romance. And Fanny speaks the truth, Agnes, about Seth."

"I can't disagree with you both at once," Agnes said, and she had a sudden inkling that maybe, just maybe, everything would be all right. The dangerous moves of the murky characters who'd ruined her life at the orphanage seemed as far away as though on a different continent. Little Persimmon Hollow and its people were becoming home.

Chapter Fourteen

They finished the whitewashing just in time. Days later an early fall storm blew through and curtailed all but the most necessary outdoor activity. Four days of steady rain hampered spirited young people and taxed the patience of adults. Agnes sloshed back and forth to the Academy and used all her resources to keep pupils' attention focused on lessons as rain lashed against the windows and kept everyone cooped up.

"I'm at my wit's end," she told Fanny on the second day of rain as they shared a lunch of sandwiches and slices of lemon pie. "Even calisthenics aren't keeping the children settled. They need an outlet for all that energy." She looked out the window. "And this rain shows no sign of stopping."

"Oh, yes, I do understand—you should see me trying to keep them on task during Latin lessons," Fanny sympathized. "This weather is most unusual. I have never seen it rain like this in fall except for the storm of '77, and that was a hurricane of fierce winds. This rain has similar bands of heavy and lighter rain, but the winds are minimal—enough to be a nuisance but not strong enough to be a hurricane, thank God."

They munched in silence and watched the rain grow more intense. "I could easily fall asleep," said Agnes. Seconds later, a loud crash broke through the steady patter of raindrops against the metal roof. "Not anymore!" Agnes said, her muscles suddenly taut and on alert. Fanny patted her hand across her chest as she, too, rose.

"Miss Alloway, Miss Foster!" Billy's shout accompanied the thud of his footsteps down the hallway toward the teachers' office. He burst in without knocking, his face pale and etched with alarm. "Come quick. Polly slipped an' fell on a wet spot on the floor an' some desks got turned over an' I think her arm is hurt."

Agnes knocked over her chair in her haste. "Where?" Fanny was right behind her. "In the auditorium," Billy said, already leading the way.

Shortly afterward, a shaken but uninjured Polly was settled in a seat looking like a proper little lady. Agnes and Fanny lectured on the perils of playing hide-and-seek indoors then decided to combine their afternoon sessions. Most of the students were in the auditorium already, anyway. Fanny rounded up the rest.

"I propose a theatrical presentation with spirited marching, patriotic songs, and elocution exercises," Agnes said. She stood on the tiny stage and scanned the thirty or so already fidgety youngsters who were further animated by the change in routine.

"A wonderful idea," Fanny said, clapping her hands and standing next to Agnes. "Miss Bight, I'll thank you to stop pulling your sister's hair. Miss Polly Todd, please pay attention instead of chatting with your neighbor, unless your news is worthy of sharing with us all. Master Taylor, is that a slingshot I see in your hand?! Deliver it to me at once! Listen, everyone, we need to see immediate improvement in deportment, or I shall request a visit and lecture from the principal."

As principal, Eunice was known for stern lectures to misbe-having youngsters and for handing out chalkboard writing assign-ments to transgressors. The mention of her name quieted even Billy. He relinquished the slingshot with an "aw, shucks" expres-sion that failed to soften either Fanny or Agnes.

"Now that I have your attention," Agnes said and paused to ensure that she did indeed. "We shall review exercises from Mr. Lucius Osgood's *Progressive Fifth Reader*. As a reward for good behavior—if I see evidence of good behavior—you shall be allowed to help select the exercises and help plan the presentation."

The rain continued into the next day and the one after that. The weather allowed ample time for rehearsal, participation, and a growing excitement about the program, especially after Eunice pronounced it good enough to perform publicly for the town. By the time the sun broke through the clouds Friday afternoon, the program was in place and the pupils even more excited, if possible, than when they began the project.

"I get to recite Patrick Henry's 1775 'Speech Before the Virginia Delegates,'" Billy told Seth with no small amount of pride that evening. They had gathered with Agnes, Polly, Fanny, Eunice, and Clyde on the Alloway porch to drink in the freshened air and savor the hint of coolness that had washed in with the rain.

Seth stretched his legs out and leaned back in the porch swing, where he sat next to Agnes. "The whole thing?" he asked.

"I dunno," Billy said, scratching his head and petting Lumpy, who thumped his tail in reply. "But I'm gonna definitely say the 'give me liberty or give me death' part." He stood up to recite the last words with a bold delivery and senatorial stance.

"He's practiced that line quite well," Agnes said.

"And I'm to recite from Mr. Washington Irving's 'Manners in New York in Early Times' so people can learn about where I come from," Polly said from her perch on a wicker chair where she sat stroking the family's newest addition, a tiny kitten. "Did you know people here are from so many places?! Even the West Indies! I didn't even know where that was until Agnes showed me on a map."

"Hmmm, perhaps we can stage this at the meeting hall instead of at school," Eunice pondered aloud. "It's larger than the Academy's auditorium. We could charge a small fee to raise funds for the school."

"And Polly's comment has just given me an idea!" said Agnes, leaning forward. "She's right, how most people here are from many different places. What if we have a community potluck dinner before or after the presentation, with everyone contributing a dish that represents their home or the homeland of their ancestors?"

Clyde rubbed his hand over his stomach and smacked his lips. Seth nodded and said, "Mmmmmm, I like that idea."

"We could contribute Great-Aunt Lucinda's peach cobbler, my specialty," said Fanny to Eunice.

"I could introduce people to the type of food Michelangelo and Dante ate," Agnes said.

"Who?" asked Billy and Polly in one voice.

"Famous artists from Italy. Michelangelo was a painter and sculptor, and Dante was a poet. They lived during the Renaissance. You'll learn about them soon enough in school."

"You're not gonna make us eat anything weird, are you?" Billy asked.

Agnes laughed. "No. I was thinking of pasta—that's a kind of noodle—and homemade tomato sauce."

"I reckon me 'n Billy could rustle up some greens and cornbread," said Seth. "I'm getting hungry already."

"An' maybe Tustenuggee would bring the Seminole pumpkin he grows back in the woods!" Billy said. "He sure makes it taste good."

"As long as the parson agrees to all these plans, although I can't imagine him disapproving," Eunice said.

The scent of ripening citrus drifted over the porch. Seth and Agnes looked at each other as if of one mind.

"I'll make some marmalades and...," she began.

"...that could be introduced to people at the dinner," he finished.

"Spoken like true companions in life," Fanny said with a sigh.

Agnes blushed.

Seth took her hands in his. "I'm ready when you are," he said in a lowered voice. She knew he wasn't talking about citrus marmalade.

"Are you going to services Sunday?" she asked in a quiet voice.

He fingered his hat, which rested on his thighs, and then met her gaze. "Yes," he said. "I am." He held up a hand at her look of surprise. "I think it's time I ask God's forgiveness." He took both her hands in his.

"Would you mind if I joined you and the Alloways in your seats?" he asked.

"I'd be delighted, and I'm sure Fanny and Eunice feel the same," she said.

Agnes felt such a connection, to him, to the others on the porch, to the little town of Persimmon Hollow, and to the Lord who made it all possible. For the first time in months, a blanket of peace and safety draped her world. She counted her blessings. *Thank you, God,* she prayed, *for leading me here.* The only thing that could make things better were if Seth planned to attend a Mass. *All in due time,* she thought. And this time she believed it would be.

*   *   *

Sunday dawned sunny and cool. Seth, Clyde, and Billy escorted the Alloways, Agnes, and Polly to services. "What a beautiful morning!" Agnes said. She thought, but didn't voice, her wish about what would make the morning even brighter: that they were walking to a Catholic church for Mass.

"We'll be the first to the meeting hall, I believe," Eunice said. "After all that rain, I was ready to set out walking last night."

They all agreed and soaked in the sun's early rays as they walked across the main boulevard to the meeting hall. They entered the building in good cheer then halted as though stopped by an invisible wall.

"Mercy!" cried Fanny.

"When did this happen?" Agnes asked.

"I didn't hear anything fall," Polly said. "Wouldn't a roof falling in make a loud noise?"

They hastened over to the far end of the hall where Parson Pierce stood in his shirtsleeves surrounded by wet hymnals and staring at the collapsed corner of the building.

"Rain must have pooled or else a leak gave way," the parson said. "I couldn't get over here during the storm. Was trying to keep the hotel food garden from flooding. Reckoned all was good as could be here."

"Nobody would have seen this, it being in the back corner," Clyde said. "The live oaks hide the view from the street."

Seth assessed the damaged roof with a critical eye. "I'll tackle this roof right after the service. Can get you some new benches too," he added, looking at the warped boards of the first two rows of benches.

"Are you a skilled roofer?" the parson asked as though such a thing were too much to wish for.

"A man learns a lot on a homestead and grove, parson," Seth said. "I helped my brother build our house."

Agnes sensed a shadow falling over Seth when he mentioned his family. She was glad other churchgoers started to arrive. Everyone had the same shocked reaction. The hall was soon full of astonished people and multiple conversations.

Seth and Clyde helped the parson move the pulpit down the aisle to an undamaged part of the room. Churchgoers squeezed into benches in the rear two-thirds of the building.

"Let us praise God for protecting this portion of our church," the parson said as he welcomed everyone to worship. "And for allowing such damage to occur in an unoccupied place and not in a home with people inside. We are thankful. Now let us bow our heads in prayer."

At the end of service, the parson announced Seth's generous offer to fix the roof. "I'm sure he would welcome help from..."

"No need to bother anyone," Seth said, standing up. "It's something I'd like to do as my way of asking the Lord's forgiveness for staying away so long."

Murmurs of surprise and approval rippled through the congregation. Agnes thought her heart would burst from joy, and she squeezed back tears. "Isn't that wonderful?" she said to Polly and took her hand. Fanny beamed. Even Eunice smiled, something she never did while at worship. "It's about time," Clyde said just loud enough for Seth and Agnes and the Alloways to hear.

"Why…," the parson began then stopped and blinked, "why… welcome home, Brother Taylor!"

Everyone applauded, and many called out "Amen!" and "Welcome home!" Seth sat back down, clearly uncomfortable with the attention. Agnes clasped his hand, and the smile he gave her spoke more than words could. She saw the truth of his declaration in the expression he wore. No longer closed and suspicious, it was open, calm, and certain.

The parson's wife bustled up to where her husband stood. "This calls for a celebration. If you don't mind waiting, I'll send back to the hotel for some lemonade and cookies."

"Seth…," Agnes said as they walked out together toward the picnic tables by the live oak while others dawdled in conversations or extended a hand in welcome to Seth. "What a wonderful change of heart," she said. She wanted to ask how it came about but, for once in her life, managed to check her impatient tongue. *Thank you, God,* she said silently as she swallowed the question.

"Did a lot of thinking while waiting for the rain to stop," Seth said but didn't elaborate.

"God bestows grace in his own way at unexpected times," she said.

"He sent a helper," Seth said and stopped to look down at her. "You." Their gazes met, and she felt a stirring inside that was deeper and richer than just physical attraction between a man and a woman.

He lifted her hand and kissed it. "I plan to meet with the priest next time he visits from Palatka. I have a lot to say. And you'll have to help me remember the parts of the Mass."

"I can do that!" Agnes said. "We can start right away."

"Good," he said. "Here come the Alloways. I'll leave you with them. I'm going to check out the roof and see what supplies I need."

As he strode off, she heard a rustling of clothing behind her and turned to see Adelaide walk up, a little ahead of the Alloways and coming from a different direction.

"You believe everything you hear?" Adelaide asked in an arch tone that implied superiority.

Agnes was puzzled. "Why do you ask?" she replied.

"You know Seth Taylor is lying, don't you? He doesn't give a hoot about God. He's just trying to make people forget about his past."

Adelaide gave a little shake of her head so that her ringlets bounced. "You silly thing," she continued to Agnes. "You believed him, didn't you?" She trilled a sharp laugh. "You'll find out in due time," she added and then shrugged her shoulders as if bored. "I'm not waiting around for silly old lemonade. I've more important things to do." She walked off just as the Alloways and Clyde arrived. Agnes was glad Polly and Billy were playing with the other youngsters and were out of earshot.

"The nerve of that woman," said Fanny indignantly. "I heard every word. I think she wanted me to hear every word. She wanted all of us to hear! I declare!"

"It's the work of the devil to spread doubt where none exists," Eunice said. "If ever there was a time to accept Seth's words as God-sent, this is it."

"Amen to that," Clyde said.

Seth made his way back to them. "It's not as bad as it looks," he said. "A mess of shingles are gone, but the weak spot in the truss ain't too bad."

"*Isn't*," Agnes said automatically and then put a gloved hand over her mouth. They all laughed.

"Okay, *isn't*," Seth said.

The parson's hotel wagon rolled into the yard, and Billy and other young men unloaded a small barrel and rolled it under the vast shade of the oak. Mrs. Pierce carried over a platter and uncovered it, revealing a mound of cookies. The beverage and food quickly became focal points of the gathering.

"How come you said you were away so long?" Polly asked Seth as their small group sat together on a blanket Fanny pulled from her large wicker bag.

"Hush, Polly, it's not polite to question adults," Agnes reprimanded her.

"No, let her be," Seth said. "Young'uns have a right to know why a person would be fool enough to turn against God's ways. These two," he said, gesturing toward Billy and Polly, "are old enough to know. Might help them avoid making the same mistake when they face a rough spot in life."

Billy's face wore a guarded look.

"You, especially, Billy, have a right to know, seeing as how this involves your mother and father," Seth added.

"God rest their souls," Fanny said.

Seth squatted where Billy and Polly sat at the edge of the blanket. "It's like this," he began, but he looked over and met Agnes's gaze briefly, and she understood he spoke to her as much as to the children.

"I thought I knew everything when I was a young man," he said.

"How old are you now?" Polly piped up.

"Polly!" Agnes said.

"I'm thirty," Seth answered. "No longer a young man. But when I was younger, I thought I knew everything. My parents worked hard to feed and clothe me and my brother, to raise us right. Sometimes we went hungry because there wasn't enough food. We didn't own our land. My pa was in Florida during the war. Afterward, he claimed a homestead and moved us all here to the land the grove is on now. He and my ma were getting on in years and weren't as strong as they had been. We had some hungry times while waiting for the citrus to come into bearing. We lived in a one-room cabin with palm fronds for a roof. My brother and I wanted to build a decent house for the family to take shelter in, but money and supplies were scant. I'm not proud that I did some moonshining to get cash."

Agnes gulped down a gasp. Moonshine? He'd made it?

"Like I said, I ain't—I'm not—proud of the fact," Seth said after he saw the look on Agnes's face. "But it brought in enough money until we started shipping out citrus on a regular basis. I quit the moonshine business soon as I got a little older and saw the foolishness of what I was doing. By that time, my brother and I had built the house—four rooms and a tight roof. Things were looking up. We were able to keep Ma and Pa comfortable until they passed. My brother married a nice girl, our citrus gained a good reputation, Billy was born, and I started thinking it was time for me to settle down."

He quieted.

"What'd Billy look like as a baby?" Polly asked.

"He was a fat fellow with chubby cheeks," Seth said and tousled Billy's hair.

"Just about when Billy was toddling around, railroad men started nosing around, looking at the land and asking if we'd sell. They made a nuisance of themselves, especially when we said the land wasn't for sale and wasn't going to be. First, they offered a lot of money. Then they tried to be tough and said they 'owned' the circuit judge and could get him to seize our land. The biggest loudmouth was a fellow named Lester Little. He and I almost came to blows one day, and I told him never to set foot on my land again. He fixed an evil stare on me and said that I hadn't seen the last of him."

Agnes shivered, even though the day had warmed. Lester Little reminded her of Rufus Smith. She realized she hadn't thought of the past in several days. Persimmon Hollow had started to heal her, and she was grateful.

"I forgot about Little until a month later when I found myself in a jail cell, accused of selling bad moonshine to a drunken tramp passing through town," Seth said. "The guy died from drinking it. The marshal apologized when he came to take me but said the jug had my name scratched on it. Said he had to detain me until he and his men had time to unravel what happened."

Seth took off his hat, ran his hand through his hair, and put his hat back on. "I told the marshal exactly where my old still was, deep in the woods, and suggested he go look at it. One quick look would tell anybody no moonshine had come out of it for years. The equipment was overgrown with Virginia creeper and maypop, the pipes were broken and twisted in some spots, and the vats were rotted half through. Plus, the Taylor name was known in town by then and had a good reputation. Tustenuggee vouched that he and I had been on a hunting trip when the tramp supposedly bought liquor from me. I told the marshal that maybe someone dug up an old bottle or added my name to a newer one. He said he and our sheriff, once he got into town, would check out all angles. Meanwhile, I was left in jail to stew about it."

"The entire town was in an uproar," Clyde said. "Most folks backed the Taylors. 'Course you always have your malcontents, stirring the pot. Gossip was going around."

"And it spread fast," added Fanny. "Fueled by people breaking the Eighth Commandment."

Polly nudged Agnes and whispered, "I forget which one is the Eighth."

"You shall not bear false witness against your neighbor," Agnes whispered back. "It means don't speak untruths about anyone, don't tell lies about them or spread stories by gossiping."

Seth shrugged. "I wasn't aware of the uproar in town. I was in the jail in Lemon City, the next town south on Black Bear Trail, because Persimmon Hollow had no place to detain me. I lay around for two days only to wake up one morning and see smoke billowing in the sky in the direction of the grove. I busted down the door and took off."

"Whooeee," Billy sat up. "You escaped from jail? Uncle Seth!"

"This is no tall tale like what you might have read in *Robinson Crusoe*," Eunice said. "This was real. This is how your parents died, William."

"Oh," he said. "Oh."

Seth's voice had become uncertain and his face haggard. Agnes scooted closer to him and laid a hand on his arm, willing strength into him. He clasped his hand over hers and continued.

"I was too late," he said so low it was hard to hear. "By the time I got back, fire had destroyed the cabin and killed my brother and his wife." His grip on Agnes grew stronger, as though seeking support.

"Billy, you were toddling around the yard with old Murphy dog guarding you. You're too young to remember that dog. He died in his sleep of old age about a year later. You were young and in need of mothering. I was incapable of anything except remembering I hadn't made it home in time. Your mother's sister in Jacksonville came down and took you home. It was temporary. You were the only family I had left, and I wanted you with me, raised the way your father would have raised you. So I soon went north and brought you back. It didn't take long to figure out I knew less than nothing about raising young'uns. The Gomezes hadn't yet settled on the land, else Señora Gomez would have been there. You ran wild, too wild. After you nearly drowned in the cistern, I sent you back to your aunt, for your own safety."

"It was mighty hard to do that, to send you away," he said to Billy, who nodded in adultlike understanding. "That's why you visited back and forth so much after Señora Gomez was around to improve my poor child-raising habits."

"Did the sheriff figure out who did it?" Billy asked in a small voice.

"We all knew something more than a regular fire had happened," Seth said. "Sure enough, the sheriff discovered my brother—your dad—had been hit in the head. We figured your mother must have left you with Murphy—he was an old guard dog—for a moment to run and help her husband inside the cabin. We think someone tossed a lighter knot in the window or brought it in and was startled by my brother's appearance. No one really knows. We do know that the fire caused a jug of kerosene to explode, and the flames and fumes killed them both. We're fairly certain the fire was set. If only I had..."

"What happened, happened," Eunice said clearly and firmly. "Who knows what might have transpired had you been there. Whoever did it might have knocked you out, too. Then who would be looking after Billy today?"

"True, to a point," Seth said. "But I was bitter, and I felt responsible for the whole mess. I had a gut feeling Lester Little had been involved and that maybe things wouldn't have gotten so bad if I hadn't ordered him off the land at gunpoint. But he was long gone. I swore I'd get revenge someday. Anger ran through me when I heard he was nosing around town again. But, to get back to answering your first question, Polly, the reason I stayed away from church was because I turned away from God after everything happened. I felt like God had abandoned me. So I abandoned him."

"God never abandons us," Agnes said softly. "He is our rock during times of despair. God sees us through the dark times." She recited the line from Jeremiah 16:19 that had helped her: "O Lord, my strength and my stronghold, my refuge on the day of trouble..."

"I didn't have you here to remind me, at the time," Seth said.

"We tried, son," Clyde said, to affirmations from Fanny and Eunice.

"I know," Seth said. "Like I said, I thought I knew everything, even if that meant questioning God and ignoring the advice of my elders. Times got so dark I thought about selling out and heading West."

"The sheriff did clear your name," reminded Fanny.

"Yes, he said everything you had told him was true," Eunice added.

"It was too little, too late," Seth said. "I felt sorry for myself, angry at the world, and alone, so I poured myself into the grove. I was as mad at folks in town as I was at God. Wanted nothing to do with Persimmon Hollow except to forget it existed."

"It's true some people dragged down your name," Fanny said. "We did our best to stop the talk. It certainly wasn't fitting behavior for the town our father founded on his ideals."

"Water under the bridge, now," Clyde said, as if to break the uncomfortable silence that threatened to blanket them all.

"Yes, we're here, together, and times are good," Fanny agreed.

"Reckon we ought to be heading back?" Clyde said and gestured at Polly, who had fallen asleep with her head in Agnes's lap.

"Your mother was the angel sent to save me," Seth said to the sleeping girl.

"Even I'm glad of that," said Billy. He scrambled up and tugged on Polly's hand to wake her up. "Miss Agnes makes fine pie. Hey, c'mon, Polly, get up. I just remembered. We gotta go check to see if the squirrels ate all the peanuts we put out before the service."

"And I have a roof to fix," Seth said as if glad for the excuse to change the subject.

"Oh, mercy, in all the excitement we forgot to ask the parson if we could have our school program here!" said Fanny.

"And the dinner, too!" said Agnes.

Seth looked up at the roof and back at the little group, the only ones left in the churchyard. Everyone else had drifted home.

"You know Parson Pierce will insist on paying me for the job," Seth said. "You know what he's like. And you know I don't want payment. So I'll suggest another form of thanks. I'll tell him I know some ladies who'd like to stage a school recital and community dinner. That'd be all the payment I need."

Chapter Fifteen

$\mathcal{B}$arrel sat outside the lopsided palm-frond shelter. It was built against a wide live oak limb that stretched out horizontally, low to the ground, for twenty feet. The makeshift camp had become a temporary home.

"Least it done stopped raining, boss," he said to Lester. "Been nice for a coupla days."

"About time," came the grumbling reply from inside the tent-like lean-to, which was still damp from the recent rains. "I'm getting moldy."

"What next?" Barrel asked. "Don't we got to get out to the depot and ride up to St. Augustine? And find out what the boss man wants us to do next about this Taylor guy and his land?"

"How we going to get there with no horses, you idiot," said Lester from inside the lean-to. "It's a good five miles out from here."

"This hiding in the woods and spying on people ain't fitting for a man like me," Barrel said. "I say do your business out in the open and duke it out if'n that's what it comes to."

Lester snorted. "Like you did at the Land Inn? That's what got us into this mess."

"But, but, but, just a minute, those men insulted me and…"

"And now we're living in the woods like animals, and the townsfolk think we're scum," Lester said. "Let me think on it a minute. Only thing the guys in St. Augustine can do is give me more money for this job. It's a darn site harder than I expected. I'm thirsty. Go find us some water. Gotta be a spring around here somewhere."

"Where's your fancy lady friend? Can't she send us some vittles and something for my scratchy throat?" Barrel grumbled. He ignored the order to find water. "I'm going to puke if I eat squirrel meat one more time."

Lester snorted. "You mean Adelaide Land? She says she can't let on in refined company that she knows us," he said as he came out of the shelter, stretched, and scratched. "But for once you're right, Barrel. Unless she wants us to talk loud and long about her shopping debts up north and cut off the money supply that feeds her fancy-clothes habit, she better start getting mighty friendly. I'll remind her again how much she owes us."

He tapped his fingers on the bark. "I sure could use a good meal," he continued. "Might be time to show up at Land Inn again and pretend we're coming back through town from some business trip. I hope Addy's been making herself useful spreading dirt about Taylor so folks stop talking about us. I couldn't frame Taylor or burn him out of his land, so maybe we can run him out of town. Heh, heh, heh."

"I dunno, boss, he's smitten with the schoolmarm. Plus he's got that kid. And the Injun friend. And that Mexican family or whatever they are."

"You seen any of them in the past week we been out here?" Lester asked. "Me neither. We're squatting on his land, and he don't even know it. What are you still doing here? Thought I told you to go find us some water. Oh, forget it. Break down this camp. Then we'll find us a spring. I need a bath. Got leaves and mud all over me. Gotta look respectable if we're heading back into town. We also got to borrow some horses so we can get out to the depot and head to St. Augustine to see if the railmen can cough up some more cash."

"Ain't no kinda life, boss, I'm telling you," Barrel said as he started yanking down fronds and branches. "I'm fixin' to maybe get respectable with a real job."

"Right. Stuff it, Barrel. I got to think. There's a spring around here somewhere, I remember from when I was here before. We just got to find it."

* * *

"Ready?" Seth stood at the front door of the Alloway house, a bouquet of ironweed flowers in his hand, and spoke through the screened door. "It's perfect weather to show you the spring."

"We're ready!" Agnes called. She beckoned him inside as she tied her hat ribbon under her chin. She took the bouquet with a shy smile and went in search of a vase.

"We're so happy to see the sun shining again, that famous Florida sunshine," Fanny said as she walked into the parlor toting her flowered carry bag. "Eunice, Billy, and Polly are already over at Clyde's getting the wagon ready. Seth, I believe I haven't been out to the spring on your land in some years now. This is a treat!"

"I've heard a lot about it," Agnes said as she came back into the room carrying the flowers in a blue vase that set off the purple of the blossoms. She set the vase on the mantel. "It sounds beautiful."

"It is," Seth said. He held open the door for Fanny and Agnes, called a goodbye to Estelle, and escorted the two across the street to the yard of Clyde's store. "I imagine you'll say you feel close to God there," he added to Agnes.

"You sound as if you already feel that way," she said.

"I might, without realizing it," Seth acknowledged.

The horses were hitched, and the travelers were soon settled. Clyde urged his team out, and Seth mounted Silver and rode alongside as they headed out of town and toward his grove.

"Wow, having this school day off is great!" Billy said. "I sure am glad the caretaker had to clear out those nesting squirrels and seal up the holes before we can go back inside."

"Me, too!" echoed Polly. "But of course I love my lessons. Agnes, you know that."

"Seeing the beauty of nature is always worth our time," Agnes said. "And I could fit a lesson or two into the excursion, if you two wish," she teased and laughed at their emphatic nos.

They soon turned onto the road through Seth's grove. The sunlight, warmth, gentle breeze, and steady rhythm of the horses' hooves lulled Agnes and the others. They traveled in peaceable silence until Seth called out to them.

"Clyde, head off through this row of trees," he said, pointing toward the east. Agnes thought the rows all looked the same. Each was lined with oval-shaped trees with dark-emerald leaves that nearly touched the ground. Each tree was lush with heavy globes of orange citrus.

"Near about ready for harvest, ain't you?" Clyde commented.

"Yeah, getting close. Tustenuggee is rounding up a work crew."

"Can I help?" Billy asked.

"Me, too?!" Polly chimed in.

"Better ask the schoolmarm," Seth said.

Before Agnes could answer, Eunice did. "We traditionally suspend classes or adjust lesson times during harvest seasons," she said. "Many of our pupils have to help in the groves."

"Perhaps we can make the experience educational," Agnes said. "I'll work on some lesson plans." Billy groaned so loudly everyone laughed.

"There are many lessons to be learned," Eunice said. "Money-handling, crop cultivation and harvest, sorting and packing methods, distribution to market. I think Miss Agnes's idea has merit." Billy groaned even louder.

They reached the far edge of the grove, which ended on a gentle slope adjacent to a hammock of thick oak, hickory, palmetto, and magnolia. Seth led the way into a narrow wooded path, just wide enough for the wagon. The land around them changed as they traversed from a high sandhill downward to a shaded, overgrown nook.

"The air is changing," Agnes said after they'd ridden a while. "It's cooler, and lighter, not as heavy as it can sometimes be. It feels...refreshing. It smells earthy and welcoming."

"We're getting close to the spring, that's why," Fanny said. "I hardly even need my fan!"

Polly and Billy knelt at the side of the wagon, studying the woods. "Persimmons," Billy yelled, pointing at tall trees with small orange-red orbs of fruit with a skin much smoother than a citrus fruit. "Yup, we must be getting close. Wild persimmons grow all around the spring."

"What's a persimmon?" Polly asked.

"A yummy fruit but you gotta eat it at the right time or else it makes your mouth pucker. It's sour as can be if it's not ripe," he said.

"They look ripe," Eunice and Clyde said in unison.

"Let's pick some on the way back," Fanny said. "Agnes, you will love cooking jams and jellies with them. They are delicious."

"I'm beginning to love everything about Persimmon Hollow," Agnes said.

She marveled at the beauty of the world around her. The flora was so different from that in the orange grove. Ferns, mosses, and tangled sprays of Spanish moss fed the lushness of the landscape. Sprays of palmetto grew between and around the trees.

"Look, there's a little stream," she said, pointing to the rivulet carving a path parallel to the road. "It's so clear it sparkles!"

"Runs for a long way before it disappears into the ground," Clyde said.

"Disappears!" Agnes, Polly, and Billy exclaimed.

"Yup, goes plumb underground into limestone caves. Them caves is where all of Florida's rainfall collects," he said. "It bubbles back up in springs or when we tap into it by drilling an artesian well into the limestone. Finest tasting water you can find anywhere."

Seth, who had maneuvered so that he rode ahead of the wagon, stopped as the path ended and opened up into a small clearing. He sat there, hands resting on his thighs, and looked first at the scene before him and then at Agnes as though waiting to see her reaction.

She was speechless as Clyde pulled the wagon up next to Seth and dropped the reins.

"Welcome to Green Spring," Seth said.

"Is it real?" Agnes whispered, astonished at what lay before her. "It's the most beautiful, enchanting place I've ever seen." Talking aloud seemed disrespectful to such a stunning display.

The spring was a round, green-blue-tinted jewel of water in a natural basin. The sandy bottom sparkled in the rays of sun that dappled the water. Ferns and young palmettos grew on the sloping sides of the water. Higher above, live oaks, palms, hickory, magnolia, and cypress lined the tops of the banks. The oaks' massive limbs stretched across the basin so far a person could sit atop one in the middle of the spring and dangle their feet into the water. Tiny resurrection ferns awash with the recent rains sprouted along the rain-darkened limbs. Spanish moss draped from limbs of all sizes and shapes.

"For where your treasure is, there your heart will be also," Agnes whispered Matthew 6:21 as they all sat there and felt the beauty and power of the small corner of the woods.

"Let me show you," Seth said and dismounted. He helped her climb out of the wagon.

"God is sharing a sliver of paradise, a sliver of Eden," she said. They all disembarked, stretched their legs, and walked toward a break in the bank that provided access to the water. Billy and Polly ran ahead. Seth slowed down until he and Agnes lagged behind the others.

"I'd like to share my humbler plan," Seth said. Agnes leaned on his arm so as not to stumble on the uneven terrain.

"The sulfur and mineral content of the spring waters provide some healing properties, and I've thought of building a boarding house here where sick folks could take the waters," he said.

"An excellent idea," Eunice said, calling back to them over her shoulder. She held onto one of Clyde's arms, and Fanny had the other. All three nodded in approval at the idea.

"I like it, too," Agnes said.

"We'll see how this year's harvest goes," Seth said. "Got to do the store first. One thing at a time and it'll get done." Lowering his voice, he spoke so that only Agnes could hear, "And I'd love to share it all with the pretty, warm-hearted, woman of faith and love by my side, when she's ready."

"Oh, Seth," she whispered, her heart seeming to swell with feeling. "I...I..."

Billy's yell startled everyone into a halt. "Hey, somebody else is here!" he called, from just inside a thickly wooded area where he and Polly had gone to pick persimmons.

They hurried over. Sure enough, just inside the area the brush was trampled and footprints evident.

Seth tightened his grip on Agnes's arm, and Clyde pulled a pistol from his overalls.

"Out of here, now," Seth said tersely to the youngsters, who scrambled out and pressed close to Agnes and the Alloways.

Seth and Clyde squatted and checked the footprints. "New prints," Seth said.

Clyde nodded in agreement. "New enough to make me think they're still around here," he said.

They stood up. "Sorry to call it a day, ladies and young'uns, but you need to get back to the house while we clear this up," Seth said. "Probably harmless travelers squatting for the night, but you never know."

His face was tight, and Agnes suspected he knew more than he was saying. They climbed back into the wagon and retraced their route without mishap. Clyde urged the team toward the house, and Seth rode off to find Tustenuggee.

As soon as they were gone, a panting Lester and Barrel crawled out of the thicket. "Woooo, boy, was that close," said Barrel, puffing.

Lester looked at the retreating wagon with narrowed eyes. "I hate to see happy families," he said, his thin lips pressed together. "Got me an idea, I do. Just might work, too. Once and for all, the railroad will get the land, and I'll get a big wad of cash. Yeahhhh."

He rubbed his hands together and chuckled in a thin, sinister tone.

Chapter Sixteen

*S*eth rode in to pick up Billy after classes ended the following day. He had a spring in his step that Agnes hadn't seen before. She wondered why, considering how yesterday's events had been troubling.

"His spirit is healing, thanks to you," Fanny leaned over and whispered as they stood at the Academy doorway, saying goodbye to youngsters who filed out in order and broke into a run as soon as they cleared the steps.

"You mean thanks to God," Agnes said.

"Yes, and to his helper, Miss Agnes," Fanny added. "I am certain he sent you here on a mission."

"Perhaps," Agnes said. "I sometimes wonder myself."

Billy raced to Seth's wagon, and Polly skipped along. "I'm going with Billy and Mr. Taylor, okay, Agnes?" Polly called over her shoulder.

"Yes, and watch where you are skipping!" Agnes called back, expecting Polly to stumble any moment if she didn't pay attention. The young girl already had a skinned knee from running and jumping and occasionally tumbling, and she was getting freckles from being outdoors with a bonnet that hung down her back instead of staying perched on her head.

"How many times do we have to tell her that bonnets belong atop the head?" Agnes wondered aloud. Polly's bonnet once again hung by its strings tied loosely around her neck.

"The child is thriving," Fanny observed. "Let her be for now. I see how you instruct her in deportment, needlework, and cookery. Trust me, she won't forget. There's room for her to enjoy her playmates and the outdoors, and to also learn womanly skills."

Agnes frowned. "I hope so. I don't want her disappointed when it comes time to rein her into a woman's sphere."

"A sphere that widens with each decade," Fanny pointed out. "We're almost on the verge of a new century. Just imagine, the twentieth century. Who knows what it will bring for all of us." She chuckled. "Perhaps even the vote."

They watched as Sarah's three school-age children begged Seth for a ride. The oldest, Pansy, stood a head and shoulders above her sisters, the twins Nuby and Nettie. Seth nodded, helped them in, and then bounded up the walkway toward Agnes and Fanny.

"Parson Pierce not only likes the dinner-fundraiser idea," Seth said, "he's so happy about the roof repair he insists the menfolk of the church repay the favor by helping me raise the frame of my store." Seth pushed his hat back on his head and grinned.

"I declare, Seth Taylor, it's a happy day and a blessing to see you once again become part of this community," Fanny said. She placed her hands on either side of his face and pulled him toward her for a matronly kiss. "It's about time!"

"I admit it'll be a big help," Seth said. His smile curved downward. "No time to waste in getting the store up and running. It'll raise the value of my land and let anybody who's eyeing it know I'm serious about staying put."

"Anybody? Meaning the railroad?" Fanny asked.

"You got it. Tustenuggee and I are sure somebody's spying on us. I think the railroad's behind it, at least some of the bastar...uh, some of the men. A group of investors are behind the Flagler line's plan to run that new spur past my place. They want to grab all the surrounding acreage. The government will give every parcel that isn't claimed, but they want it all."

"I'm not sure I understand," Agnes said.

"It's an incentive," Seth explained. "The government gives the railroad and its investors hundreds of thousands of acres of land in exchange for extending the rail lines. The state gets access for the tourists and settlers new rail lines bring in, and the railroad gets land to sell to those settlers and the businesses that serve them."

"Everyone around here knows about the healing waters of springs," Fanny said, pulling her fan out of her bag. "Do you think the railroad wants Green Spring, too?"

"Well, it's part of my land," Seth said. "I wasn't aware they knew about the spring."

"You think the evidence in the woods yesterday was a sign of railroad spies?" Agnes asked.

"They've done it before," Seth said.

"Oh, that's worrisome," Agnes said.

"Well," Fanny said briskly. "We as a town are not going to fall into any traps they set. We'd like the railroad to come into town, of course, but on our terms."

"They can play a mean game," Seth said. "Not all of them, but enough."

"Be careful, Seth," Agnes said, placing a hand on his arm.

"I am," he said and looked down at her. "Got a future to prepare for."

Fanny started humming the wedding march.

"We haven't set a date yet, Fanny!" Agnes said. "I'm still getting used to the idea of being betrothed. And…of saying good-bye to St. Isidore's Home," she added. She tried to keep the pain out of her voice.

Fanny and Seth exchanged glances.

"Everything will work out for the best," Fanny said, and Seth nodded. They waited, as if needing her agreement. She nodded, but her heart was heavy when it should have been joyful. If only there were a way to fit everything together in a neat package.

"Would you ladies like a ride home?" Seth asked, changing the subject. He tipped his hat and offered a gentlemanly bow. "I could rearrange that passel of young'uns raising a ruckus in the wagon right now."

"Mercy, no," said Fanny, laughing. "It's a fine day for walking."

"I'll walk with Fanny," Agnes said. "We have to start planning recipes if we're to help you stock the store. Sounds like you'll be in business sooner than we expected."

"Yeah, it's a busy time," Seth said. "Crop's rolling in, store going up…wedding to plan…and an orphanage up North to help Agnes support."

Agnes's smile spoke her thanks.

"I always say it's better to be busy than bored," Fanny remarked, and she and Agnes set out for home. Seth escorted them as far as the wagon.

"You are staying for dinner, yes?" Fanny said just before taking her leave.

"Oh, can we, can we, can we?" Billy pleaded, looking imploringly at Seth. "Polly said dinner is gonna be meat loaf and fresh green beans and grits." His cohorts in the wagon joined in begging to stay for dinner, too.

"Looks like the decision's made," Seth said and climbed aboard the wagon seat.

"Ask your parents for their permission first," Agnes told the Bight children.

"It'll give their mother a break," she said to Fanny, as the wagon rattled off.

"Sarah shoulders so much," Fanny said. "We'll send enough home to feed the rest of the family. Their finances are always tight."

Eunice walked out to meet them as they reached the walkway to the Alloway house.

"Clyde just told me the men who started the fight at Land Inn have returned. They ate a meal and are already gone," she said. "They claimed they were passing through town on their way north. I find their behavior odd. So does Clyde. No one stops in this town for a meal and leaves immediately afterward. We're not on a thoroughfare."

"I'm glad they're gone," Agnes said. She remembered how the sight of them discomforted her outside the church that day. A chill passed over her.

The three stayed at the edge of road, talking long enough for Seth to arrive and unload six youngsters, one more than the five he started with. The addition was Sarah's second youngest, too young for school but old enough to tag along with his three older sisters.

"Mamma said yes!" little Toby Bight, Jr., crowed as the six youngsters climbed out of the wagon and headed for the back-yard. Sarah's eldest, Pansy, ran to catch up with Toby.

"Mamma said she and Pop would be happy to have a quiet dinner with the baby—he's real cranky, the baby is—and Mamma said to say thank you," Pansy said shyly to Agnes as she passed.

"I took them by the house to check about dinner," Seth said. "Sarah was sweeping the yard and was so happy to send them over that she added Toby Jr. to the party." Seth maneuvered the horse and wagon across the road into the mercantile yard.

Clyde stomped out the mercantile's back door just as Seth hitched Silver to the post and started to groom him.

"Clyde wasn't upset like that a half hour ago," Eunice said. "I wonder if we should go over."

They couldn't hear the conversation but watched Seth hitch his thumbs in his back pockets and rock back and forth on the heels of his boots as he listened. Clyde emphasized his comments by pointing his index finger into the palm of his other hand over and over again.

"Yes, let's go," Eunice said, and the three women hurried across the street.

"Anything we can do?" Eunice asked.

"Too late for that, Ennie, though I thank you for asking," Clyde said, calling Eunice by the nickname he had started using more and more often. "Those two lowlifes I told you about have run out of town on stolen horses. Just got word from the livery."

"And we're going after them," Seth said. "They'll have to stop at some point, and we can catch up." Minutes later, the livery owner, the parson, Sarah's husband Toby, and a handful of other men rode hard around the corner and stopped in front of the mercantile. Agnes coughed from the dust kicked up by the horses and pulled her handkerchief from her skirt pocket and put it over her mouth. Seth grabbed her a ladle of water from the well, made sure she was all right, then unhitched Silver. Clyde saddled a horse, and the two men joined the posse and headed out.

Two hours later, the men returned, leading the stolen horses. The criminals were nowhere to be seen.

Agnes, Fanny, and Eunice watched from the Alloway porch. Seth and Clyde tethered their horses, waved off the others, and walked over.

"That was quick," Eunice said.

"We've got dinner warming for you on the stove," Fanny added.

Agnes tried to catch a sense of what happened by watching Seth, but he remained unreadable.

"Found the horses abandoned at the depot," Clyde said. "Ain't typical."

"No, it isn't," Seth said. "Those two creeps are on some kind of mission. I am pretty darn sure it involves my land. We have to figure out what the rest of their plan is."

* * *

Miles away, Lester and Barrel sat in the back of the train and listened to a newfound friend ramble. Rufus Smith had just disembarked at Persimmon Hollow when Lester and Barrel raced up to the depot, dismounted, and nearly collided with him. They warned the stranger that if he was smart, he would flee town with them, else dangerous, crazed townsfolk hot on their trail would think he stole the horses. Rufus lost no time getting back on the train. He ingratiated himself with his newfound companions.

"Looking for my wife," Rufus explained in a smooth, practiced voice about why he had come to Persimmon Hollow. "She ran off. Got my little girl with her." And he described them in detail. In the process, he painted himself as a wounded, innocent husband.

"Gee, boss," Barrel said. "Sounds like that schoolmarm."

"Sure does," said Lester, fingering his mustache.

"What schoolmarm? You know them?" Rufus asked. He leaned forward, too eagerly.

"What's it worth to ya?" Lester asked.

Rufus pulled out a wad of bills and rippled it with his fingers. "Name your price."

Barrel's eyes widened. "It's our lucky day," he squeaked.

"Why you so crazy to find 'em?" Lester asked, suspicious. "Schoolmarm's been around a while now, and you're just showing up?"

"Like I said, I didn't know their whereabouts," Rufus said in a mournful tone. "I just want my family back together again."

Lester looked at the wad of money again.

"What you waitin' for?" Barrel said in a high-pitched voice. "Take some," and he reached to grab some money, but Rufus was faster and pulled his hand out of reach.

"Keep it quiet, Barrel. I'm thinkin'," Lester said.

After a few minutes, he gave Rufus a calculated stare. "Stick with us, and we'll lead you to them when we go back to town, for a good price, that is. We can figure out the money later. But I'm warning you. Don't try to double-cross us."

Rufus leaned back in his seat, gave Lester a self-satisfied smile, and nodded. "I'm a patient man."

* * *

The next two weeks flew by in a mix of lessons, recital rehearsals, party planning, and recipe selection. Agnes reveled in cooking, canning, and creating and told herself Polly was equally enthralled with their project. With lesson times adjusted at the Academy, the two of them had extra free time to devote to the project. One sunny morning, they, Eunice, and Fanny drove the Alloway barouche out to Seth's grove to pick up fruits for the marmalade and other goodies needed for the recipes Agnes had laid out on the Alloway kitchen counter.

Harvest was in full swing. As they rolled up to the house, they could hear the *thunk, thunk, thunk* of oranges, lemons, and grape-fruits rolling into field crates. The fruit pickers yelled to each other as they harvested fruit, scrambling up and down tall ladders set against the full, round trees. Each tree was covered with bright globes of citrus on branches that drooped almost to the ground.

"Wow," said Agnes. "Look at all that fruit!"

Each picker had a thick, heavy canvas bag slung over his neck and shoulder. With speed and dexterity, the men picked fruit and placed it into the bag, descending the ladder only when the bag bulged with citrus. They emptied their sacks into large wagons, which then were sent to a section of the yard behind the house. There, the fruit was sorted and packed into wooden boxes.

Seth scrambled down one of the ladders and came over to them.

"Look! There's Billy!" Polly yelped, pointing toward a tree where the youngster was high on a ladder hard at work. "Oh, boy, I want to help!"

"Not this time, young lady," Agnes said firmly, putting a hand on her shoulder. "This is men's work."

"When I grow up, I'm gonna do whatever I want, ladies' work or men's work," Polly said and crossed her arms over her chest in stubbornness. She pouted and looked at Seth with pleading eyes as he reached them, but it was to no avail.

"Too rough and tumble out there for little ladies," he said, patting her on the shoulder. "It isn't a game. Tell you what, you pick whatever fruit you want from that crate right there, and I'll show you how to drink the juice from it the way the Indians do."

Her eyes lit up. "Oh, goody!" and she scampered off to inspect the oranges in the crate he indicated. She picked up and judged each selection with earnest diligence.

"How much fruit do you get from a harvest?" Agnes asked. "The marmalades, jellies, and candies we could make from just a portion of this will stock all the shelves of your store no matter how large you build it."

"Each bag the men carry weighs thirty pounds full," he said. Agnes tried to imagine lifting such a weight as effortlessly as these workers did. "Each crate holds ninety pounds. Ten crates fill one of those packing boxes," he said and pointed to a huge box already secured on a flat wagon hitched to four horses.

"Depending on a tree's age, it'll produce five hundred to two thousand fruits. I ship most of it north, but some stays in town. I'll clear a few thousand, enough to get the store built and fully stocked, with some left over for the hotel I plan to build at the spring."

Polly ran back to them with a perfect orange in her hand. She gave it to Seth and watched with eager eyes as he cut a small round hole in the fruit, pulled a piece of thin bamboo from his pocket, and inserted the bamboo into the hole. "I carry a few of these bamboo pieces in my pocket all during the harvest season," he said. "Comes from that clump of bamboo near my house. Now, put your lips on the bamboo and squeeze the orange," he instructed. "The liquid will come up the bamboo and right into your mouth."

After a few attempts, Polly perfected the technique. "Yum," she said and wiped juice off her chin. "Here, Agnes, you try," she said and skipped away. Agnes put her lips to the bamboo, followed Seth's instructions, and tasted a burst of fresh, sweet orange flavor.

"Best citrus in Florida," Seth said, standing a little taller.

"Best I've ever tasted," Agnes said.

"You select whatever fruit you want," he told her. "I see Fanny is already hard at work." They looked over to where Fanny alternately directed some workers to set aside a certain quantity of fruit and inspected different crates of citrus with Polly as an able assistant.

"Billy can help you haul it into town," Seth added. "I've got to get back to work."

An awkward silence enveloped them despite the noise that surrounded them and the crush of people tending to their chores. Seth lifted Agnes's hand and gave it a gentle kiss.

"Could you get used to living here?" he asked, not releasing her hand.

She looked around in awe. "I think so," she replied, and his hand tightened on hers. "It's so different from anything I've ever known. All of Persimmon Hollow is... I've never seen anything like this. City life is all I've ever known."

"This grove will be surrounded by a town someday, you mark my words," Seth said.

"I grow to love all of Persimmon Hollow more and more each day," she said.

"All of it?" he asked, watching her intently.

"Yes," she said and smiled. "All of it. And everyone in it."

Chapter Seventeen

After morning service on Sunday, Agnes hurried back to the house. She wrapped the ties of a flour sack apron around her waist and set to work in the kitchen. Sunday was Estelle's day off, and Agnes had the large, airy room to herself. She propped open the door. Such a gorgeous day! The breeze was scented with a mixture of grass, wildflowers, citrus, and a hint of sea air from the ocean some twenty miles away. She'd seen the Atlantic Ocean a few times during day outings at the orphanage, and the city was always a few steps from water's edge. Here, she'd heard that the ocean fronted mile after mile of empty beach bordered by thick vegetation with names she hadn't heard before and couldn't remember now. Maybe someday she'd get to visit and see for herself.

Fanny bustled in from church and inhaled. "Ah, yes, Florida is beautiful year-round, but in fall the weather is supreme," she said. The two of them stood by the doorway and let the breeze flow over them as they heard Eunice enter the house.

"Fanny doesn't even need to use her fan so much," said Eunice when she reached the kitchen. It was as close to making a joke as Agnes had yet heard from her. "I gave Polly permission to go to the Bight homestead to play with Pansy. Billy tagged along."

Fanny lifted her sunhat off the hat tree by the door and grabbed a basket from the shelf. "I know it's Sunday, but the Lord calls one outdoors on days like this. I'm going to do a light picking of the beans, unless you need me, Agnes," she said.

"Same here, Agnes," Eunice said. "I want to check the chickens again. Looks like a fox tried to get in the coop last night. I might get Clyde to take a look."

Agnes waved off their offers of help, and Eunice departed as quickly as she had arrived. Agnes drummed her fingers on the table as she watched her go. "Fanny, is it my imagination, or are Eunice and Clyde sweet on each other?" she asked. She started organizing her utensils and measuring cups on the butcher-block table. "Have you been playing matchmaker again?"

"Dear, dear," Fanny said and chuckled as she adjusted the hat's ties under her chin. "I adore seeing a true spark between good people, and yes, I'm not averse to helping one or the other become aware. But I make no claim to this one. I have been watching them for quite some time now. Feelings have been growing between the two of them. My dear sister deserves another chance at love. You know her fiancé died at Gettysburg, don't you? She stopped smiling for a long time after that. She turned all her attention to her work as a missionary teacher until coming home to help our dear departed father, God rest his soul, settle this town."

"What about you, Fanny?" Agnes asked. "Don't you want romance for yourself, too?"

A flush spread across Fanny's plump cheeks. "I was never poised and composed like Eunice. Just the opposite. My curls were always flying out from my bonnets, and my clothes were always a bit wrinkled," she said.

She gazed out the door. "In my generation, many men died in the war, just like Eunice's beau. I had expected to come out, to be introduced to society, but my family considered the idea of hosting a debutante ball unthinkable during the war. Our country was torn apart, bloodied and fighting. The two sides even had different names for the conflict. The North called it the Civil War, and the South called it the War Between the States. Brother fought brother…Agnes, it was terrible, even where we lived, far from the battlefields. Most families were touched in some way. By the time the war ended, life as we knew it had changed. There were many more young women than young men walking God's earth. Hundreds of thousands of men had been killed or died of wounds or sickness. I was sweet on one town boy who hadn't joined the fighting because of a lung ailment, but his family moved out West, and we lost touch. It was more than twenty years ago, dear. I joined Eunice in missionary work in the Southwest for about ten years. When we returned, we continued living together and devoted ourselves to helping others and then to helping Father after Mother passed." Fanny was silent for a moment. "It has been enough," she added. "God has granted us many blessings."

But Agnes perceived a touch of an aching heart in Fanny. She murmured a silent prayer that God would bring Fanny a companion with whom she could share her eldest years. If anyone deserved love, it was Fanny, she thought.

Fanny's cheerful smile returned. "Well!" she said. "Off to the garden, dearie. Call if you need me."

"I will, Fanny," she replied and continued rummaging in the pie safe and pantry for baking sheets and pie tins. She fixed herself a cup of tea and sat down to re-read parts of the cookbook Fanny had selected for her from the bookshelf.

After poring over the recipes, Agnes finally decided on a marmalade. Anxious to begin, she checked the wood supply next to the stove and lined up the canning jars, caps, paraffin, towels, and utensils on the table. She could almost taste the sweet treat already.

Agnes peeled and sliced the fruit, boiled the rinds to remove bitterness, and boiled the fruit segments until they were pulpy. She wiped her face with the edge of her apron. Cooking was not just hard, but hot. After draining the rinds and pulp, she combined them with sugar, ladled the mixture into a kettle, and hovered over the cooking marmalade until it reached the jellying point.

Fanny returned long enough to say she was taking the beans down to the Bights. "Although it smells so good in here I'm tempted to stay," she said as she left. "But dropping off these beans is a good excuse for checking on Sarah and her brood. I'll bring Polly back with me. Oh, Eunice went over to Clyde's. They resecured the coop already, but he's going to build a sturdier outer fence."

By the time Fanny and Polly returned, Agnes was ladling the last of the marmalade into jars. Smudges of fruit puree dotted her apron. Jars of deep orange marmalade glistened on the table.

"How beautiful!" Fanny said. Polly peered from behind Fanny, then ventured out for a closer look. A jagged tear ran down the side of her smock.

"What happened?!" Agnes asked.

"The very same question I asked," Fanny said.

"Oh, nothing," Polly said and gestured to the tear. "It got snagged when I climbed a tree. Oh, the jars look so pretty! It smells yummy in here. Can I try some of the jelly?"

"Not yet," Agnes said. "The marmalade has to set. We'll try some at breakfast. And just what were you doing climbing trees? That's not very ladylike."

Polly shrugged. "I don't know. We were just having fun. I didn't mean to get messy. It just happened." She offered a pleading look that never failed to move Agnes then gazed around at all the jars. "How come you made so much?"

"We're going to sell some at the store Mr. Taylor plans to build at the grove," Agnes said. "We'll send a good amount of the proceeds back home to help the orphanage."

They heard Eunice come in through the front door. "Big news, everyone," she said as she came into the kitchen. "The store-raising is set for next weekend. I told Clyde and Seth that we and the other ladies would take care of the food."

"And you'll be pleased to help us," Agnes said to Polly, "instead of climbing trees or picking up a hammer and nails." She held up a hand before Polly could protest. "This will be a much bigger event than the whitewashing," she said. "We'll need every hand to help do our duty of feeding everyone."

"But...but...," Polly started to say. She scrunched her face into a grimace that conveyed her lack of enthusiasm.

"Honey, we'll find a task especially fitting for you," Fanny said. "You can help us figure it out."

It was Agnes's turn to protest. "She'll do as she's told! These are skills she needs to learn."

Polly appeared near tears.

"Maybe a lemonade stand," Eunice said with an unspoken glance at Agnes. Surprised at such an intervention from the usually sterner Eunice, Agnes bit back a retort.

"What is that?" Polly asked.

"You brew and serve lemonade from your own stand that looks like a counter," Fanny said. "We would help you."

"Can I build the stand?" Polly asked. "I like to make things."

"You mean, *may* I?" Agnes said. "Carpentry is not a suitable pastime for a young lady such as yourself."

"Billy will help me. Lemme try, please!"

"It can't hurt to learn the skill, especially if she has an aptitude for it," Eunice said. "You never know what you might be called upon to do on a frontier."

Agnes sighed. Polly was rapidly becoming a tomboy. Yet Agnes couldn't deny the relocation had done the young girl a world of good. She thrived on Persimmon Hollow country life. And the frontier did indeed require a person to have multiple skills.

"You can practice in the backyard after school in the coming days, as long as the Misses Alloway approve," Agnes said. "If you build something usable, we'll carry it out to the grove." She questioned whether Polly would complete such a project. Her enthusiasm occasionally exceeded her abilities. Agnes decided it might end up a lesson learned for the girl and help her finally see where her responsibilities lay as a young lady.

"Our first guests of the season will start to arrive a few days after the store-raising," Eunice said. "I need your word the yard will be clean and tidy by then, with all evidence of the project put away."

"Oh, I promise!" Polly said.

They heard a knock on the front door, followed by the creak of the door opening and Clyde's voice. "Y'all here?"

"In the kitchen," Eunice called.

He strode in. "Another telegram came for Miss Agnes," he said, handing it to her.

Agnes was suddenly short of breath. Telegrams to her never delivered good news. And Clyde was not smiling. He hadn't even said hello or nodded in greeting, most unusual for him.

She reached out and took the paper from his hand. The tick of the grandfather clock in the parlor was never so loud.

Agnes read it, read it again, and grabbed the back of a chair. Another brick fell from the fragile foundation of security she had started to build. She closed her eyes and was in another kitchen, another place of warmth, back at the orphanage, baking bread and making hot chocolate for the girls with Mother Superior and some of the other sisters. The room was warm and welcoming on a winter's day, and the sound of girls' laughter drifted in from the hallway. She saw the chapel, saw it full during Mass and quiet during contemplative prayer. And then empty: cold, dark, and shuttered. She had a premonition of the chapel and the entire orphanage abandoned and falling into ruin.

She opened her eyes and saw questioning, anxious faces reflected back at her.

"I can see you're pained. I'm sorry," Clyde said. He held his hat in his hands and flexed the brim as though it needed adjustment.

"Mercy, please, do tell us!" Fanny said. "Agnes, sit, dear child. You've become pale."

Agnes plopped into the chair. "It's the orphanage," she said. "It's being forced to close. They are being evicted from their building." She buried her face in her hands and gave in to the tears she couldn't stifle any longer.

A tightness pulled at her chest. What would become of the all the girls, the sisters, the helpers? Who would be their spiritual guide? She couldn't separate Fr. Tom from the orphanage. What would become of them all? What would become of her?

The hand on her shoulder was light and hesitant.

"Agnes," said Polly, her voice close to her ear and tentative. "Where will everyone go?"

Agnes sat up straight and blinked back tears. The last thing she wanted was for Polly to fret over adult problems. She pulled the girl closer and hugged her. "I don't know, honey, but I do know all will be well. I'm sure Mother Superior and Fr. Tom are coming up with solutions right now. The telegram said a longer letter has been mailed to us and that it contains full details. We have to wait until we know more. Then we'll determine how best we can serve. Right now, we wait. And we pray."

"We'll all pray with you," Fanny said. "Starting right now."

They all joined hands and said the Lord's Prayer. *Deliver us from evil*...Surely some kind of evil had infected the hearts of those who wielded unjust power over the orphanage. Agnes prayed for the misguided, that they would feel the strength of God's mercy and learn to live Jesus's Gospel message of love.

*   *   *

A fury of good intention overtook Agnes after the telegram arrived. Over the next several days, she spent every spare moment peeling, cooking, stirring, mixing, and canning citrus marmalades and candied peel. She baked orange pound cake and lemon pie and sent them over to Clyde's for immediate sales. Each slice of cake and jar of marmalade represented another few coins for the orphanage.

"Geez, Agnes, do we have to peel more," Polly and Billy protested finally, late Friday afternoon. "We wanna play outside.

We've been helping every single day after school this week. Don't you have enough stuff made yet?" They talked alternately as though in a rehearsed speech.

"I said you'll both earn a percentage of the proceeds," Agnes reminded them without looking up from the cookbook she held open in one hand. With her other hand, she held a ladle over a steaming pan of water and sugar on the stove. She stirred the mixture every few seconds. "Now, what page is that recipe on? How much simple sugar syrup do I have to make?" She set down the ladle and paged through the book.

"Agnes, you're not listening," Polly said a little louder. She flopped back in her chair in dramatic fashion. "I declare, I cannot peel another orange," she said in a falsetto voice and wiped her forehead with her wrist.

That got Agnes's attention. She glanced at the two youngsters without halting the stirring she had resumed. "That sounded suspiciously like Adelaide Land," she said. Billy snorted, and Polly giggled.

"Sure does," Billy said and guffawed. "It's a perfect imitation."

"She takes a long time to say her words, and they sound like her mouth is filled with marbles or rocks or something," Polly said. "Plus she always puts her arm up to her forehead like it hurts or something."

Billy stood up from the table and started swaggering around the kitchen. He stopped in front of Polly. "Let me help you, miss," he said in a deep voice and bowed. "Your arm must be mighty tired." Polly shrieked with laughter.

Agnes sighed. "Go ahead, get out of here, both of you." They scrambled to see who could reach the door first. "*But*," Agnes called after them before they scooted outdoors, "remember it's impolite to make fun of people, even people who try us with their habits and ways."

"Okay," said Polly just before she dissolved into giggles as she and Billy squashed together and tried to fit through the door at the same time. Just then, Seth appeared on the other side of the door opening. He carried a sack of citrus.

"Aaaaaaaahhhhh," Billy hollered, "more citrus!" He stepped back a pace and grabbed Polly's hand. The two of them bolted around Seth before he had a chance to step inside.

"Let's get outta here!" Billy hollered. "Hurry! Hurry!" added Polly. Their shouts echoed as their footsteps thudded down the porch steps and onto the bricked patio and then onto the sandy dirt lane.

"Victims of overwork?" Seth asked. He looked after them for a moment, then put his hat on the wall hook, set the sack down on the table, and sat down.

Agnes laughed. "They do think so, don't they? Actually, they've been faithful helpers all week."

"Smells good in here," Seth said, and he looked around at the products of Agnes's feverish days. "You could slow down a mite, you know. The store's not going to be that big."

"Oh, Seth," Agnes said as she moved the pan of sugar water off the heat. She wiped her hands on her apron and sat down opposite him at the table. "The more I make, the more I can sell, and the more money I can send to the orphanage. What else can I do from so far away?" She told him about the telegram. "I didn't want to bother you during the harvest."

He reached across the table and put his hand over hers. "I already heard, Agnes. That's why I came over as soon as I could. Has the letter arrived yet?"

Agnes shook her head no. "I check every day, but no, not yet. I so fear the news it will contain." She looked at the man she had come to love, and her heart constricted. She was being pulled in opposite directions, called home on one hand and, on the other, rooted to this new place and embraced by the love of a good man. How could she choose between the two? *Blessed Mother Mary, St. Teresa, St. Catherine, St. Clare, please, show the way.*

"I'll help anyway I can," Seth said.

"You already are," Agnes said. "You've been more than generous, Seth. You helped bring Polly here and are giving me the chance to sell this food. I owe you so much."

"You owe me nothing," Seth said. "But," he added and leaned forward, "you could tell me what day you'd like to get married."

Agnes burst into tears.

"Uh, Agnes, hey, don't cry," Seth said. He pulled his hand back and brushed his fingers through his hair. "What...did I say something wrong?"

She shook her head, unable to form words with her lips, and kept blubbering.

Seth got up and came around the table. Gently, he helped her rise. Then he folded her in his arms. "I'm here," he said. "I'll protect you and fix whatever is wrong. It'll be okay, I promise."

"Noooooooo," she said and sobbed into this shoulder. "How can I stay here and marry you and go back and help the orphanage fend off threats to its very existence?" She looked up at him. "Did I tell you they have to find a new location? Right away? I know my help will be a pittance, but it'll be something. I owe so much to St. Isidore's...I want to leave, but I don't want to leave. I want to be there, but I want to be here with you and the Alloways and the school and..." She hiccupped, gulped, and gave in to tears again.

Seth didn't say anything. He held her and let her cry herself out. She relaxed into him and savored his firm strength, his scent of the outdoors, and the feel of his arms around her. From this small taste, she knew she wanted more, much more. Tilting her head up, she looked into his eyes and saw the depth of emotion in them and the spark of desire. She felt the same. She stepped back. But she held onto his hands.

"Better?" he asked.

"Yes and no," she whispered. She released his hands and dabbed her face dry with the edge of her apron.

He was quiet for a few moments. "Do you want to pray about it?" he asked finally.

Was he joking? Pacifying her? She searched his eyes for any hint of evasiveness. Seth wasn't the type of man to speak falsely just to soothe a person. She knew him well enough already to understand that. The look he returned to her was earnest and direct.

"Will you pray with me?" she asked. "Really pray?"

"If you think it will help," he replied.

She shook her head. "Prayer has to come from the heart," she said. "It's not something you do to please another person."

"Might help you figure out what to do," he said and shrugged.

"I've been praying all week, Seth," she said. "I ask the Blessed Mother, St. Francis, St. Anthony, St. Teresa—oh so many more saints, too—I ask them all to pray for me. I seek guidance from God. The only way I can even calm down and get to sleep each night is to say a rosary. Still, I can't see my way clear. I'm confused and disheartened." Tears began to pool in her eyes again.

"I think you're exhausted, not confused," Seth said. "You teach, rehearse the young'uns, then cook half the afternoon and into evening. In this heat, no less. You haven't given yourself a break. If you keep cooking and baking at this pace, we'll need every wagon in town to cart the goods over to the store. You'll collapse before the building is framed. If you make yourself sick, you won't be any help to anyone."

She gave him a wan smile. "Cooking and baking help me think and sort out things," she said.

She waited and hoped he might offer to pray again. When he didn't, she stepped forward took his hands in hers. "Dear Lord," she began and felt his hands stiffen and then relax. "Hear our prayer from your Word, from Isaiah, chapter fifty-eight, verse nine: Then you shall call, and the Lord will answer; you shall cry for help, and he will say, Here I am."

"Amen," Seth said, even before Agnes had the last word out of her mouth. Prayer always helped soothe her spirit. She was still conflicted about which direction to turn. But God had answered one of her prayers, she realized. Seth had started to find his faith again, and it came from his heart, where it had been all along.

Chapter Eighteen

"Agnes, what *exactly* is a store-raising?" Polly asked as they dressed the next morning in the bedroom they shared. Agnes braided Polly's hair, wound the braids around her head, and tied a kerchief atop her hair. The sun hadn't yet broken the horizon, but through the window Agnes could see that the pearl-gray pink of dawn lightened the sky with the promise of a perfect day.

"It's the same thing as a barn-raising," Agnes said. "There, you're finished." She set down the comb and dimmed the kerosene lantern as the room brightened with morning rays.

"Uh, what's that?" Polly asked.

"Well, I've never been to one," Agnes said. "But the Misses Alloway and Seth explained it well. They said people from throughout the community come together at a predetermined time and day. Everybody pitches in to help a person build a barn, or in this case, a store."

"Everybody?" Polly asked.

"Everyone who is able," Agnes said. "The men handle the construction, and the women prepare and serve the meals. Boys help the men, and girls help the women. "

"Oh," said Polly. "An' I'm gonna make sure everybody has enough lemonade, right?"

"That's right, sweetie," said Agnes and gave her a kiss on the top of her head before tying a bonnet over the scarf. "Put your shoes on while I fix my hair." She pinned up her tresses and covered them with a scarf, then put on her bonnet.

They both turned toward the sound of footsteps on the landing.

"Yoo-hoo, almost ready?" Fanny called. Minutes later she stood in the doorway.

"Almost," said Agnes. "Come in. We'll only be a few moments. How is Mrs. Land? Is everything all right at Land Inn? I retired early last night, before you returned from visiting. It seemed odd for you to make such a late call on someone."

"She still hasn't fully recovered from the fright of that day," Fanny said and frowned. "I could tell by the way she called for support so late in the afternoon and then begged Eunice and me to stay and keep her company just a little while longer. It turned into quite a long time. But she improves, bit by bit. She is a nervous woman, though. Much given to anxiousness."

"She appears to be nice, if a bit timid," Agnes said. "Is Adelaide being any help to her?"

"I'm afraid not, from what I understand." Fanny glanced out the window, where a rising sun cast a beam that cut an angled path across the room's heart pine floors.

"Let's discuss happier subjects," Fanny said. "I did a quick inventory downstairs. I don't know how we're going to fit all your citrus creations into the wagon with all of us. We may have to make two trips. What do you want to bring out first?"

Adelaide was obviously an ungrateful daughter. Well, Agnes wasn't surprised. Not at the implications of Fanny's sentence, nor at Fanny's reluctance to speak ill of anyone.

"Definitely the orange chiffon pie," Agnes said. "That has to go with us. I promised Seth I'd bring it." She helped Polly tie on a work apron.

"Miss Fanny, does everybody work at a store-raising?" Polly asked.

"Yes, child, everybody from the tiniest toddler to the oldest granny. The whole community comes together to help one of their own. Just like Miss Eunice and I went to sit with Mrs. Land last night. Neighbors always help neighbors. It's what makes a community."

Her gaze met Agnes's over Polly's head. "This store-raising is an especially fine thing," Fanny said, "because it represents a man who has come home to the Lord as well as to the community."

"Oh, you mean Mr. Seth, don't you?" Polly said. She skipped over to the corner of the room, plopped unceremoniously on the floor, and started to put on her high-button shoes.

"Polly! Walk, please. And young ladies do not sit on the floor like that." Agnes sighed at Polly's lack of decorum. Frontier or no frontier, there were certain protocols for young ladies. But this wasn't the time or place for a lecture.

"I've always believed that young people are more aware of the world around them than we adults give them credit for," Agnes said. Fanny nodded in agreement.

"In fact, when I told Polly what happened when Seth was here yesterday, she wasn't the least bit surprised."

"Happened? What happened? Do tell," Fanny asked.

"When you and Eunice were already gone to Land Inn—Seth asked me if I wanted to pray."

"How wonderful!" Fanny said and nodded in approval. "God works in his own special way."

"Seth still struggles with his faith," Agnes added. "He still faces demons."

"Yes, but he is on the right path," Fanny said.

"Let's go!" Eunice called up the stairs. "It's time!"

They trooped down, drawn as much by the smell of coffee brewing as by Eunice's reminder.

"The coffee and ham biscuits are in the basket, so hold those appetites," Eunice said when they reached the kitchen. "We'll eat when we get there."

Agnes could have drunk an entire jug of coffee then and there, so warm and rich was the aroma. Her head was clouded by the tension caused by the tug between the orphanage, calling her back, and her feelings for Seth, beckoning her to stay. She put her arm around Polly's shoulders, grateful for the blessing of her presence. Her heart ached for everyone coping with the troubles at St. Isidore's Home. *Please watch over them and keep them safe,* she prayed silently as they gathered their things and went out to where Clyde sat in his wagon waiting for them in his usual patient way.

The sun rose higher in a pastel blue and rose sky as they rode silently through the mist-shrouded town and out toward the grove. The early morning chirps, coos, and calls of warblers, finches, mockingbirds, and mourning doves drifted on the gentle breeze, and in the distance two owls alternated hoots. The squeaking wheels and clip-clop of other horses and wagons soon joined the background noise, and by the time they reached the road through Seth's citrus grove, a caravan had formed.

"It's such a thrill to see everyone coming together," Agnes said to Polly, who nodded and waved at Pansy Bight in the wagon behind theirs. Agnes took note of the sparkle in Polly's eyes and the brightness in her cheeks.

The sun broke through fully just as their wagon neared the house. "Over here," Billy called and waved. He directed the drivers toward the far side of a live oak beside the house. Seth and Tustenuggee were already at work amid stacked lumber in the yard. A banked fire smoldered in a clearing, and it scented the air with a bracing mix of pine and oak. Near the wagon area the men had set up rows of boards on log horses as tables and had fashioned benches of palm trunks with boards laid across them.

"There must be a hundred people here!" Polly exclaimed after all the wagons had pulled in, the horses had been turned out, and baskets of food and piles of tools had been unpacked. The parson led the group in morning prayer, and finally the breakfast baskets were opened. *Not a moment too soon,* Agnes thought. She watched with barely contained impatience as Eunice poured cupfuls of coffee and Fanny dished out breakfast fare of ham and biscuits.

"Food always tastes better in the outdoors," Clyde said. He ate a ham biscuit in three bites, wiped his mouth, and took a gulp of coffee. "I thank you, ladies," he said as he rose. "That will sustain me just long enough." He smiled, doffed his hat to them as he put it on, and headed to where the men were gathered by the lumber pile with blueprints spread on the ground around them. Sawing, hammering, and the thump of tapped nailheads soon drowned out the morning birdsong except for the loud antics of some raucous crows, who assessed the breakfast remains until the women shooed them away. Agnes watched, fascinated, as the men moved in unison as though they worked together all the time.

They hardly needed to confer, except for the occasional "one, two, three, up," and "over here, down a few inches," as logs were lifted, hauled, and fitted into place.

She noticed that Polly, too, watched, but with barely contained agitation.

"Why can't I help them?" Polly asked.

"Because you have a different job," Agnes said. "Come, Mrs. Bight and I will help you and her girls get the lemonade ready." She nodded in the direction of Sarah and her family, who were tidying up from breakfast.

"That is, unless you'd rather be on cooking duty," she said, hiding a smile while she nodded toward Fanny and Eunice, who were already supervising the cooking of Brunswick stew. Polly hadn't yet embraced any of the culinary arts, although Agnes saw indications of a budding baker in her. Polly shook her head in an emphatic no at the offer.

She and Agnes watched the stew preparations. Agnes had never seen such a large kettle. No one else was surprised when three men hoisted the cast-iron vat into place over the fire a short while earlier. Fanny sat at a table near it, amid a pile of ingredients. She scraped kernels from a mound of corn cobs, another woman chopped tomatoes and peppers, a third cut up squirrel, and Eunice added items to the stew and stirred.

Agnes noticed the woman who had come up to her at school to offer congratulations on her betrothal to Seth. The woman poured cornbread batter in large cast iron skillets on a separate fire. That conversation seemed so long ago. A warm feeling came over Agnes as she imagined a future she still didn't dare hope for. Looking around for Seth, she found him hammering nails into the frame as another man steadied the lumber. The store-raising, the grove, the people, the delicious aroma of food, the feel of the sun and breeze, the coming together of community—together they touched her in a deep way. *I could live here,* she thought and remembered Seth asking her that very question. *If only…*

Thoughts of the orphanage intruded, as they always did. She couldn't help but compare the dreary future of the Home with the happy scene in front of her. Some of the day's brightness dimmed.

Not wanting Polly to see her sudden dismay, she turned to her with a forced smile only to find that Sarah and her girls had walked over and stood beside her. Agnes welcomed the intrusion. She briskly led the way to Clyde's wagon, where lemonade ingredients were still packed.

"Is something troubling you?" Sarah asked. They trailed the girls to the small stand Billy and Seth had helped Polly build. The girls were laden with jugs, cups, and bags of lemon. Agnes carried the tightly wrapped cone of sugar.

"God blessed me by leading me to Persimmon Hollow," Agnes said. "But the news about the orphanage troubles me so deeply, Sarah. Such a large part of me feels a duty to return. More than duty, really. Part of my heart is there."

Sarah shifted baby Noah on her hip. "You and Polly will be at risk if you return."

"Yes, but…"

"No but," interrupted Sarah. "Another path will open. God always opens a new door when he closes one." She stopped walking and put a hand on Agnes's arm. "Do you really have no idea what your and Polly's presence in Persimmon Hollow has done? Think for a moment of something other than yourself, my dear Agnes, and I mean that in the kindest way. You have not only helped a lost man find himself, you and Polly have brought joy into the lives of the Alloway sisters. Surely you see that."

"Oh, no, I hadn't," said Agnes. She was stunned. The Alloways had helped her. She never imagined she had done anything for them.

She and Sarah resumed walking.

"They consider you the daughter neither of them ever had," Sarah said. "Many of us have noticed that. And there's something else, too, that has come to mind. Agnes, have you considered that God put you here expressly because it is the best way you can help the orphanage? You'll do more good selling foodstuffs and sending money to the orphanage than you would do sitting up there with them and fretting. You are already helping."

"Yes...you're right," Agnes said. "But I don't like being so far from them. The distance troubles me. To be physically with someone, to join in communion with them in their suffering, is also a way of helping. It's the closeness of assistance and understanding."

Sarah nodded. "I understand, but I still think you're doing more good than you know. Has the letter they promised arrived yet?"

Agnes shook her head no as they reached the stand and the cluster of youngsters who surrounded it.

"Agnes, how many lemons do we need in each gallon?" Polly asked. She stood in the center of the group. She and Pansy were poised to place whole lemons in a jug.

Sarah and Agnes laughed. "You ladies have to squeeze the lemons first and put the juice in the large jug," Agnes said. "Then you pump a small amount of water from the well, heat it, add it to the lemon juice, and stir in some cane sugar until it dissolves. Then you pump more water and add enough to fill the jug. Finally, you slice some fresh lemon and float the slices in the lemonade. Some peel, too."

"And you cut slices and float one atop each cup of lemonade you serve," Sarah added. "Miss Agnes and I will show you how to make the first batch."

The girls looked from one to the other then at the older women and giggled as they stepped aside and set down the whole lemons. Sarah gave Noah to Pansy, where he waved his fists and jabbered as though overseeing the work. Sarah and Agnes demonstrated the lemonade procedure step-by-step and let everyone sample the result. Sarah took the squirming Noah back, and she and Agnes supervised Pansy and Polly until the girls were able to brew lemonade to perfection.

"Good job," Agnes said. "Now I suggest you carry over a jug and some cups to the building site and leave them for the workers. I'm sure they're thirsty."

Polly and Pansy displayed maturity in the seriousness with which they carried out the task. "They're growing up so fast," she said to Sarah as they started to walk toward the cooks by the stew kettle.

"Yes." Sarah nodded in agreement. "Both will be fine young women, if I say so myself. Polly has much to be thankful for in you. Again, I see a woman whose help is going unnoticed by herself, even as she proffers it."

"Sarah!" Agnes said. "I'm just doing my small part. Actually, I'm stumbling through my small part. Polly wasn't supposed to have to flee here. Yet Persimmon Hollow has proved a blessing for her."

"Your plan to help from here has always been a good one, Agnes," Sarah said. "Remember the words of the apostle John. We may make the plan, but God shows us the steps."

* * *

"Yeah, that's her," Rufus Smith snarled out of the corner of his mouth. He chewed on a tobacco wad, spit out the juice, and peered through the thicket of wild grapevine.

"You're sure about that?" Lester asked, smoothing his mustache.

"You questioning me?" Rufus snapped. He kept his gaze on Agnes. "Think I don't know one of my own girls?"

"Back on the train you said she was your wife," Lester said.

Rufus gave him a glance that was like black ice.

Barrel, for once, was quiet. He stared at the scene through gaps between the vine's leaves and the cherry laurel trees that supported the vine. The scent of freshly sawn wood mingled with the aroma of Brunswick stew, cornbread, and coffee. His stomach rumbled. Upwards of fifty people were gathered around tables. They ate, laughed, and talked in a jumble of noise that reached him as a mixture of happy voices. On the far side of the group, the new, two-room store rose from the cleared hammock lands. Youngsters played hide-and-seek and their laughter mingled with the adult voices. For a few moments, Barrel was transported to a memory of a long ago time that resembled the scene before him.

"Ha! There's the little brat," Rufus said and pointed to Polly. She walked around one of the tables and poured lemonade for eager takers.

"They raised that store building up fast, too fast," Lester grumbled. "Next thing, the fence will go up. We got to take action, and soon, if the railroad's going to get this land and I'm going to get my money."

"What're we going to do, boss?" Barrel piped up at the sound of the word *money*.

"I think it's time we showed our faces again," Lester answered, "and acted like regular townsfolk looking to settle. We took a room at a respectable boarding house in town when we first came in. That showed us in a good light, like proper folk. Now we'll do that again. Barrel, you'll have apologize for your behavior with the gun. That's what proper folk do."

Rufus snorted.

"You stay in hiding," Lester turned quickly toward Rufus. "You ain't going to show your face yet."

"Says who?" Rufus said, hand on his hip as though to draw his gun. "No man tells me what to do. Especially not you."

"Whoa, whoa, guys, stop. We don't want to blow our cover," Barrel said.

"Yeah, you ought to know," Lester said, "seeing as how you done messed it up once."

"Speak your piece," Rufus ordered. "What's your plan? Why do I hide?"

Lester looked at him long and hard before he spoke. "Like I said before, me and Barrel will act like we're back in town to buy land. We'll act like regular townsfolk. I say we start right now. We leave here the way we came, loop back around, and come in on the main road. We act like we're making a special trip to bring the mailbag that fool conductor paid us to haul into town from the station. I remember right where we ditched it."

"But, but, but, boss, then we can't make them pay to get their mail like we was planning," Barrel objected.

"Yeah, yeah, I know. But it'll show us in a good light. Make it look like we're the helpful kind. We got to make up for your foolishness, causing a ruckus the way you did that day."

"And then what?" Rufus asked. He spit out another stream of dirty juice. "You hicks ain't too smart, far as I can see."

Lester and Barrel bristled. Rufus ignored them and watched the townsfolk.

"I'm thinking of luring Taylor by using the woman and the kids as bait," Lester said. "Make him give up his land in exchange for them. After I'm done, you can do whatever you want. Just wait your turn."

"Why would I want to do that?" Rufus asked.

"Cause it's a plan that'll work, that's why. You won't inspire trust in nobody if you go out there among those church folk and start in cursing and spitting. You'll be run out of town. Not to mention the woman will recognize you. You figure on that?"

Rufus grunted. "How you going to get her and the girl and boy?"

"Kidnap them," Lester said.

"What?!" Barrel squeaked. "I didn't sign up for no kidnapping of women and children."

Rufus and Lester ignored him.

"I like that," Rufus said and nodded. "Makes it easy for me to take the girls back with me."

"Only after I get what I want," Lester said. He nodded toward where Seth stood as he checked the new building. "After I get the deed to the land, you get the woman and the girl."

They shook hands on it.

"Let's go, Barrel. Like I said, we circle back around, pick up the mailbag, and ride into the grove like we just arrived. Good thing they're done building, or we'd have to do that, too," Lester said and grimaced.

"Meet us back at the hideout at dusk," he told Rufus, who ignored him.

Barrel and Lester snuck back to where their horses were tethered. They rode quickly and silently around the far side of the property to the main road, hastened toward town, pulled the mailbag out of the woods, and returned to the grove by way of the main entry.

Everybody looked up as they entered the clearing.

"Howdy!" said Lester with a false brightness. "Got a mail call for you folks. Picked up the bag at the station. The sickly lady at the hotel told us you all were out here. What's her name? Uh, yeah, Miz Land. Yeah. She said she was resting her nerves but that we should ride on out here. We come to help build, too, but I regret to see you've already finished." He threw down the mailbag. Agnes froze at the sight of Lester and his sidekick, and her heart thudded as the bag thumped to the ground. Was there a letter from the orphanage in it?

"Boss, that sick lady didn't say nothing of the kind," Barrel whispered. "She didn't even come out of the sickroom. Adelaide told us about this here event." Lester poked him in the ribs to shut up.

Seth, who had sat down next to Agnes, glared at Lester. His smile faded. A ripple of murmurs went around the table. "Those two caused the fight and shootout at the Land Inn," Clyde said in a low voice.

"We come to help, seeing as how we left on some bad terms before," Lester continued, when no one stepped forward or offered a welcome. Barrel smiled and nodded.

"Chow sure smells good," Barrel said.

"Well, by all means, help yourself," Fanny said finally. She stood and waved her hand in the direction of the food but didn't move from her place at the table. It was far from her usual friendly invite to strangers.

"Thankee, ma'am," Barrel said. He slid off his horse and almost rolled over to the food.

Seth stood up as Lester dismounted.

"Not so fast," Seth said.

Everyone looked. No one said a word.

"You and I have some differences to settle," Seth said. He stepped out and away from the table.

"Differences? We ain't got no differences. You jest," Lester said, his tone light but his eyes narrowed to slits.

"No, I don't," Seth said. "We're going to settle this score right now." He advanced and started to roll up his shirtsleeves.

Lester sized up Seth's larger size and his muscled arms. "We kin talk this out," he said, stepping backward.

"No we can't. You're the reason my family is dead," Seth said.

Agnes gasped. She wasn't the only one.

"Seth!" Clyde called out. "Not here and not now."

He was beside Seth in seconds. In a lower voice, he said, "This ain't for the women and children to see, son."

Seth turned to him. Clyde nodded for him to look at the women, the children.

Agnes reached for Sarah's hand and together they started to softly pray aloud. The parson paged through his Bible with one hand and waved everyone together with the other. Eunice and

Fanny ushered people into a group and called out to the children to stay away from the adults.

Seth dropped his fist and labored to slow his breathing.

"I'm not finished with you," he said to Lester, who continued to step back.

"I'll just return to town now," Lester said and hopped back on his horse. Barrel looked up from his food as Lester turned his horse around and started to ride out of the homestead.

"Hey, wait up!" Barrel said. "Don't leave me here." He stuffed cornbread into his pockets and gulped down a few more bites of food before he ran for his horse. He scrambled on and thundered after Lester.

"Nice work, son," Clyde said. He stood close to Seth but kept his hands in his pockets. "Your job right now is to take care of the living."

Seth nodded, but his breathing still came short and hard.

"People here need you," Clyde said.

As the excitement died down, Billy dug into the mailbag and started to hand out letters and packages to folks.

"Here, Agnes! I got it! The letter!" he called. He held up the envelope.

Agnes hurried to meet him halfway. "Yes, it's from the orphanage," she said as soon as she got a good look at it. Her knees were weak as she walked back to the table. Sarah, Fanny, and Eunice hovered like protective angels as she sat down and opened the envelope. The thin sheets of paper inside trembled when she couldn't keep her hands steady while unfolding them.

She read as fast as her eyes would allow and as much as she could before tears blotted her vision.

Eunice put a hand on her shoulder, and Sarah pulled her close.

"Agnes, what's it say?" Polly asked. She edged in between the women, close enough to see the spidery handwriting that filled the pages.

"It says they have to find a new home," Agnes said. "They never owned the land the orphanage stands on. The landowner died, and his heirs are selling the property." She looked up. Seth stood opposite, watching her with concern. Clyde and the parson completed the circle around her.

"Whether or not they have a place to go, the doors close as soon as the home is sold. They'll be on the street if they don't find another location," Agnes said. Despair tugged at her heart and showed in her face. She tried hard to control her emotions in front of the children.

"They're not going to be on the street," Seth said in a voice that brooked no argument. Agnes glanced at him questioningly.

"We're going to build them a new orphanage right here, on my land," he said. "I've got plenty of space and plenty of timber."

Clyde clapped him on the back in brotherly solidarity. "Taking care of the living," he said low enough for only Seth to hear.

Agnes's mouth was an astonished oval. "I...I..." She couldn't get any words out.

"Yippee, yay!" Polly said exuberantly, clapping her hands and starting all the youngsters clapping and dancing around. Billy whooped, and the other boys joined in.

"Marvelous!" said Fanny, and she fanned herself furiously. "How marvelous."

"I couldn't have thought of a better solution myself," said Eunice. She gave Seth a glance of admiration.

The commotion was oddly distant to Agnes. She heard and yet didn't hear any of it. She was focused on Seth and saw only Seth. She read love, desire, and protection in his gaze and the promise of a strong commitment to the future.

"God chooses the steps," Sarah whispered to her.

Agnes nodded and stood up. She stepped past everyone clustered around her and walked around the table to where Seth stood. He had already taken steps toward her. He put his arm around her, and together they faced the crowd.

"This brave lady knows what an orphanage needs. I'm sure she'll tell us what do to next," he said, and everyone laughed.

"God will tell us," she said.

"Amen!" said the parson. "Now let us pray."

Chapter Nineteen

*R*eady for business, aren't you?"

Agnes turned at the sound of Seth's voice and smiled. He stood in the doorway of the new store, but she was already inside and immersed in display ideas.

"I guess you could say I'm a little anxious to get started," she said. She continued to arrange rows of fruit jams, marmalades, and cordials on the shelves, which smelled of new wood. "Fanny and Eunice shooed me away from cleaning up and packing the dishes and leftover food. Billy and some of his friends unloaded the cart for me and carried everything in here. So, I thought, why waste a minute when I could be organizing?"

Seth chuckled, walked in, and stood beside her. They stood together and looked over the array of products. Agnes grew ever more aware of his nearness, his solid strength, and she fought back a desire to be in his arms. She was too conscious that they were alone together, despite the short distance between the store and the people outdoors. She moved away slightly and adjusted the placement of jars already in neat order. She pushed one back an inch from the edge, then pulled it forward again. Sunlight streamed in the open window spaces and glinted on the jars so that the citruses' jewel-like colors sparkled. Snippets of conversations and laughter, the clinking of china and tools being gathered, and the lingering, light smoke of pine and oak drifted through the door and window openings.

"About time for the winter folks to come in," Seth said. "Could start to see them this week." His voice was strained, as though he fought to keep it in a neutral zone.

Agnes frowned. "What if we sell out of all this right away? I won't have time to restock quickly even if I work through the nights. Fanny and Eunice won't be able to help because they'll be busy with winter visitors. Seth! I need to keep a brisk business going to help get the orphanage built and..."

Why such agitation? She could cope with such a good problem. She willed her rapid heartbeat to slow, to no avail.

Seth put a hand on her arm. A calming sense of power came from him, as well as a heated yearning. Never had she been so aware of his maleness, of how strongly she was attracted to him.

"Slow down," he said. "Tourists and winter folk arrive slowly this early in the season. The train tracks haven't been extended this far yet, Agnes. People right now will have to make a special trip to reach the store."

"Well...we'll just have to make sure they all know about the store, that's for certain!" she said. She spoke too fast and too brightly. A jumbled mix of emotions whirled inside her, and she strained to stay focused on safe ground. "Clyde said he'd put a sign up in the mercantile, and Billy plans to offer buggy rides back and forth. After classes and on weekends, of course."

"Yeah," Seth said. "About Billy and school..." He took his hand off her arm and ran his fingers through his hair. He stepped far enough away, back against the doorframe, that Agnes felt able to take a full breath again. Her head cleared.

"Yes? What about Billy and school?"

"Agnes, don't worry about funding the orphanage." He glossed over her question as though it hadn't been asked. "I've got the land and the lumber. Every man out here right now is willing to help build it. All you have to do is make sure the orphans get here from up north. Money's already coming in from the harvest. I can forward the funds they need for travel."

"You're a special man, Seth Taylor," she said. She couldn't resist. She took a light step, pecked a kiss on his cheek, and stepped back. Her cheeks flushed.

She knew this moment, the entire day, in fact, belonged as much to the Lord as to her and Seth. "So have no fear; I myself will provide for you and your little ones," she murmured, quoting Genesis 50:21.

"Huh? What did you say?"

"The thought of Joseph came to me. He opened his heart to those who had done him wrong."

Seth looked at her, perplexed.

"Joseph, in the Bible. In Genesis."

"Oh," said Seth. "I can't keep up with you and the Bible."

"I've been reading more Scripture recently, especially here where I don't have a priest or nuns nearby for spiritual guidance," she said. "But you, Seth, you also live according to the Bible's teachings. You help others in need. You even turned away from that horrible Lester man, too. You turned the other cheek, just like Jesus counseled us all to do."

"Hold on a minute," Seth said. "All I did was delay the inevitable. I don't forgive him, and I won't turn away from evening the score. It's for another time and place, is all."

She took a breath.

"Forgiving is hard."

"I'll never forgive him, Agnes." The intensity in Seth's eyes darkened them. "Forgive? Could you forgive what he did if it were done to you? I doubt it."

Sympathy, love, and tenderness welled up in her. "Honestly, I don't know, but I would try, and I would pray," she said. "I would seek spiritual counsel. And I would pray some more, until my heart was at peace. If you hold hatred in your heart, all it does is consume you. It doesn't affect the person you hate. They don't know or care."

Seth paced the floor between the shelves and the still-empty counter.

"I won't rest until justice is done," he said. "And I aim to help it get done."

"We'll all rest better when those evil men are stopped from harming anyone," she said and remembered the chill that crept upon her when near them. "I beg you, don't do anything you will regret or that is wrong. Or that will hurt you. I want my husband-to-be to stay safe and sound." She spoke that last in a lower tone.

He stilled, and their gazes met.

"Maybe we could plan our wedding for right after everybody from the orphanage gets here and settled in?" she said as sudden inspiration struck. "It could be a double celebration! A welcome home and a wedding! Oh, Seth!" She clasped her hands together at the idea. "What do you think?"

"Whatever makes you happy, Agnes," he said. He leaned, relaxed again, against the doorframe and watched her. "Tell me where to be, and when, and I'll be there."

Joy bubbled in her. Her eyes sparkled, and her lips curved into a mischievous grin. "You mean you don't want to help me, Polly, Sarah, the Alloways—all of us—with wedding plans?"

She laughed aloud at the grimace that crossed his face.

"Truly, we'd be surprised if you did want to help," she added.

His face lost its tenseness. "Whew," he said. "Wasn't sure if you were fooling with me or not."

Suddenly, they were in one another's arms. Agnes wasn't even sure how she got there, how they closed the few feet between them, who moved first. All she knew was the warm touch of his lips on hers and the deliciousness of his arms around her as he pulled her close. His kisses became harder and more demanding. Her body yearned toward him as her lips responded. Her arms reached midway around his back, and she was conscious of the firmness of him, the feel of him, and of the need that burned within her body and soul. The edge of the counter pressed on her back as she leaned into his firm hold on her.

"Oh, *yuck*! They're *kissing*!" Billy's yell was so loud it overrode all else. The bustle, chatter, and activity outside the store stopped so abruptly that the ensuing silence seemed to have sound. Agnes and Seth broke apart. Seth's breath was heavy. Agnes put her hand to her throat, shocked at her own behavior. Billy and Polly stood in the doorway and stared at them.

"Oh, yuck!" Billy repeated. "What were you guys *doing*? Uncle Seth! Miss Agnes! How can you do something so yucky as *kissing*?"

Polly stood next to him. Her eyes were wide, and her mouth was a big O.

Chuckles and laughter drifted in from the clearing outside the store as Billy's chatter drifted out to them.

"Y'all need a chaperone in there?" Clyde called out.

Agnes's cheeks grew warmer, and she knew a blush crept up her neck and face.

"Oh, dear, we should go," she said in a fluster and ushered Polly and Billy back down the steps and outdoors. She kept close behind them. Seth followed and chuckled.

People applauded as the foursome reached the clearing. Fanny dabbed her eyes with her handkerchief and smiled. Even Eunice looked charmed.

"Set a date yet?" someone else called out.

"As a matter of fact…," Seth said. His comment drew instant attention. Sarah walked over and put an arm around Agnes. "Congratulations, Agnes. I'm so, so happy for you," Sarah said.

Seth came and stood beside Agnes on the other side, placing an arm around her shoulders. Billy and Polly stuck near them. Sarah stepped back a few paces, her smile wide.

"You want to tell them?" Seth whispered.

"I don't think I can speak and make any sense!" Agnes said.

"We're here to help you!" said Fanny. She, Eunice, and Clyde walked over. Even Tustenuggee stepped forward and clapped Seth on the back.

Everyone looked at Agnes. She gulped.

"Go ahead," Seth urged. "Tell them what you told me."

She took a deep breath and said a silent prayer.

"First, I want to thank God for leading me to the dear, wonderful extended family I have found in this community," she said. Amens rippled through the crowd.

"And I want to especially thank God for leading me to this wonderful man I will be proud to call my husband." More amens, plus some cheers and applause.

"Seth and I decided we'd like to have a double celebration—a wedding and a welcoming for the orphans when their new house is built here."

"A wedding!!!" Polly squealed. "Ohhhhhh, how exciting! Can I be in it?"

Agnes smiled down at her. "You are the flower girl," she whispered. Around them, amid louder cheers and applause, conversations bubbled about dates, places, buildings, food, drink, fashions, and countless other needs and wants.

The parson, not known as a loud man, spoke in a voice that rang clear above the others. Conversations quieted.

"I believe the first business at hand then, after we offer a prayer of thanks, is to build an orphanage," he said. "Seth, I know you refused payment for the roof repair. Perhaps you'll agree that the planned fundraiser for the Academy can instead be a fundraiser for the orphanage. We're good as new with our new roof at the hall."

Seth barely had time to nod his thanks before excited chatter rose again from the crowd.

Agnes looked down at Polly and Billy and saw in them both excitement and a touch of apprehension. The news meant big changes in both their lives. "Did you hear that?!" she asked. "Great news, don't you think? We've got some busy times ahead of us, and I'll need your help like never before. You both have important roles to play in everything that's coming up. Right now, we have to focus on our recital program. We will present the best recital Persimmon Hollow has ever seen! We'll practice every single day, beginning this week."

* * *

"What do you mean Billy won't be at school today?" Agnes leaned in to hear Polly's answers after she set her little scholars to work on their presentations.

"He told me before we left the grove yesterday that his Uncle Seth needs him to put up a fence on the land," Polly said. She looked up from her poem. "He probably won't be here for a week."

"I see," Agnes said not seeing at all. She suddenly remembered that when she and Seth were in the store the day before, he neglected to finish the comment he started about Billy and school. She'd even asked, and he hadn't answered. "And now I know why," Agnes grumbled under her breath. Her chest grew tight. Had Seth deflected the conversation? Had he brought up the orphanage to avoid an unpleasant scene about schooling? And had she fallen for it?

"What did you say?" Polly asked.

"Nothing, honey." Yet it was something. It was very much something. Agnes couldn't take action at the moment, either. She had a job to do. She straightened, inhaled, and looked around the room. This was her mission right now.

"All right, children, let's do a first presentation practice. Line up by height…yes, you may bring your papers with you right now, yes, dear, you may read your work today but not the day of the actual event. You'll have to have it memorized by then."

Chairs scraped across wood, and shoes and bare feet scuffled and shuffled across the floor. Her pupils organized themselves and lined up in a neat row. Agnes walked in front of the line that stretched across the blackboard and inside wall and surveyed her group.

"Are we going to have to dress up?" asked Pansy. She twisted her hands around her paper. She wore a faded, hand-me-down dress with sleeves that didn't reach her wrists.

"No," said Agnes. "I expect everyone to be in clean clothes, however, with washed hair and clean face, hands, and feet. I will make sure to get some fresh ribbon for all the young ladies to put in their hair. Gentlemen, I expect all of you to wash and comb your hair for the presentation. Understood?"

"Yes, Miss Agnes," they chorused.

"Good," she said. "Now let's begin. Pretend this is the church meeting hall and it's filled with people. Each one of you will step forward, one at a time, with the smallest going first, and will present your oration. We'll practice this so many times, you'll be champions by the time presentation day arrives."

Anticipation, anxiety, bravado, and fear washed across the little faces. "Put yourself in God's hands as you step forward and trust in his care," she said, more gently, and noticed ease cross faces.

Sarah's youngest school-age children, little Nuby and Nettie, were the first ones up, and they lisped their way through the first stanza of Psalm 136 with much coaching and coaxing from Agnes.

O give thanks to the Lord, for he is good,
for his steadfast love endures forever.
O give thanks to the God of gods,
for his steadfast love endures forever.
O give thanks to the Lord of lords,
for his steadfast love endures forever.

"Excellent!" said Agnes, and she and the class applauded the twins' effort. "Next!" called Agnes. One by one the youngsters stumbled their way through their chosen pieces, with many starts and stops, revisions, corrections, and repeated efforts. Two hours later, Agnes dismissed the group for lunch and went to find Fanny. Her ire resurfaced as she stalked down the hall.

"Seth has kept Billy out of school to help build a fence," she announced when she entered the office. "I'm going out there right after school today to set him straight."

Her irritation increased when she considered the valuable practice time Billy was missing. "Recital practice is an opportunity for my pupils to learn from one another's work, as well as being an exercise in memorization and a practice in elocution. How could he?!"

She paced back and forth in the small office she and Fanny shared.

Fanny sighed. "Folks pull their children out of school all the time to help with crops," she said. "But I see you're not going to take no for an answer, not in this case. I'll take your class this afternoon if you must go. Rain clouds are forming. I would rather you ride out now and return as soon as possible, before a storm moves in."

"Fanny! Thank you!" said Agnes. She grabbed her rain poncho from the wall hook. "I'll take this just in case. Why are you humming?" She looked at Fanny, perplexed.

"Oh, those are the angels singing," Fanny said with an air of innocence. "Happy angels. They sing about how you and Seth won't have sharp words. About how you will refrain from letting impatience get the best of you."

Agnes sighed and gave Fanny a sheepish smile. "Yes, I hear you...and the angels," she said. She departed in a brighter mood than when she had arrived. She untied the horse from its tether and on impulse unhitched it from the wagon.

"No need for the wagon today," she said aloud to the horse. "I've had enough practice on horseback, and I know the route. We'll do fine, you and me, right, Bessy, won't we?" Bessy was the oldest and gentlest of the Alloways' horses and, in many ways, a companion animal more than a work animal.

She mounted and arranged her skirts. Only a spark of apprehension surfaced when she picked up the reins and nudged Bessy forward. Agnes was still a little wobbly on the back of a horse, but she straightened her back and squared her shoulders. She was on a mission. Riding horseback was faster than going by horse and cart.

The grove was quiet when she arrived. She slid off Bessy, gave the horse some water, and tied her loosely to a hitch near the porch.

"Yooo-hoooo," she called, but no one replied. She strained to hear past the cicadas and other insects and could pick out the sound of hammering in the distance. As she stood there wondering whether to walk toward the sound or wait for someone to return, she heard hoofbeats. Seth emerged from a wooded path behind the house. He looked so handsome she was tempted to let his actions slide. "No, that won't do," she murmured and remembered what led to her excursion.

"Nice surprise, seeing you here," Seth said. He dismounted and was by her side in seconds, a wide smile on his face.

"No more surprised than I was when I saw that Billy missed class today," she said. She crossed her arms over her chest and tapped her foot. *Your charm will get you nowhere today, Mr. Seth Taylor,* she wanted to say.

"I see the schoolmarm has visited, not my fiancée," Seth said. He was somewhat bemused, but then he grinned.

Agnes's irritation quickened.

"This is no laughing matter, Mr. Seth Taylor," she said. "Yes, I am here as the schoolmarm. It's my duty to look after my pupils' education. Billy is not getting an education if he's out in the woods with you."

"I'll argue that point, ma'am," Seth said in a formal, polite manner. "He's learning how to put up a fence. Any man running a grove, cattle, a farm, anything, needs to know how to fence."

"Understood," said Agnes with equal formality. "But not on my time."

"Your time?"

"Yes, my school time."

"Is that so?"

"Yes it is, Mr. Taylor," she said. She pulled herself up as straight as she could. "Any man running a grove also needs to know how to figure, to write, to speak well, to…"

"Hold on," Seth said, and he put up a hand for her to stop. "Agnes, listen to me. Yes, he needs those skills. He's got time to learn them. Right now, we've got to get the fence up before those strangers try anything else to get this land. Understood?"

He acted like school-learning was less important. It rankled her.

"This is important to me," she said. "It should be to you, too."

"The fence is important to me," he said. "And to you."

"Me?"

"Yes," Seth said. He placed his hands on her shoulders and twirled her around so that they both faced the same direction. "This is all yours, Agnes. I'm making this safe for you and me both."

"You're a hard man to argue with," she conceded. "But I still say Billy can help after school. There's still a great deal of daylight after school."

He dropped his hands. "There are some things women just don't understand."

"The same goes for men!" she retorted.

"Looks like we have a difference of opinion," Seth said. He gazed around, up at the sky, down at the ground, anywhere but at her.

"Yes, indeed," said Agnes. She put her hands on her hips. "How do you propose we solve it?"

"With a kiss?" Seth asked only half-jokingly.

"Don't you try to distract me, Seth," she said, but she could feel her irritation start to diffuse, although her determination remained strong. "As Persimmon Hollow's schoolteacher, I'm concerned that Billy will fall behind in his recitation practice for the recital. We did quite a bit of work today."

Seth looked at the position of the sun, a small bright spot buried in clouds. "Looks like you should still be doing it," he said. "It's only about one o'clock."

"Fanny took my afternoon class so I could fetch the errant member of my little flock," she said.

"It's that important to you?" Seth asked. She nodded with vigor.

"I have an idea," they both said at the same time then laughed, and the tension between them broke. She let her hands relax.

"Maybe he could attend class half a day until the fence is built," Agnes started to say.

"He could head to the Alloways for lessons after dinner, if you'll have him," Seth said at the same time.

"I'd be happy to have him over for lessons," she said, "although he'll have to recite amid the flurry of cooking in the kitchen."

"He won't mind, as long as he doesn't have to peel oranges," Seth said.

"And gets to sample the treats," Agnes added.

"It won't take us more than a week to get the fence in, Agnes. Less than that, even, if we work sunrise to sunset. I've got to protect my land. You're the schoolmarm. What's better for Billy? To miss a week of full days and catch up, or to do some learning each day?"

"Oh, he must attend to schoolwork each day," she said in earnest. "The best way for him to learn is to repeat each day's lessons before he forgets them."

"He'll be over to the house tonight," Seth said, "and will be in class for the last part of the school day tomorrow and the rest of the week. That's the best I can offer."

She met his gaze levelly. "I accept your offer, and I thank you. He will be expected to work hard to stay abreast of what his class-mates are learning."

"Hard work never hurt anybody," Seth said. "It builds char-acter. Speaking of work, I've got to get back to it. I rode in to pick up another coil of wire." He checked the clouds. "Rain's moving in soon. Wait here and have Billy ride back with you later."

"No, I'll be fine," Agnes said. "I want to return before school ends so I can give Fanny a ride home. I took the horse and left the wagon."

Seth kept his gaze on the clouds and frowned. "I'd rather you stayed," he said.

"I've become a semi-accomplished horsewoman since I've arrived in Persimmon Hollow, and I've got my rain slicker,"

Agnes said. "The schoolmarm is perfectly capable of taking care of herself."

"Agnes...," Seth began.

"Bye," she said. She kissed her fingertips and touched them to his lips for a few seconds and then slid them away.

"You haven't been caught in one of our storms here," he said. He took hold of her hand and kissed it.

"What? What? I can't hear you," she bantered and edged toward the horse. She smiled, unhitched Bessy, and mounted with undue pride at her skill. As she headed out, she looked back to see if Seth noticed her improved horsemanship. He watched her go, a scowl on his face.

Chapter Twenty

The first raindrops fell in big, wet splats before Agnes reached the far side of the grove. The water was cold and surprisingly hard, and she slowed Bessy while she twisted, fumbled, and tried to pull her slicker from the knapsack rolled in the blanket behind her. By the time she tugged out the slicker and draped it over her, the rainfall was so hard and fierce she was soaked and visibility was limited to inches. Thunder cracked, and lightning arced in bolts too close for comfort.

Agnes wished she hadn't been so headstrong as to completely ignore both Fanny's and Seth's warnings. Their experience with Florida weather far outpaced all but her impatience. Wind gusted and drove the rain sideways. It lashed her face.

"Oh, Bessy, I'm so sorry you're out in this," she said to the horse. She patted its neck as it tucked its head down as protection against the driving rain.

Agnes looked around for shelter but could make out nothing more than the dark shapes of the trees that lined the trail. She knew better than to seek shelter under a tree during lightning, and citrus trees were hardly the type of trees a person and horse could hide under, anyway.

It was time to abandon her plan to get back to town.

"Time to turn around, Bessy, return, humble my pride, and admit I made a mistake," she said, and they started back to the ranch house. She was shivering by the time she reached the house. But not only had the rain stopped, the sun shone. All around her, raindrops glistened and sparkled on leaves and shrubs, and a rich, earthy scent rose from the humus on the ground.

"Florida rainstorms are like nowhere else," she said to the horse. Movement off to the side caught her attention, and she watched three distant figures disappear into the woods far behind the house.

"They must have worked on the fence right through the rainstorm," she said and slid off the horse. She took off the rain slicker, shook it out and hung it over a shrub, and wiped down the horse with a towel she found on the porch. She took off her shoes and stepped inside, only to find Seth, Billy, and Tustenuggee seated around a table, their wet slickers drying on a rack in front of the wood stove. The three looked as though they'd been there for hours.

"How did you get here so fast?" she asked. "I just saw the three of you go off into the woods, minutes ago."

Seth jumped up. "Agnes! Get over here by the stove. You're soaked!" he exclaimed. "Billy, get her some clothes from the trunk in the back bedroom." He took an afghan off the back of a chair, wrapped it around Agnes, and sat her in his chair.

"What's that about seeing us?" he asked. "We've been inside since the first lightning cracked. Got caught only in the start of the rain. Darn, look at you. You should have listened to me."

"I know," she admitted. "I figured that out. But I just saw the three of you when I rode up on Bessy, not ten minutes ago. Not long enough to get this size of a fire going," she said, scooting her chair closer to the stove. The warmth caressed her like a blanket. She rubbed her hands together.

Seth and Tustenuggee exchanged glances.

"I'm no longer surprised," Seth said. "They're getting bolder and more desperate. There's going to be a showdown, and soon."

"That wasn't you out there, was it?" Agnes asked needlessly, as the truth became evident to her. "I saw three people, not two."

"That means they've brought in an accomplice," Tustenuggee said, and Seth gave an affirming nod.

Billy staggered back, hidden by yards of material. He carried three women's dresses, a shawl, and a towel. "Here, Miss Agnes," he said, his voice muffled by the fabric. He dumped the pile on the settee near the table.

"Women's clothing," Agnes said and remembered how there had been dresses here the day she fainted during the picnic. She looked questioningly at Seth. "Your late sister-in-law's, right?" she asked quietly.

Seth gave a curt nod. He glanced at the clothing as though it pained him. A stiff silence filled the room.

"I will go check on our unwelcome visitors," Tustenuggee said. He shook his head no when Seth got up to accompany him. "Billy, you will go refill the stove box with wood from the porch. Now," Tustenuggee said to Billy, who jumped up to obey

"Why did you keep the clothes all this time?" Agnes asked in the quiet that followed their exit.

"Didn't know what to do with them," Seth said. "And didn't want anybody else here messing with them. Seemed disrespectful."

"I can take them back with me," she said. "We can turn the fabric into quilts and weave any leftover pieces into rag rugs."

He gave a quick, hard nod of assent and looked relieved.

"Seth, I don't mean to tell you what to do. But I have to suggest: Put your faith in God and the message of Jesus. Try. Just try." She squeezed his hand. He closed his eyes. "The Holy Trinity is a circle of love. Let that love flow over you and heal you," she said.

She willed the strength of her beliefs to him and prayed that God would grant him grace and that his soul would feel peace. She prayed that the Blessed Mother would intercede to help his journey.

Seth kept his head bowed. "Amen," he said after a little while. He opened his eyes. He seemed calmer, more at ease.

"I'll step outside while you dress by the fire," he said. "We need you out of those wet clothes before you catch a chill. Then Billy can ride with you back to town. I know a schoolmarm there who says he needs to do extra lessons." He smiled at her.

Agnes took Seth's other hand, and he helped her rise from the chair. Then he leaned down and kissed her.

"I can't wait until you're my wife," he said. The calm in his eyes turned to heat.

"I can't wait until you're my husband," she said and leaned in for another quick kiss before she stepped back. She was suddenly acutely aware that they were alone, without a chaperone of any kind. Seth followed her glance at the door. "On my way," he said and strolled out, whistling.

* * *

Deep in the far side of Seth's land, Lester, Barrel, and Rufus hashed out the final details of their plan.

"They got some kind of school program happening soon," Lester said. "If it runs into the night, it'll be easy to grab the kids and the woman."

Rufus snorted. "Yeah, and the whole town will form a posse and hang us."

"I got it, I got it!" Barrel said. He jiggled with excitement.

"Barrel has an idea. Imagine that," Lester said drily.

"All we do is create a diversion," Barrel said. "Like start a small fire or something. Then when everybody runs to put out the fire, we grab the kids."

Lester and Rufus paid attention.

"What about the woman?" Rufus asked.

"She'll run after the kids," said Lester. "We can nab her while there's a lot of confusion."

"I ain't hurtin' no women or kids," Barrel said.

"All you'll have to do is guard them, so stop squawking," Lester said.

"Might work, but I'd like it a whole lot better if she and the kids were outside before the rest of the folks," Rufus said. "But seeing as I'm ready to get out of this mosquito-infested backwater, I'm willing to go with what we got."

* * *

Excitement ran high throughout town as the day of the recital and dinner neared.

"Just look at what's on this list!" said Agnes. She, Sarah, Fanny, and Eunice sat at the Alloways' dining room table and pored over the potluck contribution list that had been posted on the community board at Clyde's store.

"It's like every woman in town plans to participate and some of the men, too," Agnes said. "And look here," she said tapping a spot on the page. "I bet Toby's smoked turkey is delicious."

Sarah smiled in confirmation, but her lips were tight. "Yes. We thank Mr. Williams for his generosity," she said with a nod toward Eunice. "He is providing the bird from the game he buys from regular suppliers. He specifically requested they bring a nice-size bird for Toby to smoke."

Sarah's thin shoulders were so tense they seemed to bunch under her dress.

"Well, I'm getting hungry just reading this list," said Fanny, and she fanned herself. "What a delight this will be for our boarders, too. A few more are due to arrive just before the big day."

"How are the students doing?" Sarah asked. "My girls spend hours practicing their selections." The women looked out the window to the backyard, where Polly and the Bight girls took turns rehearsing. When he wasn't making sandy mud pies in a wet patch of yard, Toby Jr. sat on a log and watched. The girls took turns adding ladles of well water to his tiny reservoir.

"They're all doing wonderfully," Agnes said. "But that reminds me, please put hair ribbons on the mercantile list," she said to Eunice. The older woman added a notation to her list of materials needed and chores to be done.

Polly ran inside.

"Agnes!" she called.

"Walk, don't run," the women all said in unison before the little girl had a chance to speak another word.

"Yes'm," she said. "Agnes! How long 'til the recital?"

"Five days," Agnes said.

Polly squealed. "Ooooooh, we must practice lots more!" and she ran, not walked, out.

"It's hard to believe she's the same child who stepped off the train with a timid walk and city clothing," said Agnes. "She has blossomed here. I'm so glad we're staying."

"So are we, dear," Fanny said. She leaned over and tapped Agnes's arm with her fan.

"All of us," Sarah added, and Eunice nodded in affirmation.

"But no one is happier than that young man who's expected any moment now for dinner, I believe," Fanny said. "He certainly knows how to time his visits when he brings Billy here each evening for lessons."

Agnes frowned. "Yes, but Billy is still falling behind in schoolwork. The way things worked out, he attends morning session, works with Seth in the afternoon, then comes here for a few hours of more schoolwork. It's a lot even for a strong youngster like him."

Eunice looked up from the task list. "That's because his chauffeur distracts the schoolteacher for half the evening."

Agnes blushed, everyone laughed, and she had to admit there was some truth to the statement.

In an effort to forestall more comments, Agnes quickly changed the subject. "Oh, look at this!" she said and gestured to the menu list. "Adelaide from Land Inn has listed herself as contributing a dish 'a la Parisian.' But she doesn't write what it will be. Any ideas?"

No one had a clue. "Knowing she has fine tastes, I imagine it'll be something costly," suggested Fanny.

Sarah didn't say much, just bent her head low over the piece of paper on which they were plotting how to arrange the food on a long table. She wrapped one arm around Noah, perched on her knee, and gave studious attention to the penciled chart.

"Sarah?" Agnes asked. "Is something wrong?"

"I wish I could contribute," Sarah whispered in a fierce tone, but low enough—she thought—for only Agnes to hear.

"You do contribute!" Agnes said.

"You are contributing right now!" added Fanny. "People share according to their means."

"And don't forget Toby is smoking a turkey," said Eunice.

"Mrs. Sarah Bight, I am mighty surprised at you," Fanny said. "It's not like you to give in to self-pity."

Sarah's eyes blazed.

"It's not self-pity," she said. "It's just that, sometimes, you work and work and work so hard and can't ever seem to get ahead. Sickness comes in, or an animal dies, or crops fail, or another child comes. Oh, I pray for guidance. I know God only gives us what we can bear. But sometimes the burden is mighty hard."

She set down the pencil, buried her head in her free hand, and started to cry. Noah patted her with baby taps, his eyes wide.

Agnes picked up the baby and sat him on her lap then reached over to hug Sarah. Fanny got up and rubbed the back of Sarah's neck. She, Agnes, and Eunice exchanged worried glances over the top of Sarah's head. They all knew the Bight groves were too young to bear enough fruit to support the family and that the death of Sarah's grandmother had drained the little money they'd set aside. The small income her grandmother brought in by sewing was now gone. Property loan payments would soon be due.

"Has the Lord blessed you in the family way again?" Fanny asked almost hesitantly.

Sarah shook her head no but didn't raise her head. She kept her face hidden in her hands.

"No. But Toby...he's such a good man, but he's not a farmer. His heart's not in it. Oh, he grows enough to feed us but...we were fixing to grow extra to sell. He tries and tries, but it's not his

God-given talent. But he can look at something for a minute and turn around and build it. Anything. And explain what he's doing so well even the twins understand."

Agnes remembered the pie safe, bedstead, and other wood furniture in Sarah's cabin.

"We might have to move back to Georgia," Sarah whispered.

"Oh, no!" Agnes said, and she half-rose and handed Noah to Fanny, who sat back down, plopped him in her lap, and cooed to him. Agnes had come to feel real affection toward Fanny and Eunice, and she doted on Polly, but Sarah was the closest thing she had to a friend near her own age.

"You can't leave!"

"We don't want to," Sarah said. She looked up with a sad smile. "But we might have to."

"Hurrumph!" said Eunice. She rose at the sound of hoofbeats outside. "Not if the rest of Persimmon Hollow has anything to say about it."

Agnes sat down again and willed her brain to concentrate on possible solutions. She didn't care that no one had asked for her advice. She'd do anything to help Sarah and her family in a way that would allow them to help themselves. She knew they would refuse charity.

Seth, Billy, and Sarah's husband, Toby, walked into the house.

"Here's your pupil," Seth said. He steered Billy by his shoulders toward Agnes's seat at the table.

"I tell you all, Toby's the best woodworker this side of the Mississippi," Seth said. "He sure can build a fence. He's agreed to work full-time with us until the fence is finished. The schoolmarm can have Billy back full-time now."

Billy didn't look happy. "Aw, shucks, can't I do the fence one more day?"

"Sorry, son," Seth said. "A strict schoolmarm told me in no uncertain terms I had failed in my duties when I kept you out of class."

"The other youngsters are out back rehearsing, if you'd like to join them," Eunice said. She pointed toward the window and door. Billy shuffled out, looking none the happier.

Toby went over, kissed Sarah on the top of the head, and tousled Noah's soft tuft of hair. Seth looked around the table.

"Now that Billy's left the room, may I ask why you women look like you've been to a wake?" he asked.

Sarah gave Agnes a small, pleading nod that begged without words for her to stay silent. She then made the same mute appeal to Fanny and Eunice.

Each of the four of them started to mumble at once. "Oh, nothing's wrong, truly." "No, nothing." "Really, all is well." "We're okay." Noah clapped his hands.

"I know a unified front when I see one," Seth remarked to Toby. "We'll get nothing from any of them."

He looked at Agnes. "I know you'll have an answer for this, though: How big an orphanage do you need? It's off-season for Toby's crops, and lucky for us, he's willing to help us build."

Agnes saw Eunice raise her eyebrows at Seth's comment about the off-season. Agnes, in her short time at Persimmon Hollow, had learned that crops of some kind could be grown year-round in Florida. A flush of love, respect, and admiration for Seth ran through her as she realized he spoke in a manner to spare Toby embarrassment about his failed crops.

"Oh, goodness," she said, "I don't know. Big. It has to be big enough to house a lot of children. Plus we need living quarters for staff members and…I don't know. I had expected a number of sisters would move here and that we would need a convent, but I'm no longer sure of that."

"Let's start with the orphans," Seth said. "How many are there? All girls? Girls and boys? Does the orphanage need to have workrooms? You know, places where the girls can learn house-keeping, sewing, and other skills? Places where boys can learn woodworking, farming, and other trades?" Seth ticked off the questions. "Of course, they'll all go to your school so we won't need classrooms."

"That's it!" Agnes said and jumped up in such haste she nearly knocked over her chair. "Why didn't I think of it before?!"

"What?" Seth asked. Toby, Fanny, Eunice, and Sarah looked at her.

"Mr. Bight, I understand you are a master carpenter," she said to Toby. Before he could answer, she turned toward Sarah and said, "Sarah, you are one of the most creative housekeepers I've ever met." Sarah looked back at her, perplexed.

Agnes swirled and faced Seth. "The orphanage is a large building that has common rooms in the center and two wings of dormitories, one for boys and one for girls. There are about thirty youngsters."

She continued at a rapid clip, her eyes bright.

"In the last letter I received from the orphanage, I learned that most of the sisters—the religious women—would not move here with the children. The bishop asked them to stay and continue operating the hospital that is also part of their mission. A couple of sisters will move south, but Mother Superior wrote that they are young and not yet skilled enough to assume directorship responsibilities for the entire orphanage. She asked if I would consider assuming that responsibility until she can establish a full convent here. I wrote back that, of course, without a doubt, I would be happy to assist with the orphanage and children."

Seth looked a little alarmed. "My new wife is going to come with thirty children attached?" he asked.

She shook her head. "Not if Sarah and Toby would consider being houseparents, with help, of course, from me and the sisters. I can't think of better role models for youth than you two," she said to them. "And think of the skills you both could teach those youngsters in need."

"I reckon it's something we could think about," Toby said. He kept one hand protectively on Sarah's shoulder. She reached up and clasped it with her free hand. With the other, she again held Noah, who had crawled back onto her lap.

"God works in wondrous ways," Sarah whispered. She glanced up at her husband. He met her gaze and squeezed her shoulder. Then he picked up Noah and swung him high before sitting him snugly on his shoulder. The baby giggled and played with Toby's hair.

"Well, that's settled, then," Seth said. "Agnes, you need room for about fifteen girls and fifteen boys?" he asked and started to figure calculations on the menu list. "Quarters for the sisters. Separate quarters for the Bight family. How many children do you have, Sarah? Six? Seven?"

"Hey, that's the menu!" Agnes exclaimed and snatched the paper from underneath Seth's pencil. Fanny laughed and found him another piece of paper from the sideboard. Sarah gently corrected him about the children. "We have five, Seth," she said. "It only seems like seven sometimes."

"How soon can you have something built?" asked Eunice.

"Let's see, it's November now," Seth said. "We could get the basics up by the New Year, as long as Toby is looking to pick up some extra work and can devote himself to it. Nothing fancy, but shelter, until we can go back and do amenities."

"Happy to help," said Toby. "I'm much obliged for the work."

"Thirty orphans?" Seth looked at Agnes as though he understood for the first time what it would mean to have an orphanage nearby.

"It won't always be at capacity," Agnes said, "although sometimes it might be over. I'm not sure how many children are moving south. What does it matter, Seth? You will love them as I do, I'm sure of it."

"Think of all those scholars at the Academy," Eunice said.

"And future homesteaders!" Fanny said.

"Future carpenters," Toby added.

"Good thing we're almost done with the fence," Seth said. "We have a lot of work ahead. You ladies know I work best on a full stomach." He sniffed. "Is that sweet potato pie I smell?"

Agnes smiled at him, and he grinned, and her heart did a little skip as a flush of warmth ran through her. "No," she said. "But it might be green tomato pie."

"Which you may have as dessert, after dinner," said Fanny, as prim and proper as a schoolmarm reprimanding youngsters. "You all shall stay to eat, too. We only have a few boarders in so far, and we don't want them to feel lonely at the dinner table."

"No chance of that in this household," Seth said. "But thanks for the invite. Can't think of a place I'd rather be than next to this special lady." He lifted Agnes's hand and kissed it.

Chapter Twenty-One

 *P*olly buzzed around, consumed with enthusiasm. "I thought this day would never, ever, be here!" she exclaimed to anyone who would listen. She bounced up and down on her tiptoes, unable to stay still, as she stood next to Agnes and watched guests flow into the meeting hall. Savory aromas from the home-cooked meals mingled around them.

"Aren't you excited?!" Polly grabbed Billy's arm as he walked up to them.

"I can't wait for the stupid program to be over so we can eat," Billy said. He slouched, hands in his pockets. "I can't believe I can't eat yet. Everything smells good, and I can't eat any of it."

"Come on, we can practice in the meantime," Polly said. "It'll be fun."

"Nah," he said. "That's the last thing I want to do."

Seth called from farther inside where he and other men were putting benches into place for the performance. "Billy, get over here. We need another hand."

"See ya," Billy said to Polly.

"Come back as soon as you're finished," Agnes called after him. "It's almost time for all students to line up on stage."

She turned to Polly. "Use up some of that restlessness by doing a quick review to see that each food dish has a sign next to it that explains what it is. Then hurry back."

"Okay!" Polly said and scampered off.

Agnes drank in the scene while she waited. The stage was an empty space at the front of the room, marked on the floor with lines of chalk. In the corner, Toby Bight tuned his mandolin, while fellow musicians did the same with their banjo and fiddle. Near them, Sarah tended to her brood. Fanny neatened cedar boughs that decorated the wooden shutters. Clyde adjusted the kerosene lanterns on the wood planks that served as tables behind the benches set up for the performance. Eunice and the parson were conversing about something on the printed program Eunice held.

"Agnes, this kind of reminds me of big meals at the orphanage," Polly said when she returned. Agnes winced at the tug that ran through her. She would likely never see St. Isidore's Home again, at least not in the building she knew. She said a prayer of gratitude for the joys she had right now and for all that had graced her life in the past. She squeezed Polly's hand.

"Yes, it does," she said. "And we're blessed to have a new family here."

"A family of people who love the two of you," Seth said as he and Billy came up to them. Seth took Agnes's hand in his. She leaned in and savored the thrill of being near him. He slipped his other arm around her and pulled her close for a moment before he stepped back.

"They're getting gushy again," Billy said to Polly. "When do we get to eat? What kind of food did you bring?"

The four of them strolled over to the long table laden with food. Agnes pointed to a large bowl of noodle-like strands topped with a tomato sauce.

"Looks like nothing I've seen before," Billy said.

"Remember a few days ago, when you came for lessons and I mixed flour, eggs, and water into a dough, rolled it out on the table, and then cut it into strips?" she asked.

"Sure do," Seth and Billy said in unison. "Those strips were draped over every chair and all across the table," Seth added. "You said they were 'drying.'"

"Well, here they are," she said. "The noodles are now covered with a sauce made from tomato and basil. It's an Italian dish I learned from the lady who cooked at the orphanage."

"Now, what did you bring?" Polly asked Seth.

Seth steered them toward a Dutch oven filled with pieces of chicken, vegetables, and rice. "Chicken perloo. Billy and I made it yesterday."

"We had help from Tustenuggee," Billy said. "And he made the bread." Small, round, flat breads were piled in a basket next to the stew. "It's called Seminole flatbread."

"Is he coming?" Agnes asked. "I don't see him."

"When we left, he hadn't decided," Seth said. "Not exactly his favorite thing, this kind of event. Or mine, either."

"It's for a good cause," Agnes said. "And look how this food tells about the people of Persimmon Hollow. How we're all from different places but are together here."

They reviewed the foods and their labels. A group of dishes fronted by a sign reading "Florida Settler" included Seth's perloo and plates of swamp cabbage and baked sweet potatoes. Sausage sat on a bed of pickled sauerkraut on a dish labeled "Oktoberfest." A crock of baked beans was adjacent to a kettle of boiled meat, carrots, and potatoes near a sign that stated "New England." A "Kentucky" card was propped by a pot of squirrel burgoo and a platter of cornbread.

"Look out, coming through," said Clyde. He stepped closer, carrying a tub of frog legs. "Fellows outside are frying fish and gator tail," he added as he set down the tub.

Fanny bustled up. "It's too warm to let the food sit out while we do the program," she fretted. "We must eat first and then have the program."

"I'll make an announcement," Agnes said and headed to the front of the room.

"May I have your attention," she called, but her voice barely carried over the chatter.

"May I have your attention!" she called, louder, but to no avail.

Seth put two of his fingers in his mouth and whistled so loud everyone froze into silence.

"Thank you kindly," he said and gave a mock bow. "I give the floor to my fiancée, Miss Agnes Foster."

"Welcome, ladies and gentlemen," she said. "Thank you for joining us for the first Persimmon Hollow recital, community dinner, and frolic. This event is to raise funds for an orphanage to be built just outside town. If you brought a dish, you are welcome to eat for free. If not, we request you make a small donation according to your means. Miss Eunice Alloway, who is seated at the table by the door, will be happy to accept your contributions." She pointed, and Eunice waved. Clyde brushed his hands on his denims and went and sat with her.

"We invite everyone to partake of this meal after the parson leads us in a blessing," she said. "Afterwards, we'll call your attention to the start of our very special school presentation. We hope you will be delighted with the work done by our intelligent youngsters. Thank you."

She stepped off to one side as people politely applauded. Parson Pierce stepped forward.

"We are gathered here from many places and backgrounds," the parson began. "The words of our Lord as expressed in Psalm 107 speak to this gathering. Please bow your heads in prayer and hear the words of our Lord:

> O give thanks to the Lord, for he is good;
>> for his steadfast love endures forever.
> Let the redeemed of the Lord say so,
>> those he redeemed from trouble
> and gathered in from the lands,
>> from the east and from the west,
>> from the north and from the south.
> Some wandered in desert wastes,
>> finding no way to an inhabited town;
> hungry and thirsty,
>> their soul fainted within them.
> Then they cried to the Lord in their trouble,
>> and he delivered them from their distress;
> he led them by a straight way,
>> until they reached an inhabited town.
> Let them thank the Lord for his steadfast love,
>> for his wonderful works to humankind.
> For he satisfies the thirsty,
>> and the hungry he fills with good things.

"Amen," said Agnes. Seth, by her side, let out a low whistle.

"That could have been written for Persimmon Hollow!" Seth said.

"God's word always speaks to us," Agnes said and squeezed his hand. "We just have to listen."

"Can we eat?" Billy asked.

"Let's chow down," Seth said, and Billy wasted no time getting in the food line.

"You'd think he hadn't eaten for days," Agnes said.

"Looks that way," Seth said, intent on fixing his own plate.

"Where did the time go?" Agnes asked as she ladled samples of several selections on her dish. "Look, the sun is setting already." The tinted sky filled the open shutters with rose-blue and orange brilliance, and a welcome breeze rifled the air.

"It's going to be a late night in Persimmon Hollow," Seth said. "May I have the first dance after the show?"

"It's a recital, not a show," she said. "And I don't recall that we planned a dance. But if we had, you certainly could have filled my dance card."

They found seats at a table already crowded with the Bights, the Alloways, Clyde, and a few other folks and dined together in community as Toby Bight and his friends filled the room with ballads and bluegrass music.

*　*　*

Outside, as the sun dipped lower, three shadowy figures on their horses sat in the woods across from the meeting hall...and waited.

"How much more time you figure we have to sit here," Rufus grumbled.

"Dunno," Lester said. "Could be a couple of hours."

"Sure smells good over that way," Barrel said.

"Everybody know their business?" Rufus said. "We don't want any screwups."

"How many times we got to go over this?" Lester demanded. "Barrel will create a diversion by lighting a fire over yonder." He nodded toward a pile of brush in the rear of the yard, where someone had piled twigs, leaves, and small branches after sweeping the grounds clean.

"You and me will untie the horses while he's setting the fire," Lester continued.

"We'll untie the horses first. Gives us more time to get into position to grab the right kids and the woman when everybody comes running out," Rufus said.

"Sure, whatever," said Lester. He drummed his fingers on his thigh.

"We have to move quickly after we get them," Rufus said. "You got enough rope?"

"I done checked three times," Lester snapped. "Got rope and got blankets to throw over their heads, and bandanas and rags case we need them. Even got us a rowboat hid out by the river."

"Okay," Rufus said. "Barrel, you better set one heck of a fire. Big enough to raise a commotion. Not big enough to kill nobody. If anybody dies, we won't be able to bargain for ransom. Set the fire, then catch up to me and Lester around the far corner of the building, where they won't see us."

"I still ain't happy about messing with no woman and children," Barrel complained, sniffing the food aromas that drifted on the breeze. "Ain't my line of work."

Rufus ignored the comment. "Everybody know who they're

supposed to grab, like we talked about?" he asked. Lester and a reluctant Barrel nodded.

"Sure wish we had time to get some of that chow in there," Barrel said.

"Ain't even worth telling him to shut up," Lester said to Rufus.

* * *

Agnes reached her seat just as the second half of the recital was about to begin.

"My little ones performed beautifully!" she whispered to Seth as she slid next to him on the bench. "I'm proud of them all." She watched Fanny supervise the second half of the presentation, which featured the upper-level students. "Oh, look, she's lining them up in reverse height order...that means Billy goes first!" Agnes leaned forward and gave him a nod of encouragement.

Billy took a deep breath and looked as though he would rather be anywhere else on earth.

After a slight stumble when he started to speak, he gained confidence and persevered through the entire speech. He didn't miss a word. When he straightened from giving the audience a deep bow, he beamed with a wide smile of relief and satisfaction and basked in the applause.

"Well done," Agnes mouthed the words to Billy. Like a proud mother, she smiled with a satisfaction that reached deep inside as well as radiated outward. She had a sudden insight into what lay ahead for her as Seth's wife and as mother of a family that included Billy and Polly. What a wonderful, special gift. She reached over and placed her hand in Seth's.

"Look, it's Polly's turn now," Agnes said a little while later. Polly walked to the front of the marked-floor stage with her head up and shoulders back. Her recitation gave evidence of hours of practice, and afterward, she curtsied and almost floated back to her position in line with the others. She grinned at the generous applause.

After each child had recited, the group reassembled, sang "Amazing Grace," and walked off the stage in a neat line while receiving a standing ovation. Moments later, the young performers reverted to noisy youngsters.

"We're going outside to play, okay, Agnes?" Polly said. She was already headed toward the door with Billy and the Bight children, all of them overexcited.

"Wait a minute, it's dark outside," Agnes said.

"They're in a meeting-hall yard in Persimmon Hollow, Agnes," Seth said. "They'll be all right." Eunice, Clyde, and Fanny nodded in agreement.

Agnes's protectiveness warred with her understanding of their words. Something felt amiss, but she couldn't say what.

"You stay right in front of the windows so I can see you in the moonlight, you understand?" she told the children in a tone she hoped indicated that she expected total obedience. They nodded yes and ran after their friends.

"And leave the door open so I can hear you," she called to the backs of the stampede. She heard them shout and shriek as soon as they cleared the doorway.

Agnes pursed her lips as she began to help the others clean up. She glanced out the door and adjacent window every few moments. A nagging unease tugged at her.

"It will be okay, dear," Eunice said. "We can reach them within seconds should there be an emergency."

"I know," Agnes said. "It's just that I'm not accustomed to such safety and security. Children who went out at night where I used to live faced many dangers. Look out the window! They're already disobeying my wish for them to stay where I can see them."

She stalked over to the open doorway and stood there a few minutes to watch the antics of the children. Just as she thought, they had widened the sphere of play considerably beyond the view from the window.

"Stay closer!" she ordered, hands on her hips. But they didn't, or wouldn't, hear.

"That does it," she muttered and stepped out after them. "Billy and Polly, over here! This minute!" She saw them halt in midstride, look at each other, and retreat toward her.

"Aw, please, can we stay out just a few more minutes," they pleaded as they came up to Agnes, who had reached the bottom step and moved forward to meet them.

A bright flash of light erupted in a corner of the yard, followed by the hiss and crackle of burning wood. The horses, startled and frightened, were suddenly all loose. They whinnied, snorted, and pranced across the yard. Just as Agnes reached to enfold Billy and Polly in her arms, she felt a blanket come down over her head and torso at the same time she was yanked away from the children.

Too stunned to feel immediate panic, she started to kick and shout, but the sound was muffled by the blanket. Her ankles, waist, and shoulders were quickly encircled with rope that held the blanket in place. Bile rose in her throat as she lost her balance, started to fall, and was picked up and hauled onto a horse that snorted, stomped, and started to gallop almost before she was slumped in front of someone who gripped her in a rough hold.

She heard other hoofbeats nearby. *Dear God in Heaven, help me,* she prayed.

Agnes willed herself to sip small breaths and force down the fear that churned with every jostle and jolt of the ride. She knew Seth and the other men would be moments behind them. They would put a stop to whatever nonsense was going on. She was almost as angry as she was scared. Angry with herself for ignoring her intuition, and scared that the children might be in danger. *Please, Blessed Mother, watch over them. Keep them in your care. Please.*

Agnes was wild to know if others had been kidnapped, too. She struggled to maneuver herself into a semi-seated position and felt her captor loosen the grip just enough for her to adjust herself. All would be lost if she panicked. But dread overtook her the longer they rode. *Hail Mary, full of grace...,* she silently prayed, and ran one Hail Mary into another, clinging to the rhythm of the prayer as she was carried into the unknown.

The hoofbeats slowed to a walk, then halted, and she could smell the river through the mustiness of the blanket. She heard a muffled voice. "Let me outta here, you jerks!" Agnes swallowed terror. That was Billy. On the other side of her, a shrouded sob. Polly. Agnes's heart beat even more wildly. She strained to hear horse hooves in the distance. Nothing.

She was slid off the horse. "Get them blankets off, loosen the ankle ropes, tie bandanas around their eyes, and stuff rags in their mouths," a strange voice ordered. "Listen up, you three. We're getting in a boat. No funny business. You try and escape you'll get ate by a gator."

Polly's sobs turned into hiccups. Agnes had one goal—to get to the children—and it overrode her fear. She blinked and tried to focus when the blanket was yanked off, but a bandana was over her eyes seconds later. "You will allow me access to the children," she said in a low, terrified voice.

"Yeah, lady, sure," came a higher-pitched voice that accompanied whomever was tying the bandana. "We don't mean no harm." Someone pulled her arms free of the rope.

"Then just why and what…" She felt a cloth cover her mouth, wrap around her jaw, and be tied at the back of her head. It stifled her words despite her attempt to ward off the fabric with her hands.

"Do that again, and the arms go back under the rope, and the guns go off in your direction," a third voice said. Agnes went rigid. She knew that voice. Knew the evil it contained. And knew hope, at least for her, was fading fast.

Just as her knees were about to give out, she was led into a boat and pushed to sit down. Soon after, she felt two small, tense bodies stumble down next to her. Instantly, her arms went around them, one on each side. She pulled Polly and Billy close as if she could protect them with the strength of her grasp. *Let one of these men attempt to harm either of these children,* she thought, indignation rising atop her panic. They would have to go through her first.

She felt the boat start to move through the water. After a while, Agnes finally stopped trying to determine how far they traveled by counting each slap of an oar on water. *Where, oh where, were they going? How was Seth to ever find them?*

Chapter Twenty-Two

*S*eth, Clyde, and Toby led the band of men on horseback at a rapid clip until they reached the crossroads on the far edge of town. Moonlight-dappled wilderness surrounded them, hushed yet alive with the buzzing of insects and calls of night birds. They slowed to a halt.

"I saw three horses before we lost them," Seth said. "Which way would three cowards go?" he wondered aloud.

"Reckon they're strangers who don't know the area?" Clyde asked.

"No," Seth said. "I'm close to sure who they are. But your question just gave me my answer."

He nudged Silver toward the river road.

"This way, fellows," he said. "To the old moonshine still."

"Out on the river island?" Toby asked.

Seth nodded. "The one with the double-trunk palm tree at the edge. The man I'm thinking of isn't smart enough to find a new place to hide. He tried to do me in once at that still."

"We can use the rowboat at the steamboat landing office," Clyde said as they started to ride again.

* * *

Agnes, Polly, and Billy were ushered off the boat and onto springy ground. Agnes gripped each child's hand tightly. They were pushed to sit on the ground, backs together, and she felt and heard ropes being wrapped around them.

Someone removed the bandana from Agnes's eyes and loosened the rag over her mouth. She blinked. Spanish moss dripped from large cypress trees that grew tall in the inky waters. A distinctive double-trunk palm tree stood near the edge of the island where the boat was pulled up.

Polly's trembles and Billy's tense stiffness made her roil with anxiety-tempered outrage. "Stay brave," she choked out the words through the fabric. Their mouths were still gagged. "Pray in your heart." The sound of a gun being cocked cut through the grunts of frogs and hisses of insects, but Agnes couldn't see anyone. Cold dread washed over her again.

Agnes strained to see in the shifting shadows cast by the moonlight and pushed down her panic. She swallowed. She had to stay strong for Polly and Billy. No one else seemed to be near. Slowly, she moved her arms and started to reach along the rope to find knots so she could try to untie them. If the three of them could run, they could hide.

A round figure emerged from the understory shrubbery. "Sorry, ma'am, but you best put a stop to that right now," he said.

Sorry, ma'am?

"Untie us!" she demanded in a muffled voice, still sounding braver than she felt. Something about the round man was familiar, too.

"I do the talking here," he said and waved the gun at her. But he came closer and loosened the rag even more so that it slid down to her chin. "That's the most I can do. Don't try anything funny. One loud word, and you're fixin' to get shot. And, like I said, you best stop fiddling with that rope."

Agnes stopped and sat quietly. Polly's small fingers reached for hers. Agnes strained to touch Polly's and Billy's hands while she tried to decipher what to do next. As her eyes adjusted to the surroundings, she could make out wild grapevine, smilax, and Virginia creeper. The vines crept over old barrels, copper tubing, and other debris. The tangle of vines and piles of junk would impede any attempts to run. But she couldn't just give up.

"I can and will shout," Agnes said as loud as she dared. The man pointed the gun at them and cocked the trigger. Agnes shut up.

Another figure emerged from the shadows. He was dressed in dark clothing like the round man, but a bandana covered his nose and mouth. Agnes's skin grew clammy as the second man studied her, and her breath shortened as her earlier awareness proved true. Rufus Smith had tracked her down. She and Polly both. The round man, it came to her with sudden clarity, was one of the strangers who had turned up at the meeting hall and offered to help whitewash the building.

"Go ahead, yell," Rufus sneered. "Nobody will hear you." He laughed, and the sound made Agnes want to vomit. She opened her mouth to scream, but only a low, strangled choking sound came out.

"I'll give you something to shout about," he continued. "I figure I can claim my due and get a ransom, both. Especially if I start now." He advanced toward her.

Panic clawed at Agnes. She could feel her heartbeat drum in her throat, her ears, her neck.

"Hey, you, let them be," the round man said. "I didn't cotton to messing with a woman and children to start with on this job. You stick to our plan. We trade 'em for money, and that's it. Keep your hands off."

Rufus snarled and twirled. "Stay outta my face, Barrel." Agnes saw a glint of knife blade in Rufus's hand as he moved toward Barrel.

The round man pointed the gun at Rufus, but the slimmer man was faster, and he snatched the rifle. Barrel hung on long enough for the gun to slide out of Rufus's hand and land with a dull thud.

"We'll settle this man to man," Barrel yelled, grunted, and charged Rufus, who was thrown off balance. They were both down on the ground pummeling each other.

Agnes found her voice. "Help us!" she screamed. "Help! Somebody! Anybody!" She raced to find the knots and untie the rope before the fight ended.

* * *

Lester ran into the clearing and waded into the fight, pushing the two men apart. "What the hell are you doing here with Barrel?" Lester snapped at Rufus and ran to Agnes. He yanked the rag over her mouth again and pulled the rope tighter.

"I came to sample the merchandise," Rufus said. He stood up and wiped his bloody nose with his sleeve.

"You fool!" Lester exploded. "You left the other side of the island unguarded! There's no telling who could come in that way."

"Folks around here aren't smart enough to find us," Rufus said. "Dumb as the oxen they drive, just like you and your buddy here."

Lester took a leap and jumped on Rufus. They rolled around in the sandy leaf mold, cursed, and punched each other. This time, Barrel jumped up and down and hollered at them to quit.

God help us, Agnes kept repeating to herself. What would befall them when the fighting stopped? She glanced over her shoulder each way and saw that while Polly turned her gaze away from the scene, Billy was riveted on the brawl.

On the other side of the island, the men had indeed gained a foothold into the area. They inched quietly through the hardwood hammock until Agnes's scream shot through the forest.

Seth bolted forward and crashed through the brush, the other men close behind him. Lester, Rufus, and Barrel never saw them coming.

Thank God, Agnes thought. *We're saved.*

* * *

It didn't take long for the men to free Agnes, Polly, and Billy, round up the three interlopers, and tie them up with the same ropes.

Seth wrapped Agnes, Polly, and Billy into a giant bear hug. Agnes let her shaky bravery give way to sweet relief. She didn't want to let go of Seth.

"I love you, Seth Taylor," she whispered.

"I love you, too," he said.

"Not so fast there, buddy." Rufus's voice was harsh and unpleasant.

"I'm talking to you, yeah, you," he continued. He glared at Seth. "That's my wife there you're kissing."

Chapter Twenty-Three

$\mathcal{S}$eth lowered his arms, released Agnes, and stared at Rufus. Neither man spoke. Seth turned slowly toward Agnes.

"Is that man your husband?" he asked and gestured with exaggeration.

Agnes shook her head in a fierce no. She grabbed hold of Seth's arm to steady herself as emotions roiled within her.

"Agnes, you're safe here," Seth said and stood close.

She took a deep breath and let it out in a slow exhale in hopes her heartbeat would also calm down. Seth was right. She had nothing to fear. She was protected by good people and surrounded by God's love.

"You no-good, evil man," she sputtered at Rufus. "How dare you lie like that?"

From the safety of Seth's side, the anger and frustration and fear of the past months tumbled out of her. "How dare you make up a story like that? Haven't you ruined my life enough?"

"I see sparks in the lady's eyes," Seth said to him. "You want to explain yourself? Or do you need some help from me?"

"You gonna believe a prostitute who came out of a…"

Agnes gasped, and Seth was within inches of planting a fist in Rufus's face when Clyde, Toby, and a few of the other men called out that if he wanted to fight, he'd have to untie Rufus first, no matter how unworthy the man was.

Seth acknowledged them and dropped his fist, but his hands stayed clenched.

"Take back those words now," he growled.

"Heck no," said Rufus. "I'm telling you, she's my wife and..."

"Listen, buddy," Seth said, and he grabbed the man's shirt so that he was forced to look Seth in the eye. "I know Agnes's story. The whole story. The true story."

A dart of fear crossed Rufus's eyes, soon replaced by an evil glare.

"I know about you, I know what you did to her, I know the trouble it caused, and I know what you tried to do to Polly," Seth continued. He let go of Rufus's shirt and stepped back. He paced, back and forth, then stopped, again right in front of Rufus and inches from his face.

"I know what it's like to have false witness ruin a life," Seth said in a low voice.

Rufus's eyes became slits. "It was all a mistake, you don't understand...," he started to whine.

Seth snorted. "You might want to thank God I'm not the type of man I used to be."

Seth turned to Lester, who tried to shrink into the shadow of a tree. Seth fought to control his breath and his temper as he came face to face with the man who had cost him so much.

Agnes willed Seth to feel the power of the prayer she uttered silently for him.

Seth swallowed hard.

"You want to 'fess up here or wait until you're in front of the judge?" he asked in a level voice.

"I don't know what you're talking about," said Lester. "Get me outta these ropes. I got my rights."

"You lost them when you lit that fire," Seth said. "You know what I'm talking about."

Lester sweated despite the evening drop in temperature. Seth stepped closer.

"Two people died because of you. Another became an orphan. I lost my family and my home. You need help remembering?"

"Uh uh, nobody died cause of me," Lester whined. "I didn't know nobody was in that house. I only hit that man on the head cause he surprised me. I never would've told Barrel here to set that fire if..."

"Hey, wait a minute, boss, I didn't set any fire," said Barrel. He tried to scratch his head. "No sirreee. Wasn't even there."

Anger, hatred, despair, grief, anguish—they all flitted across Seth's face as he squared off with the man whose actions had brought such tragedy into his life. Agnes held her breath. Then, without warning, without speaking, Seth turned on his heel and stalked off. The night woods soon swallowed him, but Agnes trailed behind. She gave him space but stayed close enough to keep him in view.

Seth walked a short distance on a game trail. Agnes wavered for a moment and wondered if she should leave him alone. An invisible push propelled her forward and urged her to catch up, to not let him wrestle with his demons alone.

Seth sat down under a pine tree and leaned against it, knees up. He propped his elbows on his knees and leaned his head in his hands. Agnes slid down beside him and ran her hand through the crook of his elbow. She kept silent, just leaned close and willed him to feel her closeness, her strength, and the strength and mercy of God.

"For a long time, the only thing that kept me going was the need for revenge," Seth finally said. He looked up and lowered his hands from his face. "I plotted it, planned ways to do it, and waited for the time to come. I wanted to end his life the way he ended theirs."

"But you didn't," Agnes said, "and you won't, will you?"

He shook his head no, as she had hoped and expected.

"Thou shalt not kill," she whispered. "God's commandments aren't always easy to follow. Killing him wouldn't bring back your brother or sister-in-law. Lester will serve time in the penitentiary, Seth, probably for many years. And you won't have blood on your hands."

He was silent, and something made Agnes continue to talk.

"I feel a hatred for Rufus that I wrestle with," she admitted. "It's hard to feel compassion for someone who did me such harm. I...I honestly don't have compassion for him, not yet. I try hard not to hate him. Hatred does nothing but eat at the heart of the one doing the hating."

Seth locked his gaze with Agnes's.

"You're the best thing that's ever happened to me, Agnes," he said. "You and your example of Christian love and life and your gentle prodding of this prodigal son."

"Love is better, so much better than hatred," Agnes said and tilted her face up and kissed him. He turned and took her in his arms. It was a quiet yet powerful kiss that spoke of pleasures to come.

Seth stood and helped Agnes get up. He kept an arm around her as they walked out of the woods and returned to the clearing.

Agnes pulled Polly and Billy close again and wanted nothing more than to keep them in her sight forever.

Clyde nodded his approval. "I reckon you all will make a right nice family. Get on home. The rest of us will escort these fellows into the hands of the law."

Agnes felt such relief and such a heart full of love, for Seth, for the community of people who had become like family, for tiny Persimmon Hollow itself. She wrapped her arms tighter around Seth and the children as they turned to leave. *Home.* They were going home.

Epilogue

March, 1887

Ready, Mrs. Taylor?" Seth stood in the doorway of their bedroom and watched as Agnes, seated in front of the dressing table, finished pinning up her hair and adjusting her collar. In the corner of the mirror was a wedding photo of the two of them exchanging vows in front of Bishop John Moore, who had ridden down from the Diocese of St. Augustine to perform the Mass and sacrament of holy matrimony before the entire population of Persimmon Hollow.

In his hand, Seth held a large, flat object wrapped in a towel.

"For you, Mr. Taylor, I'm always ready," Agnes said. She smiled at his reflected image in the mirror as she rose. She turned around. "Oh, Seth, I'm so excited. I can't believe the day is finally here!"

"Me neither," he said. He walked in and set down his package. "Thought we'd never get that building done in time."

"I'm so glad we changed our minds and had the wedding first," Agnes said. "Fanny had so much fun telling everyone, 'I told you so,' about us. And now, today will belong only to the children. Nothing else will take any of the excitement or attention away from them."

"Hmmmm, I'm glad we got married, too," Seth said and kissed the back of her neck.

She felt a shiver of pleasure, arched her back, and stood up. They shared a long, slow kiss and then walked over to the window and looked out to the far corner of the property. The U-shaped orphanage stood in a clearing in the pine forest, awaiting its first residents.

"I see our young'uns are already out there," Seth said. Agnes spotted Polly and Billy in the crowd that gathered as the time neared for the orphans to arrive.

"Let's go," Agnes said. "We don't want them to get here before we're outside."

She started to head for the door but stopped at the towel-covered object Seth had carried in and set on the table. "Seth, what is it?" she asked and reached for the towel to pull it off. Seth got his hand on it first.

"Not so fast," he said. "It has to have a proper unveiling." With drama, he inched the towel off what appeared to be a flat piece of wood.

"Hurry!" Agnes.

With a flourish, Seth whipped away the rest of the towel. In his hand was a rectangular piece of sanded cedar, with wording burned into it: St. Isidore's Home, South.

"Oh, it's perfect!" Agnes said, and tears pricked at her eyes.

"C'mon," Seth said and grinned. "Like you said, the welcoming committee can't be late."

They went, arm in arm, and walked across the property. Seth waved a hand toward the store, which had proved popular with winter residents.

"The railroad's going to extend the line right past the store and orphanage," he said.

"So much can happen in such a short time, can't it?" mused Agnes. "When I think back…"

"Forward," Seth said as they arrived at the orphanage, where the Alloways, Clyde, Toby and Sarah and their children, Polly, Billy, the parson and his wife, and other townsfolk were already assembled. "We look forward, not back," Seth said.

The largest wagon Agnes had ever seen rolled into view. Everyone stared at the assortment of small bodies that bobbed in the wagon as it rolled over the uneven ground. The wagon pulled up, and bewildered children looked out timidly at the unfamiliar surroundings and the strange people. Two sisters Agnes didn't know climbed down from the front seat with somber faces and wary eyes. They started to help the children disembark and urged order and silence.

Agnes ran up and welcomed the sisters, who looked young enough to be recently out of the novitiate. She clasped their hands one set at a time and gave them a squeeze. "We are so glad to see you, and we offer our firmest help and support," she said. The sisters smiled, and their faces softened.

In those few moments of distraction, one of the children recognized Agnes. Then another. And another. They fell out of line, shouted, called her, and started to mill about. Agnes swirled around, arms open wide, and tears streamed down her face as the little faces came into focus. She crouched down to be on their level. "Emily! Jonathan! Baby Sally, how you've grown! Benedict! Oh, come here, all of you!" They scrambled to be near her, eager to be close to the one familiar thing in their strange, new world, and they all collapsed into a group hug. Polly came out from the crowd, ran to them, and threw herself in the middle with hugs and kisses for them all.

Seth and Billy walked up to the wagon. Seth nodded to the sisters then opened his arms wide in front of the group. "These arms are big enough to protect you all," he said. Billy followed suit. Agnes looked up and blew them both kisses.

Behind them, applause began, soft at first, then louder and louder, until it sounded like hundreds of people clapped, cheered, and called out "welcome home!"

Agnes stood up. Her heart swelled with love for her new husband and her two children, for her newfound family community, for every orphan, for everything she had.

"Welcome to Persimmon Hollow, everybody," she cried. She sent a short, silent prayer of thanks to the Lord above as she glanced up at the sky. "Welcome to Persimmon Hollow, all of you," she said again. "Welcome home."

Gerri Bauer has a B.A. in English from Stetson University, where she works in social media and online marketing and volunteers for the campus ministry program. She was born and raised in New York City but has deep roots in Florida, where she lives with her husband, spoils her cats, and keeps tabs on a far-flung extended family. She edited *The Parce Letters: Voices from the Past*, a collection of primary sources on pioneer settlers in Florida. This is her first novel.